FICTION   Feldman, Ellen,
FELDMAN   1941-

        Rearview mirror.

DATE			

✓

REARVIEW MIRROR

OTHER BOOKS BY ELLEN FELDMAN

Too Close for Comfort
Looking for Love
A.K.A. Katherine Walden
Conjugal Rites

REARVIEW MIRROR

ELLEN FELDMAN

Delacorte Press

Published by
Delacorte Press
Bantam Doubleday Dell Publishing Group, Inc.
1540 Broadway
New York, New York 10036

Library of Congress Cataloging in Publication Data

Feldman, Ellen, 1941–
    Rearview mirror / Ellen Feldman.
        p.   cm.
    ISBN 0-385-30913-9 (hardcover)
    I. Title.
    PS3572.I38R4   1996
    813'.54—dc20   95-12742
                                                        CIP

Book design: Barbara Berger

Manufactured in the United States of America

Published simultaneously in Canada

January 1996

10   9   8   7   6   5   4   3   2   1

BVG

In celebration of formalized relationships,
for
my agent, Amanda Urban
my editor, Cynthia White
and my husband, Stephen

To fear love is to fear life, and
those who fear life are already three
parts dead.
     —Bertrand Russell

The judge said listen, Bessie, tell
me why you killed your man,
I said, judge, you ain't no woman and
you can't understand.
    —Bessie Smith's rendition
     of "Sing Sing Prison Blues"

REARVIEW MIRROR

One

SOME TIME AGO, when I was starting out as a freelancer, an editor who gave me an assignment when no one else would gave me a piece of advice as well. "I can't tell you how to do it," she said, "but I can tell you how not to. Don't misquote or cut and paste so cleverly that it amounts to the same thing. Don't take gifts from people you're writing about or people who want you to write about them. And don't ever sleep with a subject."

She stopped talking and sat staring across her desk at me for a moment, and I remembered a story I'd heard about her and an actor. Richard Burton, I think, or Albert Finney. Anyway, it was one of that generation and breed. She shook her head. Her name was Patricia O'Dougherty, and she had a curtain of silky red hair—not rusty brown like mine, but true red—that swung against her cheeks when she moved.

"If you absolutely can't resist, at least wait until the piece has run."

I was thinking of Pat O'Dougherty's advice that morning as I sat at the desk in the corner of my bedroom watching a sooty tugboat make its way up the East River. My apartment is on the third floor, and what the view lacks in sweep it makes up in immediacy. When empty tankers go by riding high in the water, I can almost reach out and touch them. Sometimes when I'm sitting in the living room window seat, a sailor waves. I always wave back to the men going to sea or coming home from it, though I rarely acknowledge the salutes of the tourists on Circle Line boats or the revelers on flashy pleasure craft with *My Way* or *Doc's Dream* scrawled across the transoms.

My profile of Dexter St.John hadn't actually run yet, but I'd delivered it to the magazine, my editor had okayed it, and the checkers had vetted it weeks ago. Dexter's plane was due in at JFK at seven-twenty that evening.

I knew I was shaving it closer than Pat O'Dougherty had recommended, but I didn't see what could go wrong. I no longer had to worry about my objectivity. As for Dexter's influence, I doubted he'd want me to change anything in the profile even if he had the chance, although I knew from experience there was no telling how people would react to what was written about them. Years ago a woman who'd worked her way from a trailer park near Sylmar to a multimillion-dollar Bel Air divorce had threatened to sue me and the magazine where the article had run not because of anything I'd said about her in print, and I'd said quite a bit, but because when I'd quoted her, I'd used phonetic spelling to show how she pronounced, or rather couldn't pronounce, the word *truth*. There were no phonetic spellings in my profile of Dexter St.John—his accent is impeccable Eastern Seaboard Establishment down to the way the word *restaurant* slides into two syllables, and his *wh*'s set up a breeze you can sail a small skiff by—but there were descriptions that might offend his vanity. I never came out and said that you knew just from watching him—at least I knew—that though he was worried about how far his hairline was going to recede, it was one vulnerability he'd never admit. I merely recorded how, at certain points in certain conversations, his hand went to his hairline, then stopped just short of patting it to make sure it was still there. And I never even hinted that for a man in his position his clothes were something of an affectation. I merely described the frayed collars of his blue oxford cloth shirts and the small hole, like a stigma right beneath his heart, in the one he was wearing the first time I interviewed him, and went on to say that it was the same Brooks Brothers style, half a neck size larger, that he'd gone off to Groton in, subsequently tie-dyed, then shorn of sleeves, and finally burned in protest so many years earlier. (I'd done my research.) As for the overtly unflattering parts of the profile, Dexter St.John wasn't exactly a public relations virgin. He'd been around enough to know the form of a piece like this. First you set the subject up as larger than life; then you marshal a few controversial quotes from colleagues and critics to cut him down to size; finally you wind up with a glowing appreciation of an exemplary-but-oh-so-human hope for the future of humankind.

As I sat watching the waves set up by the wake of the tug crash against the bulkheads of the river, I couldn't find a single reason not to break Pat O'Dougherty's rule, though I'd been living by it for close to fifteen years. It hasn't been that difficult. Unlike Pat, I find actors eminently resistible. If I wanted a child, I'd adopt one. As for the other types I tend to interview for my work, politicians are too slippery, billionaires too greedy, artists too much in love with their own creations. That leaves the knights in nonprofit armor, and though I admit to a sneaking admiration of their achievements, until now I'd managed to temper it with a healthy skepticism about their motives. You don't have to have a degree in psychiatry to realize that anyone who sets out to save the world has a dangerously inflated view of his place in it.

Which only brings me back to Dexter St.John. Notice the canonized name, please. Dexter is the founder and president of something called the Twenty-first Century Health Fund. Talk about an apocalyptic sense of self. Dexter is, in fact, the fund. I don't mean no one else works for it. There's an office here in New York, and doctors and nurses and medical missionaries toil in its name all over the world. I don't even mean that his name is plastered on literature and stationery and office doors. That's not Dexter's style. It's merely that he's the spirit and substance and guiding force behind the fund. He's the one who travels to the Far East and Africa and South America to decide whether the fund's resources will be more effective immunizing infants, or educating their mothers about how AIDS is spread, or trying to stop tribes from circumcising their prepubescent girls. He's the one who goes down to Washington and over to the UN to tell the officials what's really going on out there. And he's the one who crisscrosses the country from Park Avenue to Palm Beach to Palm Springs to convince investment bankers and movie moguls and trophy wives that his is a cause with cachet. See what I mean about knights in nonprofit armor. I was wary of Dexter St.John, or at least of my admiration for him, before I even met him.

Our first conversation did nothing to reassure me. At the suggestion of an editor for a slick monthly known for its profiles of celebrity survivors of substance or sexual or some other abuse, I'd written Dexter St.John a letter proposing an article. Dexter wasn't its usual sort of subject, but every now and then the editorial staff decides the magazine needs a little moral heft or at least a whitewash. A week or so later, according to procedure, I followed it up with a call.

He took the call immediately. It's been my experience that the name of a national magazine opens doors faster than a Park Avenue doorman a week before Christmas. I told him again how much I and, more important, the magazine wanted to do a profile of him.

"I suppose it will garner some attention for the fund," he said slowly, as if he were weighing the issue, as if he were considering refusing, as if he wouldn't have paid for the publicity. But that was all right. I'd been through this particular mating dance before. I was even encouraged. The man wasn't as perfect as his CV made him look.

"It certainly will," I agreed.

"And of course, there's always the First Amendment issue."

I rolled my eyes heavenward, though I live and work alone, and there was no one around to appreciate the gesture. Over the years I'd listened to a lot of subjects, who would eventually spill every secret they'd ever had and invent a few more to get attention, try to play hard to get, but this was the first time I'd ever heard anyone imply that his refusal to grant an interview might be an infringement of the freedom of the press. I decided I didn't have to worry about my weakness for do-gooders. Dexter St.John was going to be a pushover. And I wasn't.

"The public has a right to know," I said.

He laughed. His laugh, like his voice, was deep and gravelly. If he weren't a healer to the world, I would have pegged him as a three-pack-a-day man. "That was a joke, Hallie. Do you mind if I call you Hallie?"

I didn't, but even if I had, I couldn't have said so by that time. He'd caught me out, and he knew it.

"I love being interviewed," he said. "I love the fact that I get to talk nonstop about what I want to talk about, which happens to be the health of ninety percent of the population of this planet, which happens to suck, and you have to listen. And I love reading what I said. Hell, I don't even care if you don't spell my name right. Though for the record, there's no space between the *Saint* and the *John.*" He laughed again. "How soon do you want to start?"

We started immediately and went on for months, which is not the way I usually work. I'm accustomed to getting in, getting the job done, and getting out. For a week or two or maybe even a month the subject's world becomes my world, the subject's life my life. Then I move on. But the magazine wasn't about to foot the bill for me to follow him from a feeding center in Africa to a refugee camp in Eastern Europe to an AIDS conference in Asia, so I had to catch him when he was in town. The problem, I explained to Kay Meechum, the editor who'd commissioned the profile and who wasn't exactly a friend but through years of working together had become more than a professional acquaintance, was that Dexter wasn't in town often or for long at a time. He kept going away, and coming back, and going away.

"Sounds like every relationship I've had for the past decade," Kay said.

I laughed politely. Women who insist on characterizing themselves as victims, even in jest, make me uneasy, but Kay gives me a lot of work. Then I asked about an extension. She told me not to worry. There was no rush on the piece.

Finally, at the end of four months, I felt I had enough for an in-depth profile. There was no need for me to see Dexter St.John again. To judge from his behavior when we said good-bye, he agreed. After the last interview he shook my hand and told me to stay in touch. It's not one of my favorite expressions. It's what editors say as they're prying your name off their Rolodexes. I knew he had no intention of staying in touch. I wasn't particularly pleased, because after all the time I'd spent with him, I'd come to admire more about him than his work, but I wasn't exactly crestfallen either. If nothing else, it seemed like the safest course of action, or inaction, and not only because of Pat O'Dougherty's warning.

I am not a naïve woman, though friends tell me the fact that I keep saying that reveals my naïveté. The stories about JFK and his infidelity-a-day didn't exactly come as a surprise. The tapes of Martin Luther King weren't a disillusionment. If I found out tomorrow that Albert Schweitzer had cut a swath through the women of Gabon or Gandhi had succumbed to Lady Mountbatten, I wouldn't think less of either of them. In other words, I don't believe a sense of social mission requires, or is even particularly compatible with, celibacy. I subscribe to the theory that men, and women, with great imaginations are likely to have great appetites as well. But that doesn't mean I want to become a statistic in a revisionist biography. So I wrote the profile—and I went out of my way not to be too easy on him because by that time I knew I wasn't entirely objective—delivered it to the editor, and if I didn't exactly forget about Dexter St.John, I did go on to the next assignment.

That's one of the things I love about my work. I don't get mired in things. I can always move on to something new. I did a newsletter for an industrial convention, which was profoundly boring and unconscionably profitable; a puff piece on a celebrity apartment for an interior design magazine, which was almost as boring and not nearly as profitable; and an article on how to buy a car if you're a woman, which presumably is different from buying a car if you're a man. Now I was gearing up to write a piece on a subject that I was sure was going to take my career in a new direction. I won't say my work until now has been exactly frivolous—witness the profile of Dr. Dexter St.John, savior to the sick, the maimed, and the hungry—but given the taste of the magazine-reading, product-buying public, I've spent an inordinate amount of time in the past several years talking to junk bond barons, graduates of the Betty Ford Clinic, and people who are known by one name. Maybe it was Dexter's example, or maybe it was just intimations of mortality, but I was determined to write something meaningful or at least serious. I was determined to write a piece on the women of death row.

That was what I called them, though only one of them was on death row. Most were either serving prison terms or awaiting trial for shooting or knifing or in some way doing in their abusive husbands and lovers. Ever since I'd got the idea, I couldn't open a paper or turn on the evening news without running across another example. Even the small-town weeklies in the Berkshires and the Hamptons, which I read when I weekended with better-heeled friends, were rife with reports of domestic revenge. The situation was heating up. Women's groups were stepping up efforts on behalf of the victims, who in this case were the perpetrators. Male prosecutors and politicians were digging in their heels. The subject had immediacy, social and legal resonance, and human pathos. I was sure I had a winner.

The first two editors to whom I suggested the piece didn't agree. Then, two months after Dexter St.John and I had said good-bye, a third editor I'd sent the proposal to called.

I recognized Sugar Shapiro's voice before she identified herself. There aren't many senior editors of national magazines who sound like Shirley Temple. The voice is especially ironic because *Era,* Sugar's magazine, is geared to what are known as women-of-a-certain-age. *Old* and even *middle-aged* are still dirty words in the magazine business, no matter what the demographic studies tell the marketing geniuses about who buys their advertisers' products. Sugar herself was so completely programmed that she never even used the word *young,* because it didn't take a genius to figure out the term was relative and implied younger than something, which was of course old or at least middle-aged. It wasn't easy talking to Sugar, in more ways than one.

"Sweetie pie!" she squeaked, as if she were about to launch into a rendition of "On the Good Ship Lollipop." I wasn't misled by the term of endearment. Sugar calls all her writers, female and male, sweetie pie. When she's really twisting arms, she shortens it to pie. "I have an idea that has your name written all over it."

She also has a way of appropriating ideas. That was okay. I'd let her think the women of death row was her brainstorm if she'd let me do the piece.

"Women in prison," I said.

There was a moment's silence. I pictured her sitting behind her big, improbably neat desk in one of her gorgeous Armani suits. Sugar's voice and name might be juvenile, but her wardrobe was strictly adult. It was the kind of wardrobe my mother, a good woman with too much time and quite a bit of discretionary income on her hands, brought me up to have. On the rare occasions when Sugar takes me to lunch, I'm always sorry I've let my mother down.

Sugar sighed, and I knew I'd let her down too. She was hoping I'd get the hint. She was hoping she wouldn't have to spell it out for me. I almost felt sorry for her. Before I started to freelance, I'd put in a brief stint as an assistant editor. It's no fun spending half your life rejecting people and ideas. It's not as bad as getting rejected, but unless you're a sadist, it isn't as much fun as it's cracked up to be.

"Anger's out, sweetie pie."

That was news to me. As far as I could see, it was a free-floating, palpable presence. The other day, as I was standing in the hall trying to unlock my door, I overheard my neighbor, a perfectly contented-looking woman, howling at her husband—at least I assume it was her husband and not the handyman—that there are other ways of showing affection than goddamn grabbing at goddamn erogenous zones.

"From where I'm standing," I told Sugar, "anger is rampant."

"Maybe, but we've done it to death. Wives slicing off their husbands' penises. Daughters taking contracts out on their fathers. Readers have OD'd on it. So men beat up on us. So we're finally getting back at them. Who cares anymore?"

"I do."

She sighed again. "Listen, pie. You want to write ancient history, I'll give you a recommendation for graduate school. You want to write for *Era,* you have to stay on the cutting edge."

"Which is?"

"Something more upbeat. Positive. Hopeful."

"I can't get from my building to the corner without passing three homeless people, the entire country is awash in red ribbons, downward mobility is the wave of the next generation, and you're telling me optimism is the cutting edge?"

"I'm telling you people are tired of gloom and doom. They want to read about people who are making a difference without sacrificing their lifestyles."

"Or chipping their nail polish."

There was a moment's pause. "Do you want to hear the idea or not?" When Sugar is annoyed, her voice drops to an octave that's almost grown-up.

Now I was the one who sighed, though I didn't let her hear it. I'm not in a position to turn down assignments out of hand, not if I want to keep my freelance status and my view of the East River. I've done it occasionally, when the subject has been particularly unpromising or the idea especially lurid, but I don't do it regularly. I certainly didn't want to turn down Sugar Shapiro without even knowing what she had in mind. I told her I wanted to hear it.

"Does the name Emma Weill mean anything to you?"

The one thing you never do with Sugar, not if you want to stay on the cutting edge, is admit that you haven't heard of someone, but in this case I didn't have to fake it. The name Emma Weill meant something to me, probably more than it did to Sugar, but that was another story.

"She writes kids' books."

"She wrote," Sugar said, and the impatience in her voice was still making it sound almost grown-up, "the first truly feminist YA ever." It was lucky I knew what the initials stood for, because Sugar wasn't about to come out and say "young adult." "That was twelve years ago, and it's still selling like hotcakes. As are, I might add, all her subsequent books. There's a new crop of tortured adolescents every couple of years." Sugar's voice dropped another octave at the unhappy thought of all those y-word women nipping at her aging heels.

"True, but are they *Era*'s readers?" I knew I was on dangerous ground, but I couldn't imagine why a magazine aimed at women-of-a-certain-age would want to run a profile of a teen heroine.

"Emma Weill is a woman for all seasons," Sugar said, and I could tell from the register of her voice that she was pleased with the phrase. "She's successful, she's rich, and she's done a lot of good. In other words, Emma Weill is a woman who has it all, and if that doesn't make good copy, I don't know what does."

Sugar was right, of course. I knew enough about Emma Weill to know that she really did have it all. An enviable career. An admirable reputation for making a difference, no matter how small, in the world. And, according to a remark made by my aunt Babe, who wasn't really my aunt but had been my mother's best friend, a long-standing marriage and two beautiful—is there any other kind? Babe had asked—children. Emma Weill was as close to perfection and as far away from the women of death row as you could get. She was the woman every woman, at least every intelligent, responsible woman of the nineties, wanted to be. She was also everything, or at least a lot of things, I wasn't. I could picture Pat O'Dougherty if she heard me defining a subject in terms of myself. The practice was more insidious than sex.

"Look," Sugar said, and I knew she was looking at her watch, "think about it. I said this piece has your name written all over it, but if you're not interested, I know a dozen writers who'll kill for a crack at it." She hesitated for a split second, which is long enough to put the fear of God, or at least the competition, in any freelance writer. "Not that I'm suggesting for a minute they could give it your spin, pie. But I do want to get moving on it, so think it over and let me know in a couple of days if you're interested."

I looked at my view of the East River. I heard the roar of solid-state motors as all those other writers began warming up their tape recorders and word processors. I told her I didn't need a couple of days. I was interested.

Then, less than an hour later, Dexter St.John called from Vienna, where he was attending a conference, to say he was going to be back in town the following week and ask if I wanted to have dinner. At least that was what I thought he was saying. The phone line crackled with static, or maybe that was Pat O'Dougherty's warning breaking up the connection. I told Dexter St.John I'd love to have dinner.

Then I did something embarrassing. The next afternoon— almost a week before he was due in, but as a freelancer I've had to train myself never to procrastinate—while I was standing in line at the cash register of the local cut-rate drugstore, my hand, having a will of its own, reached out to the display of condoms, took a package off the rack, and dropped it into the plastic basket with my Nexxus hair conditioner, coated-to-prevent-stomach-upset aspirin, and paperback copies of three of Emma Weill's books. I know most of my friends would say there was nothing to be embarrassed about. I was merely acting sensibly. Safe sex and all that. But let's face it, the term's an oxymoron. If it's done right, if the emotions are in there for the scrimmage as well as the body, there's nothing safe about it. Then I went home, put away my purchases, and curled up in my window seat with a copy of *Just Don't Tell Me Someday I'll Laugh,* by Emma Weill.

Two

FOR THE NEXT couple of days I immersed myself in Emma Weill's world. I bought and read eight of her nine books. It was like being in high school again, acne and all. The books brought back every shame and insecurity I could remember, a few I'd managed to forget, some that nobody had dared talk about when I was growing up, and one or two that hadn't existed then. I understood why certain schools and libraries had banned her books. I also understood why millions of girls going through the torturous process of becoming women had embraced them. Emma Weill wrote as if she were one of them. She was either a smart and empathetic cookie or a woman whose development had been dangerously arrested.

I'd bought the eight books in paperback, but there was one more I had trouble tracking down. Sugar had been wrong when she'd told me all the books were still selling like hotcakes. One had gone out of print. It was called *Happily Ever After,* and by the time I tracked it down at a branch library and read it, I knew why it was no longer in print. The book, I saw from the jacket, had been touted as Emma Weill's first adult novel, but it wasn't an adult novel or even a young adult novel. It was a juvenile novel on, as the title indicated, the adult topic of marriage. Boy met girl happily, boy courted girl happily, boy married girl happily, and boy and girl lived, as the title indicated, happily ever after. It was entirely lacking in drama and conflict, not to mention credibility. By the time I finished the book, my mouth was bitter with the acrid aftertaste of artificial sweetener. I told myself Emma Weill wasn't such a smart cookie after all, but then I was a cynic, at least in this area.

After I'd read all Emma Weill's books, I went down to Forty-second Street to the main branch of the library to read what other people had written about her. This was the background research, the kind I could do with reference books and journals and computers rather than friends and colleagues and former spouses, though in this case there was none of the last. There was only the husband she'd married straight out of college and stayed married to for twenty-one years. Though I disapproved of the first part of that achievement, I was willing to suspend judgment about the second. There's a quote, from Auden I think, that I keep meaning to look up. Something about any marriage, happy or unhappy, being more interesting than any romance, no matter how passionate, because marriage is not the result of fleeting emotion but the creation of time and will. Every time I remember the observation it strikes me as insightful or at least intriguing. Then I recall the way some of my long-married friends pronounce the word *darling* or *honey* or even their husband's names, and remember how their husbands talk about their wives' work or lack of work or their obsessive housekeeping or disorganized bookkeeping, and think that Auden should have stuck to poetry.

Nonetheless, I couldn't stop thinking about the differences between Emma Weill and me. They went back a long way. What I hadn't told Sugar when she'd asked me if I recognized the name, because I didn't think it would seriously affect the piece, was that I already knew Emma Weill. At least I had known her when her name was Emma Bliss and she was growing up, a year ahead of me, in the same small town. Actually it was a medium-size city with a small-town mentality and a single claim to fame or at least notoriety. In the early 1950s, when Emma was a toddler and I was an infant, three commercial airplanes had plunged and skidded and crashed into a single half mile of the city within sixty days of one another. There was no connection between the calamities. They were just a series of accidents that could have happened anywhere at any time, only they probably wouldn't, because according to an actuary quoted in a copy of *The New York Times* I found when Babe and I were cleaning out my parents' house, three plane crashes wouldn't recur within a half-mile area within sixty days in the next thirty-six million years.

In any event by the time Emma and I were growing up, the local kids no longer referred to the town as Planecrash, NJ, and though the adults remembered that accidents could and did happen, they too had other things on their minds. The town was one of those smug isolated communities where scandal spread like mushrooms in the damp climate of rumor. Everyone knew everyone else's secrets and exaggerated them. Certainly everyone knew about the Blisses. In an era—the eleventh hour of an era—when the nuclear family was what people meant when they said "family," Emma Bliss was the product of a *broken home.* The communal voice draped the words in a shroud. Emma's father had *taken up* with his secretary. I can still remember the scandal. My mother talked about it endlessly, with Babe, with her other friends, even with the housekeeper who slept in and the woman who came in once a week to do the ironing. They said Mr. Bliss should rot in hell. They said mark their words one day he'd crawl to Mrs. Bliss on his hands and knees and beg forgiveness. The woman who came in to do the ironing suggested that Mr. Bliss should put it on a windowsill and have Mrs. Bliss slam the window on it. No one would say what *it* was, but by that time I had a pretty good idea. They all agreed. Mr. Bliss should be punished. And Mrs. Bliss should sit tight. Let her wait it out, they said. He'll get tired of the tramp, they predicted. At least she still has the position, my mother reasoned.

But Emma's mother saw things differently. She was too proud, some said. She was too impatient, others suggested. She was very foolish, they all agreed. She divorced Mr. Bliss, who promptly went out and realized everyone's worse fears. He married the tramp.

The women of the community shook their heads. They'd warned the first Mrs. Bliss. Now when they talked about her, there was an undercurrent of anger in their voices. The more they tried to hide it, the sharper their voices grew. Though no one ever said as much, they all wished she'd just disappear.

The first Mrs. Bliss didn't disappear. She opened a store. It was called The Silky Way and sold nightgowns and robes and bras and girdles and garter belts. My mother and her friends and my friends' mothers flocked to it. They took their trade there as if it were a moral duty. The angrier they were at her existence, a reminder of the precariousness of their own, the guiltier they felt about their anger, the more they bought. They patronized the store to show their support for the first Mrs. Bliss, and her daughter, and the sacred institution of marriage, first marriage. *Patronize* was the operative word.

I remember the women coming out of that small store carved from an old shingle house in a half-residential area clutching their purchases and their sense of generosity to themselves gleefully. I even remember the store. Inside, it gave off the aura of an overripe peach. There was peach paint and peach carpeting and peach chintz hanging tantalizingly in front of the two tiny fitting rooms. And there was the decaying aroma of heavy perfume and thick dusting powder and too much flesh packed too close together. The place was always crowded with women. Women talking and laughing and gossiping and sniping. Women hooking and strapping and stuffing themselves into shape. Fat women trying to look thin, and skinny women padding themselves into voluptuousness; sexy women strutting their stuff in flimsy lingerie, and no-nonsense women fingering garments so solid they were called foundations; older women whose cleavage rippled and wrinkled like accordions, and child-women with skin as smooth and rosy as the peach-tinted walls. And I remember, moving through it all numbly, folding merchandise and wrapping packages and ringing up sales like a sleepwalker, or just a girl who wanted to be somewhere else, Emma.

She was a thin girl made up of angles so sharp they looked hazardous to the touch. Sitting in the library, I realized with that terrible suspiciousness of our times that masquerades as psychological sophistication that Emma Bliss had probably been anorexic. She'd worn her thick black hair in a cap that fringed her dark eyes and curled forward over her cheeks. Her mouth was a wide nervous slash in her pale face. Even at that age she'd had the doomed look of a twenties movie star, or Dorothy Parker. She'd had some of the persona too. She spoke her mind, and she didn't speak to a lot of people, and in her independence and mystery I found her more glamorous than the sunny popular girls with more ordinary looks and acceptable accomplishments. As an only child who'd taken her time in arriving and the apple of my aunt Babe's as well as my parents' eyes, I didn't have much experience with independence or mystery.

It never occurred to me back there in that suffocating peach seraglio that Emma and I would end up entangled in each other's lives. Sitting in the library that afternoon, I still didn't believe it. But then I sometimes lack imagination. Or maybe only a sense of irony. For example, I never got the joke that went around among my mother's friends when Mrs. Bliss divorced Mr. Bliss. "I could never divorce him," one of them would say to another about her own husband. "I could kill him," she'd add, "but I could never divorce him." Then they'd exchange knowing looks and laugh. I didn't understand the joke. Or maybe I just found it too frightening to laugh at.

I noticed the derelict across the table smiling at me and realized in my reverie I'd been staring at him. I opened another magazine and turned to an interview with Emma Weill. In this one her husband had got in the act too. He wasn't as famous as Emma, but he'd managed to stir some minor controversy. His admirers called him a visionary, a voice in the wilderness, a state-of-the-art high-tech conscience of postmodern society. His detractors called him a crackpot.

Julian Weill was, like me, a freelance writer. Unlike me, he published serious articles about, or perhaps exposés of, the health hazards of microwave ovens and cellular phones and computers. I seemed to remember hearing somewhere—editors and freelance writers are an incestuous bunch—that he had a book under contract on the connection between electromagnetic fields and various forms of cancer.

I sat staring at the particles of dust that danced in the wedges of sunlight slanting through the high windows and thinking about Emma Weill and her husband. In a good year Julian Weill probably pulled down fifteen thousand dollars. I mention the fact not in condescension but in admiration. You don't have a brownstone in the Nineties between Park and Madison, a waterfront house on Shelter Island, one kid at Princeton, and another at Brearley on fifteen thousand dollars a year. Emma Weill was a hell of a breadwinner. Again I made the comparison I wasn't supposed to. I take care of myself, but a husband and two children? Not bloody likely.

I went back to trying to piece together a portrait of the man Emma Bliss had married. All the articles on her made the obligatory reference to his supportiveness. Julian Weill took the kids to the dentist when Emma Weill was on a publicity tour and did his share of the housework. Who were they kidding? With her sales figures, a full-time housekeeper did everyone's share of the housework. One of the articles even mentioned that Dr. Weill served up a mean vegetarian lasagna.

The title before his name rang a bell. I suppose I remembered because I'd been impressed at the time. Even in those days I'd been a pushover for certain kinds of moral and intellectual credentials. Years ago, when Emma Bliss married, my mother had sent me the announcement from the local paper. The gesture wasn't as peculiar as it seems, at least it wasn't if you knew my mother. In those days she was always sending me engagement and wedding announcements of girls I'd grown up with. She stopped doing it only when the marriage announcements began to turn into remarriage announcements. At any rate, I remembered being impressed by Emma's marriage or at least by the man she'd married. Julian Weill had returned from two years in the Peace Corps, got a Ph.D. in physics, and was, at the time of his marriage to Emma, a promising young professor at a large midwestern university.

I paged through some of the articles again. There were no references to Julian Weill's academic past. Apparently he'd jumped the tenure track for a higher, if less secure, path and never looked back. I decided his admirers and detractors were both right. He was a visionary *and* a crackpot. You'd be surprised how often the two go hand in hand.

I put away my notes and returned the books and magazines to the desk. As I made my way down the wide marble staircase to the main floor, I went on thinking about Emma Weill's professional success and her two beautiful children and her enduring marriage. Especially about her enduring marriage. If you believed the psychological studies and sociological statistics, Emma Weill was a sure candidate for divorce. But Emma Weill gave credence to another school of thought. She was living proof that the best training for a happy life is a miserable childhood. I thought about my own safe, easy youth with a mother who had more than enough time for me and a father who came home every night like clockwork. I decided not to pursue the analogy.

I came out of the library into the crowded midtown afternoon. On the wide front steps leading down to Fifth Avenue, kids ate ice-cream cones in the gritty sunshine, and the homeless slept, and the un- and underemployed watched a mime strutting up and down behind passersby, mimicking their foibles and drawing roars of laughter from the crowd. I gave the mime a wide berth and started east.

I'm an inveterate walker in the city, and I had plenty of time to walk home that day. In fact, I had nothing pressing to do at all, though I did have an invitation to a gallery opening that night and another to a wine-and-cheese party to garner attention for the plight of the white-naped crane. Freelance journalism might not provide financial security, but as long as you have an occasional by-line, you'll never lack for offers of waxy cheese, mediocre chardonnay, and bizarre entertainment. There were also friends I could call for a movie or dinner: several women, a couple of gay men, and one straight historian whose investment banker wife rarely knocked off work before ten or eleven, all of whom knew if not all about me, then a great deal, and about whom I knew as much. I'd probably end up going to one of the events or calling one of the friends, though I wasn't particularly enthusiastic about either prospect. There was nothing I really did want to do, outside of work, until my dinner with Dexter.

Don't misunderstand me. I was looking forward to Dexter, but I wasn't counting on Dexter. I hadn't forgotten the interview I'd had with his former wife while I was working on the profile. "Dex was great to be around," she'd told me over tea in the Fifth Avenue apartment she shared with her second husband and her daughter by her first marriage. "The only problem was that he wasn't around much."

As I turned up Madison Avenue, I thought of another story

from my childhood, one my mother used to tell me about Babe. During the war, which to my mother meant World War II, Babe had fallen in love with a flier. In those days you had to be out of your mind, my mother used to warn me, to fall in love with a flier. Everyone had known the statistics. Years later, when I was growing up, my mother could still quote them. The life expectancy of a flier in the Eighth Air Force was fifteen missions. The assigned tour of duty was twenty-five. Babe had said to hell with statistics and married her flier.

I made my way up Madison Avenue past Brooks Brothers and Paul Stuart and Tripler's, all the places my mother used to go to buy shirts and ties and sweaters and socks for my father.

I knew why I was suddenly remembering my mother's stories about Babe and her flier. My mother wouldn't find a man who spent his life soaring around the world for peace and health any more reliable than a man who'd risked his life flying for war and destruction. You'd have to be out of your mind, she'd say.

Three

WHEN I OPENED the door to Dexter St. John, the first thing I noticed was that he hadn't come straight from the airport but had stopped at his apartment or his office on the way. The shirt he was wearing, though slightly frayed at the collar, was too fresh to have spent the better part of a day on an airplane. There was also a thread of dried blood on his upper lip right beneath his nose where he'd cut himself shaving. Dexter's nose is his one unusual feature. For the most part he's an ordinary-looking man. In the unlikely event he ever committed a crime, the police wouldn't have much to go on. His height is average, perhaps an inch or two above. His build is average, perhaps a pound or two below. His eyes, behind nondesigner horn-rimmed glasses, are brown. His receding hair is brown. But his nose, which according to old photographs was once thin and straight and vaguely patrician, was broken and badly set during his boarding school days. The result gives him the faintly pugilistic air of an ex-fighter. The first time I saw him I knew from the way he held himself that he wore the nose as a badge of honor. Just because the milk of human kindness flows in my veins, it said, it doesn't mean there's an insufficiency of testosterone in my glands. I hadn't mentioned the testosterone in the profile. I'd merely described the nose.

We stood in the door to my apartment for a single awkward

moment. At least it was awkward for me. I'd probably spent a couple of hundred hours with the man. I'd interviewed him endlessly, sat in on his meetings, and followed him around town to appointments. I'd shared overmayonnaised takeout sandwiches at his desk, gone to dinners where he'd spoken, and once, toward the end of the series of interviews when he was late for one of those dinners, through the door to the bathroom in his office that he'd left half open so we could talk, watched him shave. There's something about watching a man shave—I don't know, maybe it's the sheer otherness of the act—that's more erotic than all the crotch-bulging underwear ads plastered on all the buses in the city. It occurred to me, remembering the incident now, that the night I watched Dexter St.John shave was the night I began thinking about Pat O'Dougherty's advice. At any rate, after all that time and all those encounters that passed for intimacies, I wasn't sure how to greet him. Until now we'd always shaken hands. I stuck out my hand. He looked at it for a moment, then took it and on his way through the door grazed my cheek with his. I wasn't going to make too much of that. I'd seen him do the same thing to any woman within reach when he was working a room to raise money for the fund.

We went into the living room. I asked him if he wanted a drink, though I knew him well enough to know not only that he did but that it would be, depending on the season, either scotch and soda or vodka and tonic. He said he did and followed me into the kitchen while I got the ice and out of it again when I carried the bucket to the campaign table I use as a bar. It was a novel experience. For the past several months I'd been following him around.

We took our drinks to the window seat and settled at either end facing each other. The buildings of Roosevelt Island burned pink in the reflection of the setting sun.

I asked him how his trip had gone. He told me. He told me about an overcrowded refugee camp, and a hospital without medicine, and a conference where it was determined that for the price of one soft drink for every person in the world the number of people expected to be infected with HIV by the year 2000 could be cut in half. Talk about sound bites. It was only one of half a dozen he gave me in the first half hour.

"Wait," I said, "I'll get my tape recorder."

His hand went to his hairline, then stopped and fell to his side. "I'm sorry. I think this job is getting to me."

I didn't say anything to that, but I was thinking maybe it was, or maybe I'd misread him. It was possible that Dexter St.John liked me and wanted to spend time with me. It was also possible that he thought he could get more media mileage out of me down the road. Perhaps the people I know, the work I do, and the worlds I move in have skewed my view, but suddenly the latter possibility seemed more likely. I remembered the small foil packets sitting in my night table. There's nothing tragic about living alone, but there's heartbreak in living alone with a packet of unopened condoms in your night table drawer. The words ran through my mind like a line from a bad country and western song.

Dexter asked me where I wanted to have dinner. I mentioned an Indian restaurant in the neighborhood and a Thai and an Armenian. Then I realized my mistake. "If you've had enough of all that for a while, there's a neo-WASP place a few blocks away. Underseasoned meat, listless vegetables, and drinks the size of Olympic pools."

He told me it was politically incorrect to make fun of minorities and said he knew a great Italian place nearby. We left my apartment and walked west into the last rays of daylight that spilled across the river from New Jersey and down the cross street.

The restaurant was dimly lit, and I had trouble getting my sight back. I was still trying to focus when Dexter asked me, in a suspiciously casual voice, when he was going to see the profile.

The idea that he simply liked me suddenly seemed downright absurd.

I told him it was scheduled to run in the August issue, which meant it would be out in July.

"It takes that long?"

"It used to take longer before they went on computer."

He leaned back from the table and crossed his legs. Maybe it's my training, but I found the careless pose as suspicious as the casual voice. "I don't suppose there's a chance you'd let me read it before then."

It wasn't that I'd never let a subject see a piece before it had run—there have been times that's been the only way to get the interview—but I hadn't agreed to let Dexter see this before it ran. On the other hand, there was no reason I shouldn't let him see it. As I said, I couldn't imagine how he could help liking it, or rather, I could imagine but gave him more credit. But there was no reason I should either.

I leaned back and tried for a casual look of my own, though I know from experience that when I force a smile, my mouth gets thinner and my long upper lip longer, and I end up looking more like an unhappy pretender to an outdated Bourbon throne than the insouciant woman I'm striving for. "Not a snowball's chance in hell," I told him. "To coin a perfectly new cliché."

"Is it going to hurt that much?" he asked, but he smiled when he said it, a more convincing smile than I'd managed to carry off, and I knew whatever else happened or, from the look of things, didn't happen between us, Dexter's reaction to the profile was one thing I didn't have to worry about.

We came out of the restaurant into the hectic city night. Akitas and Pomeranians and King Charles spaniels—there are no mutts on the Upper East Side—strutted at the ends of expandable leashes. Groups of men and women stood on corners telling each other what a good time they'd had and how they really ought to do this more often. Couples window-shopped, some with their arms around each other, some holding hands, some keeping a tense distance that warned the buyer to beware. In front of a corner greengrocer a young Korean sat on a wooden crate shelling peas. There were people and lights and good feelings, and if you didn't know how fast things could move and change in the city, you'd be lulled by the aura. Even those of us who knew could be lulled. Dexter and I walked along amiably with a couple of inches of mild spring night between us.

We were standing at the corner waiting for the light to change when I saw his head swivel away from the oncoming traffic. The abruptness of the gesture struck me, and I turned to follow his gaze.

The street was a corridor of darkness. I could barely make out a shadow. It was moving. My eyes distinguished an iron gate. The shadow was writhing against the gate. I made out arms and legs squirming in the darkness. The shadow looked as if it were impaled on the gate.

As we stood watching—I don't think it could have taken more than a few seconds—the shadow became two shadows, and the writhing turned into a struggle. At least that was the way it looked to two New Yorkers in the last decade of the twentieth century.

I took a step toward the pay phone on the corner. With any luck it might be working. With a little more luck 911 would get there in less than half an hour. Dexter wasn't counting on luck. He started down the block toward the shadows at a sprint.

"Are you crazy?" I called after him, but if he heard me, he didn't give any sign.

Maybe it's because in my work I'm accustomed to staying on the sidelines. Or maybe I'm just a coward. I know there are women who would have run after him. I know there are women who would have tried to help. I didn't. At least I didn't until it was too late.

I don't mean too late for Dexter to save himself. I mean too late for me to prove myself.

I stood at the corner watching him run. Even if I hadn't done the research, I would have known that he'd been something of a jock when he was younger. He reached the struggling shadows. I saw his hand go out to them. He's crazy, I thought, reckless and stupid and crazy. I didn't care if he had made it through Peru and Somalia and Croatia unscathed. This was East Eighty-first Street.

One of the shadows whirled around. I waited for the scuffle. I waited, nails digging into my palms, for the flash of a knife or report of a gun.

There was no glint of steel or roar of an explosion. There wasn't even any movement. There was only the shadow of Dexter and, perhaps a foot away in the darkness, the two other shadows.

Then over the hum of passing traffic, steady as waves on a beach, there was a noise. It wasn't loud, but it was shocking. It was the sound of laughter.

I started down the block toward it. Dexter turned away from the shadows and began walking toward me. We met in the middle. He was smiling and shaking his head. He reached up to smooth his hair. This time he didn't stop at the hairline but went through with the gesture.

"That'll teach me to mind my own business," he said, and shook his head again.

"What was it? What happened?"

"A couple of kids." He looked at me and laughed again. "A couple of kids necking each other up."

"Necking? It looked more as if she were being impaled."

"Impaled by love," he said. "Or at least sex."

He started walking. I could tell from the way he held himself, head erect, back straight, that the colleague I'd interviewed and quoted in the profile was right. For all his self-deprecating jokes, Dexter St.John did not take himself lightly.

He mentioned the profile once more that night. We were sitting at opposite ends of the window seat again. There was no traffic on the river, but overhead the lights of planes on their way into JFK and La Guardia cut across the night like slow-motion shooting stars. His feet were up on the coffee table—his shirts had holes, but not his socks—and his head was resting against the wall, and his eyes were closed. I was beginning to think he was asleep when he spoke.

"About the profile . . ."

I glanced over at him. He hadn't opened his eyes.

"What about it?" I heard the edge in my voice.

He opened his eyes. "You said it's finished, right? Written, accepted, set to go."

"Right."

"Isn't there an expression for that kind of thing in magazines? What do you call it? Putting it to bed?"

I told him the term usually applied to a whole issue rather than a single article, and in any event people didn't use it much anymore.

"But from our point of view," he insisted, "as far as this piece you wrote on me goes, you've put it to bed."

I thought of the copy of the final draft sitting in the small oak filing cabinet beneath my desk in the bedroom. I was not going to show him the profile, no matter what. I told him that was right. I'd put it to bed.

His mouth curled in a tentative smile I'd never seen before, not in all the hours I'd spent with him. His hand went to his hairline and smoothed his hair. "That takes care of the article. Now what do you say we do the same to us?"

It was my last chance not to let Pat O'Dougherty down. And I blew it.

That night I sat up in bed with my back against the head-board and watched Dexter St.John sleep. I did it partly in amazement because nobody except me had been in my bed for some time. Since, to be exact, shortly after the post–Anita Hill pro-choice march on Washington, which had led me, upon my return, to tell a political writer who'd spent a good part of the past four years in my bed that I felt guilty about his wife even if he didn't, which led the writer to turn up on my doorstep a week later with his laptop in one hand and a duffel in the other, announcing that he'd left his wife, which was just about the best news I'd heard since Pat O'Dougherty had given me that first assignment, but then a week later I got a crack at a terrific arti-cle that meant spending some time in Santa Fe—at least it had looked terrific at the time; no one could have guessed that I'd end up with nothing more than expenses and a kill fee—and by the time I got back, the writer and his wife had reconciled, and I was left with my rediscovered scruples.

I also watched Dexter sleep because after all those months I'd thought I'd come to know him, but of course, I hadn't known him at all. For the first time I was seeing him naked in more ways than one.

He slept in the pool of amber light cast by the lamp we'd left on, sprawled on his stomach, arms and legs spread out like a swastika. He wasn't a big man, but he took up a big space. Or maybe that was merely my perception after the past few years. His breath came and went so deeply I could see his rib cage move. An artery at his temple pulsed electric blue. He slept with the watchfulness of a slumbering animal.

One of his hands was still on my thigh. It lay stretched wide, the long fingers, tanned from God knows where, splayed dark against my skin, making it look unnaturally pallid. I shifted position. His hand began to close into a fist. The gesture hurt. I lifted his hand off my leg and put it on the bed. His fist clenched and unclenched several times.

As I went on watching him, I began to think about Emma Weill. I thought of her husband of twenty-one years, and her two children, and her successful career. Dexter's fist opened and closed again. I thought of what Dexter's former wife had said about him and what he'd said about his daughter, whom he admitted he saw too rarely and couldn't admit he didn't know well enough. I don't believe in gender generalizations, but I couldn't help noticing the difference. When women are at the center, it tends to hold. When men are at the center, they set up a powerful centrifugal force.

I turned out the lamp on the night table, turned on my side, and pulled the quilt over both of us. I put my hand over his clenched fist. His arm jerked away and disappeared under his body like a turtle retreating into its shell.

When I opened my eyes the next morning, Dexter was already awake. He was even wearing his glasses. And he'd brought in the papers. They were strewn about the bed. He knew how to make himself at home. People who move around a lot are like that.

He peered down at me through his glasses. I wondered if he was trying to place me, the same way he might try to place an anonymous hotel room he awakened in.

"How're you doing, ace?" he said.

I thought that was nice. Then I had second thoughts. Maybe it was a generic term of endearment. Maybe I really was like the hotel room. He was buying time while he tried to remember who I was. When he spoke again, it got worse.

"I have a confession to make," he said.

I wondered if I actually flinched or if it only felt that way. I lay there staring up at him, hidden behind his horn-rimmed glasses, and waited for the worst, though these days there were so many bad possibilities, I wasn't sure which I would categorize as the worst.

"I plagiarized," he said.

"What?"

"Last night. I plagiarized."

I still didn't get it. After all, I was the writer in the bed.

"That line about putting the book to bed and then us. It's from Christopher Morley."

All I could think was that no one even read Christopher Morley anymore, but that seemed beside the point.

"I've been wanting to use it . . . well, not exactly since I met you, but for quite a while. I was just waiting until you'd finished the profile."

He took off his glasses, put them on the table, and turned to me. The *Times* and *Newsday* and the *Washington Post* crackled and crunched beneath our weight, and a ship's horn sounded low and wistful beyond the windows. Then the sounds faded away, and I climbed to a place I'd never been before and hung there by a thread.

It was after ten by the time we got out of bed. I was surprised. In all the months I'd followed Dexter around, I'd never seen him not in a hurry. I mentioned the fact when he came into the kitchen, where I was making coffee. His hair was still wet from the shower, and he was wearing a monogrammed towel around his waist. My initials, HRF, ran down one of his thighs, as if he'd been branded. I thought that was nice.

He said he had just enough time to swing past his apartment to pick up some clean clothes and his office to get his mail before he caught the shuttle for Washington. His tone wasn't exactly businesslike, but I had heard him use it on a variety of subordinates during the months I'd followed him around. I'd been scooping coffee from the canister into the filter. I'd figured on several cups each. Now I began scooping it back.

He picked up the whistling kettle, which was making an unholy racket, and poured water into the filter. Most men would have just stood around waiting for me to take it off the fire. I forgave the tone.

He said he'd be back in town for the weekend and asked me what I felt like doing. My mother and Pat O'Dougherty, two of the more unlikely allies in my personal history, elbowed their way into the kitchen, but they were too late. I told him I felt like doing anything he did.

After Dexter left, I went back to the bedroom. Crumpled newspapers littered the bed. The quilt and one of the pillows had slipped to the floor. For as long as I've been freelancing, I've lived with the domino theory of self-discipline. All I have to do is leave the bed unmade one morning, the next day I won't bother to get out of my ratty old flannel bathrobe, and before I know it, I'll have turned into one of those crazy old ladies found dead in her apartment with thirty years of old newspapers and twenty-seven stray cats. But that morning I stepped around the quilt and pillow, walked past the unmade bed to my desk, sat, and took the folder with the final draft of Dexter's profile from the small oak filing cabinet.

I read it through slowly. He couldn't possibly mind the quote about the food and drugs that disappeared into dirty deals with petty officials of developing nations because he came off as noble but practical. He was bound to love the clash with the activists who'd accused him of culturocentricity because I'd quoted their tirade at such self-incriminating length that by the time Dexter opened his mouth to speak, you could practically hear the sound of a cavalry charge in the background. And the more I reread it, the more convinced I was that the quote from his former colleague merely showed his courage.

Reading the piece with Dexter's eyes made it look different, but it didn't make it look bad. I put the pages back in the folder, put the folder back in the filing cabinet beneath my desk, and put Dexter out of my mind. At least I stopped worrying about how he'd react to the profile.

Four

I MET Emma Weill for our first interview at a restaurant in her
neighborhood, which wasn't far from my neighborhood, though
in Manhattan walking a block can mean going to another planet
or at least crossing a demarcation line. My neighborhood was
cosmopolitan and vaguely transient, or maybe I only thought of
it that way because of the river. Emma's, like Emma herself, was
fiercely familial. It was crowded with private schools and over-
privileged children. It had also been recently and ferociously
gentrified. You couldn't get your shoes reheeled, or buy a needle
and thread, or get a cup of coffee; but there was at least one,
and frequently more than one, pricey children's clothing store
per block; the local bookstore carried, in addition to every juvenile and young adult book in print, an Italian fashion magazine
that sold for ninety dollars; and the entire area was awash in
caffè latte and decaf cappuccino.

The restaurant she'd suggested had been a Gristede's supermarket in a former life, and there were still exposed pipes overhead and small black-and-white tiles underfoot, which made for
a deafening racket. You'd be surprised how many otherwise reasonable people equate the level of noise in a restaurant with the
quality of food.

I was sitting at a table in a corner that I hoped would be
quiet, or at least bearable, near a long window open to the mild

spring afternoon waiting for Emma and taking in the scene. Kids in gray and blue and plaid uniforms swarmed up and down Madison Avenue, and Filipino and Hispanic and African American women pushed Caucasian babies in Aprica strollers and old people in wheelchairs along the shady side streets, and impeccably dressed matrons sporting airs of invulnerability hurried to volunteer meetings and manicure appointments and lunch.

When I turned from the street back to the restaurant, I saw Emma Weill following the hostess across the big, busy room to my table. The cap of dark hair was the same, and the wide slash of mouth, and she still had the aura of a twenties movie star, though she no longer looked doomed. She looked as sleek and invulnerable as those women hurrying past the window. She also, I noticed as she got closer to the table, was wearing the same silk and linen tweed jacket I was. I wondered if that boded complicity or competition, though I'd worked with enough women over the years to know the two weren't mutually exclusive or even necessarily separable.

She reached a thin hand across the table to shake mine. "Love your jacket."

"I was just admiring yours," I answered as she slid into the chair across from me.

"I've been living in it for the past month."

I told her I'd just got mine a few days ago. "I practically camped out in front of Joan and David till it went on sale."

A small tic, almost but not quite a smile, pulled at her wide mouth. I couldn't figure out whether she was pleased that she didn't have to wait for sales or embarrassed that I did.

"I have to ask you something before we start," she said after we'd ordered two glasses of wine.

"Anything." It wasn't entirely a lie. There are few questions I won't answer or stories I won't tell about myself if I think they'll elicit better answers and stories from a subject. Few, but not many.

"Is Hallie really Hilda?"

I made a show of wincing. "You are now one of the few people in the world who can blackmail me."

"Something rang a bell, so I looked you up. When I saw the town, I was pretty sure." She narrowed her eyes slightly. "I think I even recognize you. You look a lot like your mother."

"You remember my mother?" I was incredulous. My mother had left fingerprints on me, but I'd never thought of her as the kind of woman other people remembered.

"Actually I remembered her better than I did you. She used to come into my mother's store a lot."

"My mother used to go into a lot of stores a lot. It was before the era of professional shoppers, but no one ever accused my mother of being an amateur."

Emma Weill managed a polite smile, but I had the feeling she was thinking of something else.

"I always thought she had a lot of dignity."

I wanted to ask her if we were talking about the same woman, but of course, other people's parents are the adults we fall in love with on the rebound from our own. I'd been no exception, although Babe wasn't anyone else's parent. Suddenly I felt sorry that my mother wasn't around so I could pass on the compliment. "Dignity," I repeated. "She would have loved that."

The waiter came back and took our orders, and then I opened with my usual ploy. It's not really a ploy, but you'd be amazed how many people freeze at the sight of an ordinary tape recorder, though I doubted Emma Weill would.

"I hope you don't mind if I take notes," I said.

"Of course not."

I bent to the briefcase on the floor beside the table, took a small tape recorder from it, and put it on the table between us. "That's the way I take notes." I managed a smile, though I knew it was one of my forced Bourbon-pretender smiles. "Okay?"

"Clever," Emma said. "And okay. Preferable, in fact. That way we both know exactly what was said."

"If there's anything you don't want on the record, just tell me, and I'll turn it off. That way I can be sure I won't make a mistake and use it."

Her eyes held mine. "I have a better idea. Why don't I just not say anything I don't want you to use, and then neither of us will have to worry?"

"Fine," I agreed, but of course, the reporter in me had already begun to wonder what she had to hide. Cooked books she didn't want the IRS to know about? Bottles of vodka or vials of funny powder in the medicine cabinet? An offstage girlfriend? Only these days people didn't hide those things. They made capital of them on television talk shows. So what else could it be? Malraux said the truth about a man lies in what he tries to hide. Of course, he also said women want to be unhappy. Or was that Mauriac? I decided I was making too much of it—Emma Weill merely didn't want to come off looking foolish—and got down to work.

I started with the simple questions, the ones with straightforward, easy answers. How do you write, longhand or on a word processor? When do you write, daily or as inspiration strikes? Which of your books is your favorite?

I could tell from the way she answered that she'd been doing this for years. She wrote on a word processor at regular hours and loved all her books equally. Then she hesitated as if she were debating whether to confide something, but I knew this wasn't a confidence, merely a clever bit of business she'd picked up from some overpaid media trainer. Don't misunderstand me. I didn't dislike her. I just recognized that she was a pro. That was okay. That made two of us.

"Including *Happily Ever After*," she said. It was a good

trick. She'd brought up her weak spot before I could. "Maybe especially *Happily Ever After*."

"Then your favorite book is your least successful?"

She crossed her arms on the table and leaned toward me as if another confidence were on the way. "My books are like my children." She stopped again. "Do you have children, Hallie?"

I told her I didn't.

Her eyes darted to my left hand, then quickly away.

"No children, no husband," I said.

She seemed embarrassed that I'd noticed her glance, though it had been about as subtle as a searchlight. Apparently, certain issues were still capable of cracking the professional veneer.

"You have plenty of time." Her voice had the inane and excessive cheerfulness of a nurse encouraging a terminally ill patient to eat her dinner or take her medicine.

"If I run out on the street now, grab the first man I see, and happen to be ovulating, I have plenty of time. But it's okay. You haven't hit a sore spot."

I could tell from her too-bright smile that she didn't believe me.

"I guess I'm a throwback to another generation," she said. It was supposed to be an apology or at least a disclaimer. She hadn't meant to imply she was superior to me. Only she believed she was, and the more she said, the worse it got. "I married young." She went on. "I had my children young. And I stayed married." Her voice snagged on its own sharp little peak of triumph. I waited. I wasn't going to help her out of this. She shrugged. "So now you see why I love *Happily Ever After*. Even if other people don't. I bet you didn't." We were back to the-best-defense-is-an-offense ploy.

"I didn't think it was as honest as your other books."

She laughed. It was a light, self-deprecating laugh that probably played well on talk shows. "So people have told me. Write about teenage pregnancy and eating disorders and divorced parents, and everyone hails you for unflinching candor and gutsy realism and telling it like it is, to quote a few of my better reviews. But just try to tell a story about a boy and girl who fall in love, marry, and don't end up a year or two or ten later in divorce court or other people's beds, and everyone calls you a liar or at least a dewy-eyed romantic."

She'd outcynicked the cynic, but I didn't admit as much. I didn't say anything. That's one of the hardest interview techniques to learn. In normal conversation silence is anathema. In interviews it's merely a vacuum. Few subjects can resist filling it.

"But I'm not a liar." Emma went on, as I'd hoped she would. "Or even a dewy-eyed romantic. I'm just an ordinary woman who got incredibly lucky."

She stopped again, and this time she didn't continue because we both knew she'd said something important. I'm not suggesting it was true, but we both knew it was quotable.

After lunch I went back to my apartment to transcribe the tape of the interview, but all the time I was working I kept thinking of Emma Weill's comment about my mother and her dignity.

My mother was not an easy woman to celebrate. She'd been a spoiled girl and a pampered woman, though she had an agreeable streak and an appallingly soft heart for small children and beleaguered women and other species that didn't threaten her. But a lifetime of coddling had left her both unworldly and frightened of the world. She shrank her universe to two things, my father and me. In our current era of larger-than-life feminist heroines—fearless midwives who delivered babies, saved the mothers' souls and bodies, and outsmarted misogynist doctors at every turn; iron-willed immigrants who propped up drunken, debased husbands and raised children by the dozen against insurmountable odds; crusading firebrands who braved society's scorn so that other women could vote or hold jobs or have access to birth control—my mother doesn't quite cut it. Nor do the other women I grew up among, not even Babe with her tragedy or Emma's mother with her betrayal. Their hardships were less dire than those of the indomitable women of feminist lore. Their courage lay in keeping their misfortunes secret or at least private, their triumph in preserving the status quo. Their lives, in short, were not the stuff of which epics or even magazine profiles are made. Thank God for that, my mother would have said. Nonetheless, they'd left their marks. Emma's comment at lunch was proof of that. We read about and revered and quoted the heroines, but we lived in the shadows of our mothers.

Five

" 'UNDERGARMENTS, FOR EXAMPLE,' " Julian said without looking up from the paper. He reached for his coffee mug, took a sip, and placed it back on the wrought iron and glass table. "Fourteen letters."

Emma went on reading the first section of the paper. She didn't understand the attraction of crossword puzzles. She especially didn't understand Julian's magical faith in them. If he finished the daily puzzle within a given period of time—she wasn't sure how many minutes it was, or maybe he kept changing the number—he'd have a good day. If he filled in all the squares in the Sunday puzzle, he was slated for a successful week. It was a joke, of course, except that she'd seen the tense set of his mouth when he couldn't finish a puzzle and knew it wasn't entirely a joke to him.

Becky leaned toward her father now until her thin shoulder was touching his. "Like, you know, undies," she said.

Julian looked up from the paper at his daughter. "I said fourteen letters, squirt. Don't they teach you to count at that expensive school . . ." His voice trailed off.

Emma sat waiting. Sometimes he went on. This morning he didn't.

She picked up her coffee mug from the table. A blossom from one of the flowering cherry trees they'd planted when they'd bought the house floated on the surface of the black liquid. So much for breakfast in the garden. So much for gracious living. She fished the flower out with a spoon.

"Do you have, like, anything?" Becky asked, still leaning against her father to get a better look at the puzzle.

"*U* blank *m* blank blank *t* blank blank et cetera."

Emma folded the first section of the paper and put it on the empty wrought iron chair. "Unmentionables."

The two dark heads across the table from her snapped up, and her husband and daughter sat staring at her in surprise. Then Julian's mouth curled into a wicked smile. Years ago someone—a roommate? another girl who was crazy about him? —had christened it his lock-up-your-daughters smile. Fortunately both children had inherited it. When Emma was young, strange men were always calling to her on the street. "Smile, honey. You'd be so much prettier if you'd smile."

"Like, pretty good, Mom."

"Spectacular is more like it," Julian said. "That's why I married her. That and her body."

Becky flopped back in her chair and let out an exaggerated groan. "Daaaddy! You are, like, totally gross. A total, you know, sexist pig."

Julian turned the smile on his daughter. "That's me. Unreformed and unrepentant."

Emma poured herself another mug of coffee, picked up the financial section of the paper, and started to read again. She didn't know where the word had come from. It had just popped into her head. She reached the bottom of the column and realized she hadn't understood a word. She went back to the top of the page and started reading again.

She knew exactly where the word had come from. It was the story of her life.

"Twaddle," Julian said. "Four letters."

"Tosh," Emma answered. She looked up again. The smile

had shrunk to a smirk. He'd known the word, of course. It was a common crossword puzzle filler. She shrugged and started the article in the financial section a third time.

She was making too much of it. No one's life was as perfect as it seemed on the surface. Everyone harbored secrets. Things they couldn't mention. She thought of the mother of one of Becky's friends who turned up every now and then with sunglasses camouflaging a bruised eye or black and blue marks on her pale, painfully thin arms and nervous explanations about how accident-prone she was; of her friend Celia who insisted she worked as a saleswoman at Saks merely for the discount, because admitting her husband's financial reverses would have been acknowledging a loss of grace; of another friend's husband who was constantly making salacious jokes about their sex life, though Emma knew from the friend's wine-induced late-night confession that her husband hadn't slept with her for the past nine years. Some of the lies were self-destructive, and some were silly, and some were simply necessary to preserve the social fabric, not to mention spare other people embarrassment. No one wanted to hear about someone else's sexual or financial or criminal problems. Or if people did, it was only to gloat. So if you were smart, you used every trick you knew to keep the picture bright and intact. Sometimes Emma felt like an art restorer toiling over a Greek statue or Renaissance painting, struggling to reverse the ravages and rekindle the glow. The important thing was not to let the minor scratches and lacerations and dirt get you down. The important thing was to remember that beneath all that there was a masterpiece or at least something worth saving. Not that it was seriously in danger. That was one thing she knew for certain. Sometimes she had to laugh. All those people who thought they could pity her. Her friends who suspected, the women who schemed, even that goddamn dean. The memory of him still chafed. The bastard. The superior, condescending bastard. They all thought they knew the story, but there was one thing they didn't know. He'd never leave her, and not only because of the money.

She lifted her mug again. Now there was a bug floating in the coffee. She bet goddamn Martha Stewart didn't have to worry about goddamn flora and fauna in her coffee when she had breakfast in her goddamn garden.

The point was everyone had secrets, unmentionables, and she wouldn't be thinking about them now if it weren't for that interview yesterday afternoon. She didn't know why this particular profile was making her uneasy. She liked doing publicity. Even after all these years she still got a kick out of turning on the television and finding her own face smiling back at her, or opening a magazine and seeing her picture and her words and her achievements—most of all, her achievements—splashed across the pages. She loved having women wait in line in bookstores to have her inscribe copies for their daughters or granddaughters or nieces and to tell her how much they wished they'd had books like hers when they were young. She loved having people she knew and, more important, people she used to know see how far she'd come. Julian teased her about it, but it was a perfectly natural emotion. She remembered an article she'd read years ago about the CEOs of several Fortune 500 companies. All but two had confessed to a lingering wish to show their old high school classmates how well they were doing, and the two who hadn't had gone to the kind of boarding school where becoming anything less than president of the United States was nothing to write home about.

"You know that woman who's doing the piece on me for *Era* . . ." she began, and waited for Julian to look up from the puzzle. She went on waiting. He had impressive powers of concentration.

". . . that interview I did yesterday . . ."

Julian dragged his eyes up from the paper. "What?"

"That woman who's doing an article on me. It's not just a

one-shot newspaper interview. They want an in-depth profile. She plans to follow me around for a while. Talk to you. See all of us together. Of course, I told her she couldn't write about the kids."

"Danielle Miller had her picture in, you know, *People*," Becky said. "The headmistress wouldn't let them inside, so they took pictures of her, like, in front of school."

"Danielle Miller also has a mother who turned her husband's quadruple bypass into a best-seller," Emma said. "I do not exploit my children."

"And your husband has no intention of having a quadruple bypass. There's only so much I'll do for your career, sweetheart."

"Dad, like, stop."

"All I'm asking," Emma went on, "is for you to meet the woman. The one who's doing the article."

"I'm not the celebrity in the family," he said, and went back to the puzzle.

"Don't be ridiculous. You have a reputation in your field. She knew about you."

"She knew about me," he said without looking up, "because she'd done her research on you. Tell her I'm in quarantine with a rare disease. Tell her I'm a recluse. Tell her you haven't seen me in months."

"It'll look funny if you refuse to meet her."

He looked up. "Funny for whom, sweetheart?"

"You know what I mean."

"You mean they might think you're married to a weirdo or a cretin." He made a crazed face at Becky. She returned it. "Or that there's something wrong with you. Like maybe you're a driven career woman instead of a warm, compassionate, self-sacrificing wife and mom. Quick, Becky, get the White House on the phone. Tell them we need Hillary's recipe for chocolate chip cookies ASAP."

"I'll talk to the, you know, reporter," Becky said. "Danielle Miller will, like, die."

Julian did an exaggerated double take at his daughter. "Good Lord, I've sired a celebrity fucker."

"Julian," Emma said.

"Julian," Becky mimicked. "You're not supposed to say, like, fuck in front of me, Daddy. It, like, sets a bad example."

"I just think it's unimaginative," Emma said. "English is a rich language."

"Especially for those who get rich on it. Not complaining, sweetheart, just stating facts." Julian went back to his puzzle.

Emma told herself to drop it, at least for the moment. It wasn't that important. But something in her couldn't let it go. Besides, she'd look like an idiot after that comment she'd delivered at lunch. "I'm just an ordinary woman who got incredibly lucky." He had to agree to meet the reporter.

"Julian . . ." she began again.

"For Christ sake!" His head snapped up in time to notice the way Becky flinched. "All right." He went on in a tone so mellow Emma wouldn't have believed it was the same man if she hadn't known what he was capable of. "Okay, sweetheart. I'll meet her. I'll talk to her. I'll charm the fuckin' pants off her," he promised, and this time Emma didn't comment on his language.

"You don't have to get carried away. Just have dinner with the woman. All three of us. After that PEN party next Thursday. I have to present an award, and she wants to be there. I thought we could all go on for dinner afterward."

"Fine," he said, and bent to his puzzle again.

"You're sure you're free?"

"I said I'd go."

"It's just that I don't want to tell her you're going to be there and then have to make excuses."

He looked up from the paper and smiled the dangerous

smile. "You won't have to make excuses, sweetheart. We'll go to the party together. Couple of the year. Hand in hand. Joined at the fucking hip." He went back to the puzzle.

She sat staring at the top of his head. His hair was still thick and as dark as hers. The difference was he didn't have to do anything to keep it that color.

She glanced at her watch. She had a nine o'clock meeting with a television wunderkind fresh off the redeye who was talking about turning one of her books into a sitcom. At any given point in time someone somewhere was thinking of turning one of her books into something. She wasn't complaining. She just wished it would happen. And she just wished the people who could make it happen weren't so damn young. She didn't understand how men did it. Young women were supposed to make them feel young themselves and virile. Young men made her feel old and maternal. The last time one of those child producers from the Coast had taken her to lunch, she'd had the urge to cut his food for him.

She put the paper aside and stood. "I'm history." She turned to Becky. "And you'd better be too if you don't want to be late for school."

She waited as Becky unfolded herself from the wrought iron chair. Until a year ago the girl had been an amorphous mass of soft, rippling baby fat that oozed and flowed from one shape to another as easily as an amoeba. Emma had watched her, and worried, and sworn she wasn't going to worry. Then the metamorphosis had taken place, and Emma had found something new to fret about. She was determined not to take pride or even pleasure in the long legs and willowy body and coltish elegance, but of course, she did take pleasure and pride, just as she had worried, and Becky, who was no fool, sensed the approval just as she'd felt the disapproval, and Emma knew, damn it, that she was passing on, no matter how subtly, the same treacherous values that had been foisted on her. Once or twice she'd gotten so angry at herself for some slip—an admonition as Becky had reached for another cookie, a sigh of admiration as she'd tried on a pair of jeans or a bikini in a fitting room—that she'd mentioned her fears to Julian. Whatever else they were, they were united about the children.

He'd looked at her for a moment, then shaken his head slowly back and forth as if he couldn't believe her. "For Christ sake, Emma, lighten up."

Becky leaned over now and kissed him on the cheek. "Don't, like, watch, like, too many soaps or eat, like, too many, you know, bonbons," she said as she picked up her backpack from one of the empty chairs.

"Go to school, squirt," he answered with his eyes still on the paper. "So you can, like, get into a good college and become, like, a big success and support a husband in, like, style someday." He looked up at Emma with that fatal grin. "Just like your mama." He turned the smile on Becky. "Now tell me I'm a disgusting, sexist pig."

He held up his right hand with his fingers splayed wide. Becky slapped a high five against it, slung her backpack over her shoulder, and slouched into the house.

"Don't you think," Emma said as she followed Becky up the stairs to the front hall, "that soap opera and bonbon joke is getting a little thin?"

Becky kept going up the stairs. "Come on, Mom. Like, lighten up."

Six

***

DEXTER CAME THROUGH town again the following weekend. This time he didn't stop at his apartment or office on the way in from the airport. I knew because his jaw was dark with stubble, and his khaki trousers had twelve-hour-plane-ride creases around the crotch. He was carrying a hanging bag as well as his briefcase. If I hadn't put my winter coats into summer storage, I never would have been able to fit the bag in the front closet.

I asked him how his flight had been, though I already knew it had been a disaster. When he'd called from Amsterdam, he'd said he'd be in at five. I'd begun worrying at seven. By eight I couldn't stop thinking about those fluke accidents that had branded the town where I'd grown up. At nine I'd called the airline. At ten he'd called me from the airport. It was almost eleven now. He didn't look happy or even particularly well, though I admit he still looked pretty good to me.

"International travel is grossly overrated," he said, and moved in to kiss me hello.

I asked if I could do anything for him.

He smiled and told me I'd make some stand-up comic a great straight woman. Then he passed out.

* * *

When he came to, he diagnosed himself as having a twenty-four-hour bug. Both the evidence and the terminology struck me as medically suspect, but he was the doctor.

He said he'd limp on home. I'm not suggesting he was asking for pity, but he really did use the word *limp*. There was nothing imperious or even businesslike in his tone now.

I told him not to be ridiculous. He was in no shape to travel, even the fifteen blocks to his apartment. And I knew from the one interview we'd had there that it was no place to convalesce. An aura of divorced-man impermanence conspired with in-grained WASP taste to create a Disneyland version of a Williamsburg restoration. Besides, lightweight nursing was the one domestic task I was good at. My mother, the woman of dignity, as Emma Weill remembered her, had provided an excellent role model.

When I was nine or ten, my father went into the hospital for surgery. In those days illness was less a misfortune than a shame to be kept secret at any cost. Cancer, if it was mentioned at all, was called the big C. The phrase *female problems,* hissed sotto voce through tightened lips, covered a multitude of sins and headed off all further inquiries. And if the adults wouldn't level with each other, they certainly weren't going to spell anything out for us kids. To this day I don't know what kind of surgery my father underwent, but I do remember his convalescence in exquisite detail. It went on for some time. At least that's the way I remember it. I suspect it was really a matter of a week or two. But there's one thing about it I am sure of. It was an especially sunny moment in a generally clement family history.

My mother rose to the occasion magnificently. She canceled her shopping expeditions and her bridge games and whatever else she did to get through her days. She banished the maid from her and my father's room—she would do everything herself—cut short her endless phone calls, and even discouraged Babe

from coming to the house. She was all my father's. And he all
hers. Even as a child I knew that this was bliss.

She sang in the kitchen while she baked pies and made soups
and arranged my father's favorite meals on trays, which she
then carried to their room. She hummed while she made the bed
around him and gave him alcohol rubs. She smiled as she sat
beside his bed, jotting down his directives on the letters that
came up from his office, running interception with his clients,
losing to him at gin rummy. She was busy during those days and
weeks my father was laid up in bed, busier than she usually was,
and she moved quickly through the house, but there was an ease
to her movements, as if she were floating, as if she were buoyed
up on a sea of contentment, and sensing that once, close to the
end of his convalescence, I told my mother I wanted to be a
nurse when I grew up. My mother just went on putting the rose
from the trellis beside the back door in the bud vase and the bud
vase on my father's tray, and said no, what I wanted to be was a
wife.

Judging from the evidence, my mother and I were both
wrong, but that night I helped Dexter St.John undress and
steered him into my bed overlooking the East River. He was
asleep before I could hang up his trousers and jacket.

For the better part of the next twenty-four hours I served up
cups of tea and glasses of ginger ale and prodigious amounts of
sympathy. Dexter couldn't get enough of the last. Years ago,
when I was a junior in college, I think, an avuncular gynecologist had told me, in answer to my request for a prescription for
the Pill, that I had to be careful. I'd replied that was exactly
what I was trying to be. What he meant, he'd explained, was
that men wanted only one thing.

Even then I knew the gynecologist was wrong. The undergraduate who'd encouraged me to go to the doctor wanted
unencumbered sex, but he also wanted me to listen to his po-

etry, tell him it was wonderful, and—the last straw—type it up for submission.

That weekend Dexter wanted a wife and mother. Maybe that's a redundancy. Maybe when a man is sick, the distinction between the two disappears entirely. At any rate he cast the role, and I played it. Of course, we both knew it was only playacting. We were still at that early hopeful stage when faking it is a sign of good intentions rather than evidence of bad faith.

Then, twenty-four hours after he'd collapsed in my front hall and as he'd predicted, the symptoms passed, I found that if the avuncular gynecologist hadn't been entirely right, he hadn't been entirely wrong either.

I was in the shower when the recovery hit. The next best thing to the window seat overlooking the river in my apartment is a roomy old-fashioned stall shower with faucets around the sides as well as overhead. When I'd bought the place, with considerable help from my father's estate, the broker had joked that the shower was big enough for a small cocktail party. That was an exaggeration, but it did accommodate two comfortably.

"I thought you were sick," I said when Dexter stepped into it that night. The water cascaded over him, slicking his hair to his head and making his skin glisten. Without his glasses, his eyes were surprisingly naked.

He took the soap from me. "I told you it was a twenty-four-hour bug."

I took the soap back, but of course, that just left his hands free. "How do you know?"

"Because I'm an ace diagnostician." His hands were even better than the soap. "And because I feel better."

"That doesn't mean you're not still contagious." I was trying to be reasonable or at least self-protective, but by that time the words were slipping away.

"Trust me," he said, and though I've never trusted men who tell you to trust them, or men who have penchants for making uncomfortable love in out-of-the-way places, standing there in my old-fashioned shower, besotted by steam and heat and the sheer dexterity of Dexter St.John, I did, for a while.

Later that night, when we were sitting in bed eating the dinner I'd made off trays—he might say he'd recovered, but I still didn't think he was well enough to go out, or maybe I was just doing a good imitation of my mother—I asked him why he was back in town so soon. During the months I'd interviewed him for the profile, which at odd moments that weekend I remembered he still hadn't read, he'd usually turned up about one week out of four. "I mean, it's not that I'm not glad to see you. I'm just surprised."

"I'm flying to Caracas tomorrow afternoon. This was just a detour."

"To check in at your office?"

"To check in with you." He stopped eating and sat watching me.

I'd never had anyone take a detour between Amsterdam and Caracas to spend two days with me. It seemed like a lot of trouble for him. It also seemed like a lot of responsibility for me.

After Dexter left for the airport on Sunday, I did the same thing I'd done two weeks earlier. I took out the profile and read it through again. This time I wasn't reassured. It was one thing to deliver the goods on a stranger. It was something else to turn in a man you were having an affair with, even if you'd got the goods before you'd started the affair. I could hear Pat O'Dougherty whispering "I told you so" in my ear.

At the stroke of ten on Monday morning I called Kay Meechum. "About the Dexter St.John profile . . ." I began.

"Didn't you get the check?"

I'd not only got the check but deposited it in my account and begun spending it.

"It's not that. I meant the profile itself. There are a couple of things I'd like to change. Strengthen, really."

There was a pause while she tried to figure out what I was up to. "One of the things I've always loved about you, Hallie," she said finally, "is that you're not one of those precious writers who run from newsstand to newsstand crossing out their own words. The profile's great. I love it. Natalie loves it. The whole damn staff loves it."

"You don't think it's too harsh?"

"Harsh? It makes Boswell's *Johnson* look like a hatchet job. And before you ask if it's too soft, that was a joke. It's a good, balanced piece, so stop obsessing and start thinking up some new ideas. I meant it when I said everyone here loves it. At this point you could probably sell us anything short of your grocery list. Get out your calendar, and tell me when you're free for lunch. We'll kick around some ideas."

I got out my calendar, we set up a lunch date, and I got off the phone thinking Kay was right. It was a good profile, and if I had any sense, I'd leave it alone.

The phone rang again almost as soon as I'd put it back in the cradle. I recognized Babe's voice immediately. The guilt kicked in seconds later. We hadn't spoken for more than two weeks. And our monthly lunch was long overdue, even by my cavalier timing. I pretended the lunches were monthly, but I usually managed to stretch the intervals to six weeks, and if Babe noticed, as I'm sure she did, she didn't complain. Of course, as my father used to say, Babe was never one to complain. The way he said it made it clear that he thought she had plenty to complain about.

She asked me what I'd been up to. I said I'd tell her all about it at lunch if she was free the following week, but I had to run. "I'm late for an interview."

"With whom?"

"Remember Emma Weill. Emma Bliss to you. I'm doing a profile of her for *Era*."

"*Era*? You should be doing a profile of Emma Weill for *Sassy*. You should be writing about estrogen replacement or living wills for *Era*."

"According to the editor, Emma Weill is—and I quote—a woman for all seasons. A woman who has it all, and everyone wants to read about that."

"I don't."

"Thanks a lot."

"I didn't mean I don't want to read what you're going to write. I meant I'm sick to death of hearing about women who have it all."

"You don't find them enviable?" It was a tactless question to put to a single, childless woman, but it was coming from another single, childless woman, and I was banking on our intimacy.

"I find them fictitious. As far as I'm concerned, cookie, there's no such animal as a woman who has it all. Only a woman who looks that way to other women."

Seven

EMMA LOOKED at her watch again, then checked it against the digital clock on the night table. The watch said seven-forty. The clock said seven thirty-seven. The reception was called for seven-thirty. There were a couple of places she could call. The Princeton Club. One or two friends or colleagues she knew about or thought she knew about. But that smacked too much of harridans in unkempt housedresses and uncombed hair tracking down errant husbands in seedy bars. She'd give him ten more minutes. If he wasn't back by then, she'd go without him.

She stood and walked to the wall of full-length mirrors in the dressing room. Half an hour ago she'd liked the way she looked. Now all she could see were the shadows beneath her eyes and the lines, cruel as knife slashes, that ran from her nostrils to the sides of her mouth. She remembered the old quip from Chanel or Colette or some goddamn French actress from the fifties: "I love the lines in my face because they remind me of the men who put them there." The observation must have lost something in the translation.

She glanced at her watch again. She should have known better. She never should have let Julian see how important it was to her. She never should have set the dinner up in the first place. But what else could she have done? Especially after that line about being an ordinary woman who'd gotten incredibly lucky.

The phone rang. She sprang for it.

"Hi, Emma," a male voice she didn't recognize said. He sounded young or at least optimistic. He could be a friend of one of the kids, but then why was he calling her Emma? "This is Artie."

"Artie?" she repeated, stalling for time. She didn't think she knew anyone who called himself Artie.

"I'm glad I caught you, Emma, because there's something I'd really like to talk to you about."

Of course, he could be someone Julian knew, but then what did he want to talk to her about? She remembered that call so many years ago. But the voice had been portentous. And the dean had called her Mrs. Weill.

"I'm sorry," she said. "I didn't get your last name."

"Gilchrest. Artie Gilchrest. Joyce gave me your name."

Now she understood. Artie had written a book, and he wanted her to read it. Or worse, he had a story that was crying to be told and wanted her to tell it. She was always getting calls from friends of friends to do one or the other. Well, not now, Artie. Not while I'm late for a reception and waiting for a call from my husband and strung out because Julian is doing it again.

"The truth of the matter is, Emma, I've got a couple of bonds here that I think you're going to be very interested in. I don't know if you've given any thought to tax-free—"

He was a bond salesman! A goddamn telephone bond salesman! The nine on the digital clock turned to zero. She was sitting here tying up the phone, so Julian couldn't get through, listening to a sales pitch for tax-free bonds from a child who called himself Artie.

"Can you imagine, Emma," he sang, "what that would amount to before taxes!"

"*Mr.* Gilchrest," she snapped, "I am not interested in buying tax-free bonds. If I were interested in buying tax-free bonds, I certainly would not buy them over the phone from a total stranger. I suggest you get yourself a real job with a reputable firm. I further suggest that you stop going around calling total strangers by their first names. It's bad form as well as bad business. Have I made myself absolutely clear, Mr. Gilchrest?"

She stopped. There was a moment's silence. Then she heard the click on the other end of the line. It didn't make her feel any better.

She hung up the receiver, picked up her handbag, and left the bedroom. She shouldn't have trouble getting a cab at this hour. She could be at the reception in plenty of time to present the award.

But instead of heading downstairs, she turned and climbed to the fourth floor, where she and Julian had their studies, his in the back overlooking the garden, hers only slightly smaller in front overlooking the street.

She stopped at the top of the stairs and stood in the open door to his, taking in the glow of dark wood and the richness of old rugs and the gleaming promise of shelf after shelf of books. If it weren't for the shiny dust jackets on the books and the computer and printer on the table beside the desk, it could have been the library of an Edwardian gentleman. Standing there, she realized the resemblance wasn't an accident. That had been her intention when they'd furnished the house. She'd set out to build him a lair, a room so seductive to the eye, so comfortable for the body, so nurturing of the spirit that he'd never want to leave it.

It was embarrassing to remember now. She'd actually believed they could start over. Wasn't that why people bought a new house, or renovated an old one, or decided to have another baby when the children were grown? They saw themselves talking over the new dinner table, making love in the new bed, bending head to head over the old crib with the new baby. In this house we'll find the happiness that's eluded us. In these reordered spaces we'll find a way through to each other. In this blending of genes, this combining of selves, we'll finally and truly be one. Only it's no easier to talk over the new dinner table than it was over the old, and it takes more than a new box spring and mattress to put the bounce back in flaccid desire, and little by little this child will learn to crawl, and say no, and finally walk away too. Standing in the doorway now, she saw her efforts for the pathetic fantasies they'd been.

She crossed to the long inlaid library table she'd bought him to use as a desk. Papers and index cards lay in neat piles; pens and freshly sharpened pencils stood in a pewter mug; the computer and printer were even covered. He wasn't a messy man. Or else he never really worked here. No, that wasn't fair. He was sincere about his work. He was passionate about his work.

There was a calendar diary on his desk. It was made from recycled paper and had an environmental tip for each day of the year. Becky had given it to him the previous Christmas. Emma opened it and flipped the pages to May 17. There were several notations to call people but no appointments. He did that intentionally. She was sure of it. Once she'd even accused him of it. He'd told her she was paranoid as well as nosy. The only reason he didn't write down appointments, he explained, was that he had an excellent memory and didn't need to. "Besides," he'd added, "I don't have all that many appointments to remember. I'm not in as much demand as my wife."

But maybe it wasn't an appointment. Maybe it was an impulse. In the early days, before she'd known better, before they'd come back East and started over with Edwardian libraries and eat-in kitchens that contained only natural materials and goddamn gracious living in the goddamn garden, the impulses had driven her crazy.

"If you'd just let me know," she'd say at ten or midnight or three the next morning, and hate herself for the hectoring tone in her voice and the haggard look she knew she had by then, because she'd spent the night picturing his mugged body lying in an alley or his mutilated corpse on a morgue slab.

He'd apologize and say he'd meant to, but a couple of people in the department had gone for a drink, or a few of the graduate students had asked him to go for coffee, and the time had just gotten away from him. His eyes had been inky with contrition and his voice had made it clear that he hadn't really wanted to go for drinks with his colleagues or coffee with his graduate students, but what was an aspiring young professor to do, and she'd believed him. At least in the beginning she'd believed him. But little by little she'd stopped believing, and even before they'd had to leave, the contrition in the eyes and the long-suffering timbre of the voice had begun to drive her crazy.

"I imagine things," she'd scream. "Can't you understand that? I imagine the worst. You're out having a good time, and I'm here trying to smile and paint a goddamn rosy ass on things so the kids don't know I'm worried sick that their father is bleeding to death in a dark alley somewhere or lying at the bottom of Lake Michigan."

He'd smile then. It was funny, but the more upset she got, the calmer he grew. "You know what Freud would say about that, sweetheart."

"I don't give a flying fuck what Freud would say about it."

He'd shake his head then because she was the one who was supposed to be fastidious about language. "Nonetheless, sweetheart, Siggy had a point. The unconscious knows no negatives. You see me dead because you want me dead."

She slammed closed the datebook. She didn't want him dead. No matter what he or that goddamn Victorian misogynist said. She just wanted him here to go with her to the goddamn party and on to goddamn dinner with that goddamn reporter. She just wanted him to act, for once in his goddamn life, like a goddamn husband.

Eight

SHE SAT UP taking the sheets with her. Julian had known she would. He could have told her she didn't have to. Maybe he would if he saw her again. She was chubby, chunky really because like all of them these days, she worked out, but was not nearly as fat as she thought. She wasn't a knockout, but you didn't have to put a flag over her and fuck for Old Glory. Maybe he'd tell her now. She wouldn't believe him, at least she wouldn't believe him for long, but she'd like hearing it. Of course, these days you couldn't be sure. Sometimes it was safer not to mention appearance at all and just drop the odd comment about how our society was so hung up on lookism. Some of them appreciated that more than a compliment. Then there were the really needy ones who went for both. "Look, I know it's an egregious example of lookism, but do you mind if I tell you how great-looking I think you are?" And they bought it. But that was one of the attractions of the girls with piano legs or big asses or horse faces. Gratitude. When you walked down the street or into a restaurant, other men didn't stare at them, then look at you with envy, but the girls themselves were so damn grateful. Because they knew he could do better, but for some reason they didn't understand but were so damn glad about, he'd chosen them. And then, of course, they weren't as likely to make a fuss when it was over. They'd known all along they weren't the kind of women men left other women for.

She sat looking down at him with that beaming smile. As if they'd done something wonderful. As if they'd pulled off cold fusion. It had been a good fuck, but as Becky would say, get real.

The thought of Becky made him remember. He was supposed to take Emma to that reception. He sneaked a look past the girl at the clock on the night table. He'd never get out of here and uptown in time. But he could still meet her at the reception. That would be just as good. Only she wouldn't see it that way. Not after the fuss she'd made about his going with her. He'd have to come up with a real crisis to explain why he hadn't when he'd sworn that he would. And she still wouldn't buy it. Damn, it wasn't fair. She wanted him to go, and he was going. That ought to be enough.

It came to him then. That was the way he'd play it. He'd thought he was supposed to meet her there. He must have misunderstood. No, she was the one who'd misunderstood. The more he thought about it, the more convinced he was. They'd agreed to meet at the party.

The girl was still sitting there beaming down at him. She really shouldn't let him see her from this angle. If she were smart, she'd worry less about the sheet she'd tucked under her armpits, because her tits were just fine and there was no reason to hide them, and more about those chins. Sitting across her desk from her, he hadn't noticed the chins. To tell the truth, he hadn't noticed her face all that much, except for the big Dresden blue eyes that she hadn't been able to take off him and the way she kept licking her lips as if she thought he was good enough to eat. He supposed she had a pretty face, if you weren't looking up at it past the chins. That was probably what people said about her. She has such a pretty face. What they meant was she has such a pretty face for a fat girl.

The chins were beginning to depress him. He'd pull her down beside him, but she'd take it as an invitation to start all over again, and he really ought to get going. Even if he hadn't had to meet Emma, he wouldn't have wanted to sit around here all night, listening to her talk about her job and her life and how she'd been engaged once or maybe married but really liked being single, only she wanted a child and was thinking maybe she'd have one on her own. He wondered why the bodies were always new and different but the stories had such a depressing sameness.

"Do you still want that drink?" she asked, and now the grin grew mischievous. She'd offered him a drink as soon as they'd walked into the apartment, and he'd said yes, but then he'd come up behind her in the kitchen as she was taking the ice out of the freezer and put his arms around her and his hands on those big tits, just as a preliminary really, a little taste of what was to come after the drinks, but she'd turned around, and before he knew it, she had her tongue in his mouth and her hand in his fly, and there didn't seem to be much point in wasting time with drinks. They'd stopped only long enough for the requisite swearing of clean bills of health and the rifling for condoms in her night table drawer, which he'd noticed was a nightmarish mess of hand creams and emery boards and eye masks and night socks and notepads and pens and pencils. If he'd seen that drawer earlier, it might have given him pause.

"Sure," he said because he had to get out of there, but he wouldn't mind a drink first. Then he waited for what he knew would come next. She'd lean over and kiss him, not a sexy kiss, but a friendly oh-we-like-each-other-so-much-and-isn't-this-fun kiss and run her hand up and down his chest once or twice as if she were establishing proprietary rights. Then, keeping her back to him, she'd get out of bed and race to the closet or the bathroom, where she'd put on a robe, as if she could hide the imperfections, as if he hadn't already felt the heft of ass and the well-padded hips and the meaty thighs.

She bent over, kissed him, ran her hand up and down his chest, and practically dragged the damn sheet off the bed trying to get to the closet. When she came out of it, she was tying a terry-cloth robe around her. That was a mistake. Her body wasn't great, but it was better out of that heavy robe than in it. Come to think of it, it was better out of clothes than in them. Maybe he'd tell her that too. Women loved to hear that. Even the ones who ranted against lookism. It was a secret they could carry around with them and take out and fondle when the going got rough.

As soon as she left the room, he picked up the phone on the night table and dialed his own number, not the one in his study, but the house number. Emma would be gone by now, so it was safe to leave a message. She wouldn't get it till they got home, but it would be a nice touch.

He could hear the girl rattling ice and glasses and bottles in the kitchen. The apartment was one of those minuscule one-bedrooms with paper-thin walls that magazine girls always lived in. For all he knew there was a roommate somewhere, another girl she'd tell about him, or some gay guy. Only there was just this one bed, so there was probably no roommate.

He heard the click and the sound of Emma's recorded voice telling him that no one was home at the moment, but if he cared to leave a message, someone would get back to him.

"Hi, sweetheart, it's me. I just wanted to tell you I might be a little late getting to that reception. But I'll be there, as promised. You won't have any trouble spotting me. Look for the guy who's not making fatuous remarks. At least I hope I won't be making fatuous remarks. See you soon. Ciao."

He was just hanging up the phone when she came into the bedroom carrying two glasses. He pushed himself up and sat with his back against the wall. There was no headboard. He'd noticed that before when he'd wanted something to hang on to.

"I hope you don't mind," he said with one of his megawatt smiles. "I used your phone."

She stood at the foot of the bed with a drink in each hand staring at him with those big Dresden blue eyes. "That depends."

"Don't worry. Not Bangkok. Just a local call."

"That's not what it depends on."

Christ, she was serious.

"Who did you call?"

None of your fucking business who I called, and just for the record it's *whom*. What in hell was the world coming to? She was supposed to be an editor. "I called my wife," he said, because he was scrupulous about that. He never pretended he wasn't married. He always made it clear he wasn't contemplating a divorce. Take me as I am or not at all. He turned the smile up a notch. "To tell her I got tied up."

She walked around the bed and put the glasses down on the night table. He looked up at her. She was holding her head so high there were no extra chins.

"Don't ever do that again."

For a moment he didn't think he'd heard right. "What?"

"Don't ever call your wife from my bed again."

She had to be kidding. What made her think he was going to be in her bed again? Before this it had been a slight possibility. Now it wasn't even a long shot.

He swung his legs over the side of the bed and sat there for a moment. Then he bent slowly and picked his shorts up off the floor. He wasn't going to rush. He certainly wasn't going to lose his temper. He was just going to put on his clothes, slowly, carefully because he didn't want to go to that damn reception looking like one of those seedy has-beens who were always hanging around the edges. Then he'd leave. He took his trousers off the back of the chair where he'd hung them. He'd even kiss her good-bye. And he'd thank her. Just because she was behaving badly didn't mean he had to.

He made up his mind in the cab going crosstown. He was getting too old for this kind of thing. No, not too old. That wasn't the problem. He'd probably die before he got too old. Die in action. Like John Garfield. He was getting too smart. What was he doing screwing around with junior editors, built like fireplugs, for Christ sake, when he had a wife like Emma at home? What was that Paul Newman line? Why would I go out for hamburger when I've got filet mignon at home? And if you believe that, buddy, I've got a bridge I can give you a great deal on. Still, it was time to clean up his act. No more screwing around. Especially with the B-team. No more screwing around at all. He felt good just thinking about it. The elder statesman of the sexual wars. He saw himself at lunch with a colleague. That asshole Perlman, who thought he was fucking Edward R. Murrow just because he did an occasional television commentary. Oh, sure, I used to do that kind of thing, but then I got smart. Or at a party with a girl. Little Miss Fireplug. Sorry, sweetheart, not interested. God, it was a great sensation! He felt so good he almost had a hard-on again. He gave himself one of his own best smiles in the driver's rearview mirror. He wished he could tell Emma.

Nine

I RECOGNIZED the landscape at the reception as soon as I was inside the door. The names of the sponsoring organizations varied—the high-toned PEN (Poets, Essayists, Novelists), for which Emma was presenting an award that night, the more pragmatic ASJA (American Society of Journalists and Authors), to which I belong—but the ritual and even some of the people remained the same. Scattered around the ballroom in closed circles, tight as fortresses, the successful writers and powerful editors and almighty agents huddled, talking shop and trading gossip. Circling them like sharks were their mid-level counterparts, some on the way up, some on the way down, most going nowhere at all. And at the hors d'oeuvres table, the kids just out of school who still thought they were pursuing art rather than being exploited by commerce made a meal of greasy cocktail hot dogs, limp crudités, and all the free Pellegrino they could drink. It wasn't a scene I enjoyed. I know everyone says that, but I mean it. Not because of an excess of scruples but because of a lack of skills. I once spent the better part of one of those parties cultivating a man I thought was the publisher of a large-circulation magazine. Unfortunately I'd heard the introduction wrong. He taught journalism in a continuing education program at a community college. That was the night I swore I wasn't going to any more professional parties, but one day a few months later an editor I ran into at the Metropolitan Museum asked how I liked being out of the business. I started going to the parties again, but I've never got over the queasy feeling that assaults me as I stand in the doorway of a ballroom watching my colleagues successfully work a room. And tonight it was worse than ever. I recognized one or two acquaintances. I didn't see any friends. And there was no sign of Emma Weill. I got a glass of cheap generic wine and tried to make myself the same color as the walls.

It wasn't long before I caught sight of Sugar Shapiro. A night without at least one party is enough to send Sugar into serious withdrawal. We kissed the air near each other's ears; then Sugar glanced around at the crowd. We were standing only a few feet from a biographer who'd just survived a headline-making libel case and a publisher whose divorce had been in the columns for weeks.

"You ought to thank me, sweetie pie. This sure beats conducting an interview in the Women's House of Detention."

"I haven't given up on the idea," I told her, though I knew it was a mistake. Sugar prefers adaptability to passion.

"Do you mind if I ask you something," she said in that voice that made me think it was going to be if she could stay up an hour later. "Why're you so sold on this idea? I mean, you don't have to tell me if you don't want to, but were you ever"—she dropped her voice—"abused by a husband or lover or anything like that?"

I told her not only hadn't I been abused, but I'd been raised by a woman who was given to warning on occasion—though I can't imagine what the occasion was in view of my father's sunny disposition—that if a man so much as raised a hand to you, you walked out the door.

"I just think it's a good idea. Besides," I added, hitting her where I thought she lived, "lurid sells."

"Lurid sells," she agreed. "Squalid doesn't. Find me a

woman who comes home from lunch at Daniel, discovers her husband in flagrante delicto with his personal trainer in the private gym of their Park Avenue triplex, and stabs him with a Medici dagger she got at a Sotheby's auction, and I'll promise you an immoral fee and a sell line on the cover of the book. Until then stick to Emma Weill.''

As if on cue, Emma Weill appeared in the door to the ballroom. She stood poised there for a split second with the fierce concentration of a diver on the high board, then plunged into the room. I was still working my way toward her when a man in a rumpled tweed jacket—some pretensions die hard—moved to the podium at one end of the room and began asking for quiet. He got a whispering undertone of one-liners, which is the best anyone can hope for in a room full of literary cubs.

I tried to jockey for a better view. There were four awards on the agenda, but since children's writing is the stepchild of the lit party circle, I knew that Emma would go first.

The man in the rumpled jacket began talking about a woman who'd changed the lives of young people all over the world. In private meetings editors murmur darkly about bottom lines and unearned advances. At public presentations they speak of changing lives. He went on to introduce the woman who needed no introduction. The line told more than the tweed jacket. I was willing to put money on the fact that he'd risen through marketing rather than editorial ranks.

Emma took the few steps to the microphone. Like so many of the women I work with and lunch with and interview, she handled herself with an impressive self-confidence. I know, or at least I frequently tell myself, that those women who dress with such style and move with such ease and speak with such authority harbor some of the same fears and insecurities and needs I do, but I don't really believe it.

Emma began to speak. Her miked voice was strong enough to carry over the continuing undertone of whispered comments.

It's not that as a group publishing people are ruder than insurance salesmen or chiropractors; it's that they're just more in love with their own words. I was trying to listen to Emma when I heard a comment to my right.

"A single bomb to this room," the voice whispered, "would do more to save the forests than Al Gore, Bruce Babbitt, and the spotted owl combined."

I turned to tell the voice to be quiet or at least to give it a dirty look. I was face-to-face, or face-to-shoulder because he was tall and I had to look up, with a man who had the dark eyes, thick dark hair, and high cheekbones of a central casting Indian, the one who scalped the white men and raped the white women in the old cowboy movies. It wasn't a look I was particularly responsive to, but I knew a lot of women were. Then he smiled, and all the menace evaporated. No, that's not true, because the smile was a little too dangerous for comfort. The menace didn't evaporate, but it did soften a little, as if it had been tenderized. And I realized that the man hadn't been talking to another bystander, as I'd assumed, but to me. I didn't smile back, but I didn't give him a dirty look either. I merely turned back to the podium and tried to listen to what Emma was saying. She was talking about the recipient's imagination and compassion and sense of wonder.

"What do you want to bet she speaks to the child in all of us?" the central casting Native American said.

"Her voice"—Emma went on—"speaks to the child in all of us."

I turned to scowl. I found myself returning that outrageous smile. I don't know how it happened. I didn't mean to. The man was rude. And too obvious for my taste.

"Shh," I mumured, but the sound didn't come out nearly as sternly as I'd intended. There was even a touch of complicity to it.

"Sorry," he whispered, and maybe he was, because he didn't

say another word while Emma finished presenting the award. I felt prissy and faintly disappointed and furious at myself for the disappointment. I wasn't interested in this slick, predatory operator. I was recently but intensely interested in another man. So what was this atavistic need to be pursued, this pathetic Donna Juanita complex?

I tried to shut the man out of my peripheral vision and concentrate on the recipient's acceptance speech. I was supposed to be working.

She thanked a lot of people and assured us that writing was not a competitive sport. As far as she was concerned, she didn't deserve the award any more than the four other candidates she'd beaten out for it.

In a pig's eye, I thought.

"In a pig's eye," the man whispered.

As Butch Cassidy said to the Sundance Kid, or vice versa, who was this guy?

The publisher in the rumpled tweed jacket was back, and the undeserving writer and Emma were leaving the podium, and Emma was making her way through the crowd toward me. Only when she reached me, she put a hand on the arm of the man next to me, went up on her toes, and laid her cheek against his. Then she turned to me.

"I see you've met Julian," she whispered because someone else was speaking now.

I mumbled something noncommittal, and shook Julian Weill's hand, and forced myself to meet his eyes without blushing or blinking or turning away, because all the time I hadn't known who he was and had thought he was hitting on me, he'd known exactly who I was and was merely trying to ingratiate himself with the woman who was writing an article on his wife.

Ten

EMMA WAS SURE she hadn't given it away. At least not in front of Hallie. No "Where were you?" or "I was waiting for you at home," or that old saw that even she knew was no longer true, "I was worried sick." She'd simply walked up to him, as if she'd expected him to be there, as if they'd planned to meet there instead of arrive together, and said, as if it were the most normal thing in the world, which, of course, it was, "I guess you two have met." Only something about Hallie's reaction—the startled widening of those wide slate gray eyes, the quick flames of color on the pale skin that seemed too tightly stretched over the bones of her face—made Emma think they hadn't met, merely gravitated toward each other.

She wasn't going to berate him about it. At least she hadn't meant to, but the words just slipped out. "Did you know that was Hallie Fields you were talking to or—" She stopped, but it was too late.

He turned to her in the backseat of the cab. As it raced up Park Avenue, through the arcs of light and patches of dark, she watched the smile come and go. A Cheshire cat grin with a malevolent lining. It was hard to believe there'd been a time when that smile had made the muscles in her stomach contract with desire.

". . . or was I coming on to her?" He finished for her, but

there was no anger in his voice, merely an echo of weariness, as if they'd been through this too many times before.

"I didn't mean that," she said.

"Of course you did. No, I was not coming on to your little groupie. If I wanted to come on to someone, sweetheart, there were a couple of hundred women at that thing. Innocent young women who'd think I was a fuckin' seer and successful middle-aged women who'd know I was their last hope, ambitious women who'd want me to introduce them to someone and wannabe literary women with dull rich husbands who'd love to show me off to their friends, one or two knockout women whom I like to look at, which is not a crime no matter what you think, and several women whom I would in fact kick out of bed, boring women and clever—"

"Okay, I get the idea."

"So why, with all those women in the room, why in hell, sweetheart, would I go after one who's doing an article on my wife? You think I want to screw up your career? You think I'm self-destructive? Hell, do you think I'm dumb enough to shit in my own—"

"All right!" she said, because that was one phrase she really hated.

He reached over and took her hand. "You asked me to be nice to her, and I was being nice to her."

She told herself to let it go. They rode a full two blocks in silence before she spoke again.

"But how did you know who she was?"

He pulled his hand away. "For Christ sake!"

"I'm sorry. All I meant was—"

"I know what you meant. Jim Burney pointed her out to me. And in answer to the next question, I asked him to point her out because if you remember, that was the reason I was at that goddamn party. Because you wanted me to meet her. Because you were afraid she'd think terrible things about you if I didn't.

73

Coming on to her." He shook his head in wonder. "I didn't even particularly like her."

"You didn't?"

The cab pulled up in front of the house. She got out and stood on the sidewalk waiting while he paid the driver.

"What didn't you like about her?" she asked as they went up the steps to the front door. "I thought from the way you two were talking at dinner that you were crazy about her."

He pushed the door open and stood aside to let her go in first. "I give up. I really do. First I show up at that damn reception, and you tell me I was supposed to meet you here."

"I thought—"

"You thought that since one of us got his signals crossed, it had to be me. Then I'm nice to some fatuous reportette, which I thought was the purpose of the whole damn evening, and you accuse me of coming on to her. There's no pleasing you." He started up the stairs.

She followed a few steps behind him. "I'm pleased. And I'm not accusing you of anything. I just asked what you didn't like about her."

He reached the top of the second flight of stairs and turned into the bedroom. She went in after him. He continued into the dressing room, took off his jacket, and draped it carefully over the valet. Then he stood staring at her. She found she was holding her breath. He shook his head and smiled. All was forgiven. She exhaled.

"I didn't dislike her. She just struck me as . . . I don't know . . . chilly. If you ever got her into bed, and just for the record, I don't think it would be all that hard—I'm not saying I want to, I'm just saying I don't think it would be all that hard—I don't think there'd be a lot happening between the sheets." He tugged his tie loose and pulled it off. The silk made a whooshing sound in the silence. "So in answer to your original question, sweetheart, as Paul Newman says, why would I go out for hamburger when I have filet mignon at home?"

She hated that line too, or at least she knew it was supposed to offend her. Just as she knew she wasn't supposed to let him turn a perfectly innocent question about what he thought of another person into a sexual competition between two women. She'd read the books and articles, and sat in on the conversations, and even mouthed the dogma, but the truth was she liked hearing him say those things. She needed to hear him say those things.

"In that case," she said on her way to the bathroom, "I'm really grateful to you for being nice to her."

"De nada," he answered with a small bow and a quick swipe to her behind as she passed.

"Do you really think I was okay tonight?" she asked when she came out of the bathroom a little while later. He was sitting up in bed with his back against the headboard and the remote control for the television in his hand. She knew from an article she'd read recently that it wasn't just Julian; all men were incapable of watching a single channel at a time. She wondered if it had something to do with monogamy. She told herself Julian was right. She really was obsessed.

"You were terrific," he said, and switched channels. "Your speech was great. Even the business about the child within."

"I know you think that's corny."

He switched again. "Corny is what those philistines want. Corny is as much as they can handle. Like that asshole who introduced you. Bill Weaver, the grand old man of publishing. The grand old man of publishing who's never read anything more profound than a P and L statement in his life. But the point is you make it sound fresh. Hell, you make it sound believable." He switched again. "And you were terrific with that reporter too." The picture on the screen changed again. "Hallie what's-her-name?"

"Fields."

"Right. You had her eating out of your hand." He switched the television off and turned to her. He wasn't smiling now.

"But?"

"No buts."

"You were going to say something else."

He went on staring at her. The light from the bedside lamp cast the planes and angles in his face into sharp relief, almost as if the flesh had been peeled away and she were staring at his skull. "Just that sometimes I wonder."

"Wonder what?" she asked, though she knew what was coming.

"What in hell you're doing with me. You're smart. You're talented. You're a great-looking woman. And you're a hell of a lot more successful than I'm ever going to be."

"Oh, that," she said.

"Oh, that," he repeated. "That, in case you haven't noticed, happens to be the way this fucked-up world measures people."

She stood for a moment staring at him. He wasn't putting her on. He meant it. That was why he hadn't come home tonight. Not because he'd got his signals crossed. Not because he wanted to torture her. But because he had to assert himself. He had to prove that he didn't need her. That he could get along on his own. Only he couldn't. She had to remember that. Next time she got angry, next time she wanted to scream how-can-you-goddamn-it-don't-you-care-about-anyone-don't-you-even-give-a-fuck-about-me, she had to remember this Julian, the real Julian, the one only she got a glimpse of, the one only she could take care of, the one who would never leave her no matter what else he did because no matter what else he did he was the one who needed her.

She walked around the bed and sat on the side next to him. "Screw the world. We know the truth. You're smarter than I'll ever be, and more talented, and your work is ten times more important."

"That and a token will get you on the subway."

"I mean it. Sure, I make more money. So do rock stars and talk show hosts and drug dealers. If you stop to think about it, it's almost a sign of integrity not to make money in this society."

"Your nose is getting longer, Pinocchio."

"It's true. Look at half the people we know. Bob Seligman? The last time he took over a company he put several hundred people out of work. Or your cousin Alan. Product liability, my foot. The man's an ambulance chaser."

"You're a devoted little wife, sweetheart."

"I'm an intelligent woman with an enlightened worldview. Remember that line from *Citizen Kane*. 'There's no trick to making money—' "

" 'If all you want to do is make money,' " he finished for her.

"Exactly. So can we cut out the self-flagellation?"

"Right. I'm a prince among men. You're lucky to have me," he said, but she could see the sharp lines in his face begin to soften.

"And sexy too."

"Now you're talking."

"My boy toy."

He took her hand and put it on him. "I resent that."

He moved over. She got in bed beside him. They both knew the routine. These were the sweet nights, the tender nights, when he needed her—no, he always needed her, that was the point—when he wasn't afraid to show he needed her, and she realized she meant it when she told him how much she loved him. Sometimes she didn't. When they made love after a fight, she didn't love him, though sometimes she loved the sex then, when it got all mixed up with the wild surge of relief that they'd averted disaster, again. Once he'd told her she was more respon-sive then. Hell, she'd thought, but hadn't dared say because the fight was over and she hadn't wanted to start it again, who wouldn't be with her nerves rubbed raw and every wound open to the touch? She knew he loved those times, the excitement, and the intensity, and the sheer brinksmanship of it, because he'd pushed her to the edge, again, left her swinging there, again, made her prove her love, again, and then when she had, again, pulled her back just in time, again. But she preferred this, the gentleness and the familiarity and the intimacy of two peo-ple bound by time and form and habit, safe against the outside world.

Eleven

I SPENT MOST of the next two weeks talking to Emma, and eating meals with her, and following her to a book signing and a taping of a television talk show and a meeting of the board of a literacy group. Her life reminded me of one of those old B movies about writers, the ones where the tortured young artist spends the first ten minutes tearing bad drafts out of a typewriter and the next eighty writing nothing more demanding than autographs in montages of one best-seller after another. Maybe Emma was just a fast writer, or maybe young adult books didn't take as long to write, but she seemed to spend less time dashing off small classics that stayed in print forever than I did wrestling with two-thousand-word articles to kill people's time in dentists' waiting rooms and manicure parlors. It was one more comparison I wasn't supposed to make.

I also spent a lot of time talking about Emma. I interviewed friends she'd known since college and people she'd met working for a variety of good causes, colleagues who speculated on the reasons for her success, and her editor, who attested to her virtues. A lot of people had a lot of good things to say about her. She inspired loyalty as well as admiration.

But the more I got to know Emma, the less I envied her. Her achievements impressed me, in a way. I admired her success, but I didn't take it as seriously as if she'd won it writing for grown-ups. I thought it might be nice to have a happy and enduring marriage, but I wasn't sure hers fit the bill. In other words, Emma Weill had things I wanted, but she didn't have them the way I wanted them. Maybe that was why we got along so well. We shared certain interests, and endeavors, and ambitions, not to mention a past, but each of us felt just a little sorry for and superior to the other. It's not a bad basis for friendship. At least that's been my experience with a lot of my women friends. And there was a certain friendship growing between Emma and me. As long as Julian wasn't around.

Julian Weill's mere presence in a room, especially a room of women, could transform an ordinary situation into a soap opera. Part of it was the sexual heat he gave off, which was as fierce and indiscriminate as a furnace blast. It singed everything within range. But there was more to it than that, though I couldn't put my finger on exactly what.

Even when he wasn't in the room, I felt his presence hovering. Sitting in the garden talking to her, I'd hear the murmur of his voice on the phone or the faint tap of the keys of his word processor from the open window overhead. Then sometimes there'd be silence, and a few seconds later he'd come striding out of the house telling us a joke he'd just heard from a colleague, or a horror story he'd just unearthed in his research, or that he hoped we didn't mind, but he needed a break.

Of course, it wasn't all Julian's fault. In all fairness to him—and I was trying to be fair to both of them, or at least journalistically impartial—Emma was a different woman in his presence. She was always talking about how much she owed him, how she never could have done it without him, how he gave her ideas, and helped her with characters and plot, and edited early drafts. Once, when we were discussing *Happily Ever After* again, she admitted the book had been Julian's brainchild. Maybe all that was true, maybe he had made her what she was, but he also made her tense. She was more subdued when he was around, more deferential, and at the same time more maternal. I'd seen her fall silent in mid-sentence just because he walked into a room. I'd also watched her fuss over his needs and supervise his behavior as if he were a child. Sometimes I envied their intimacy; others I thought it gave off the suffocatingly sweet smell of a well-tended sickroom.

One afternoon in the garden he asked if I didn't want to interview him alone. "Find out what it's like living with the toast of America's teenyboppers," he said with an affectionate hug to Emma and a killer smile to me. And of course I did, because even the most devoted couples speak differently about each other when the other person isn't listening, differently, though not necessarily more harshly.

We set up a lunch date.

At twelve-thirty of any given weekday the lobby of the Princeton Club is filled with well-barbered men in muted gray or blue suits for as far as the eye can see. Occasionally a tweed jacket pops up, or a maverick beard, or the odd woman or two —enough variety to satisfy the Justice Department without upsetting the old boys. But mostly it's a uniform army. From a distance Julian Weill looked as if he belonged. When I got closer, I saw that he didn't feel as if he belonged. He carried himself with an uneasy watchfulness. He straightened his tie once too often and glanced in the mirror to check his appearance once, which was once more than he should have. I knew how he felt. I'd got in by virtue of my Bryn Mawr diploma, and I paid my dues once a year and my bills regularly, but I never felt I belonged either.

I held out my hand. He kissed me on the cheek. We went up to the dining room. The room was bright, and the tables were well spaced. That was one of the reasons I'd suggested meeting him there. I was counting on good acoustics and nonexistent ambiance to get the interview done. I wrote our orders on the slip, put a micro tape recorder on the table between us, and got down to business.

I asked him what he thought of his wife's books. He said he thought they were the greatest thing that had happened to teenyboppers since Vittorino da Feltre had started educating girls as well as boys in Renaissance Mantua.

"Even *Happily Ever After?*"

He looked across the table at me and shrugged. "Well, maybe not that one so much."

"Then you didn't like *Happily Ever After?*"

"Let's just say I didn't think it was as strong as some of the others."

"Does that bother you? I mean, in view of your responsibility?"

"What do you mean?"

"Emma says the book was your idea."

"My wife is too generous. All Emma's books are Emma's ideas."

I asked him what he thought of the fact that his wife wrote books.

"You mean instead of staying home and being a wife and mother?"

"Or going to an office and being the CEO of General Motors."

He laughed. "Okay, you caught me out. I admire what Emma does. I also like the fact that she's become famous and rich doing it."

"Then the money doesn't bother you?"

He stared across the table at me through narrowed eyes. "You don't strike me as an unobservant woman, Hallie. Do I strike you as the kind of hair shirt liberal who disapproves of living well?"

"No, I meant . . ." I felt my voice trailing off. This was

ridiculous. I'd asked a United States representative if it was true that he'd used campaign funds to pay for his daughter's wedding and a socialite about the rumors that she'd had an affair with her stepdaughter, but I was suddenly afraid of offending Julian Weill by pointing out that his wife made more money than he did, a fact that he never tired of pointing out himself.

"Oh," he said as if he hadn't understood, though I was fairly sure he had. "You mean, does the fact that Emma makes it and I don't bother me? No, it doesn't bother me." His voice came down on the last word.

"Are you suggesting it bothers Emma?"

"You'll have to ask Emma that." He smiled at me over his glass of wine. The waiter brought our lunches. Julian tucked into his.

I asked him about the early years with Emma. He told me about meeting her when she was an undergraduate and he was a teaching assistant finishing his Ph.D. "As soon as she walked into my section, I knew I was in trouble."

"In trouble?"

"Hooked."

He talked about being young and poor in a tiny apartment with two babies. "I know it's a cliché, but it's true. Of course, that's why things become clichés. The point is we were looking forward to the future, when things would be better or at least easier. But things were pretty good then. Things were terrific then. Everything was so new. Each other. The kids. Emma was a terrific mother in those days. I'm not suggesting she's not a great mother now," he went on quickly, "but certain women have a flair for—promise you'll never tell anyone I used the word—nurturing certain ages. Emma's at her best with kids who are small. And helpless." He paused and sipped his wine. "Then the kids started school, I encouraged Emma to begin doing something, and the rest is history." He leaned back in his chair and smiled at me.

"Is that why you started writing too? Because she was so successful at it?"

"I thought we were going to talk about Emma." Nothing in his manner changed, but my antenna shot up.

"You've been part of Emma's life for a long time."

"I got tired of being an academic. The politics were too vicious and the rewards too meager. Maybe that's why the politics are so vicious. Because there's so damn little at stake."

We went back to Emma. He talked about her intelligence and her competence. He told me amusing anecdotes about Emma the wife, and Emma the mother, and Emma the writer, and Emma who juggled all three roles. I could picture readers squirming with envy. I was beginning to feel the stirrings myself.

"Superwoman," I said.

"Oh, she's that, all right."

His tone wasn't unkind. It wasn't even sarcastic. But it was suddenly different. I waited.

"Sometimes it's a little daunting."

I waited again.

"Living with perfection, I mean."

"How?" I asked when he didn't go on.

It took him a long time to answer, and when he did, it was with another question. "Off the record?"

I switched off the tape recorder. "Off the record."

"Okay. You asked me before if Emma minded my not making as much money as she does. She doesn't care about the money. At least not primarily the money. She cares about the perception. She cares that people will think I'm a failure. More to the point, that people will think she married a failure. Emma has high standards. She set them for herself a long time ago, and woe to anyone connected to her who doesn't live up to them. And it's not just worldly success. You asked me what I thought of *Happily Ever After*. I thought it was garbage. Worst thing she ever wrote."

"Then it wasn't your idea?"

"Only Emma could have come up with a story like that."

"Did you tell her what you thought of it?"

"You don't tell Emma things like that."

"But she said she gives you all her work in progress to read."

"Just because she gives it to me to read doesn't mean she wants to hear what I think of it. Anyway, it wouldn't have helped. Emma believes in that book. She believes in it as much as she does in the ones about parents' divorces and teenage pregnancy and adolescent alcoholism, which, needless to say, are a lot more reflective of reality. She believes that's the way marriage is, or should be."

"She seems to have pulled it off. Excuse me, you both seem to have."

"Don't think it's been easy."

"According to Auden, marriage isn't supposed to be easy."

He smiled. It made me realize he hadn't in a while. "You mean that line about 'an act of will'?"

"Exactly."

"This is a bit more than that." He stopped again and glanced around the room. I followed his gaze. Most of the gray and blue suits had left. In the far corner three men sat with their heads together. Under other circumstances I would have wondered what they were cooking up. Nearby a busboy stacked dishes on a tray. Julian brought his gaze back to me. "Still off the record?"

"Whatever you say."

"You asked before why I left teaching. Why did Emma tell you I left?"

"She said you were tired of it. That you had new interests and wanted to pursue them."

"That's the party line."

"Then it's not true?"

He started to speak, then stopped again. "Christ, I don't know why I'm telling you all this."

I held my breath.

He leaned across the table toward me. "Listen, you said this is off the record."

"Absolutely."

"You have to promise me."

"I'll never use it."

"No, more than that. You have to promise you'll never even mention any of this to Emma."

"If I went around telling people what other people said, I'd have been out of work a long time ago."

His smile was perfunctory. The man was on a tear. Sometimes that happens in interviews. Sometimes the floodgates open and the information comes pouring out. It can happen with friends, too, when they're hell-bent on a confession of some sort.

"You want to know why I left teaching. I left it for Emma's sake. No, that's not fair. I left it for my own peace of mind. Because I couldn't stand her jealousy."

"She was jealous of your work?"

"She was jealous of my students."

There was something wrong with this story. I could understand Emma's jealousy—I liked to think I wouldn't have felt it in her place—but I could understand it. Being married to a man who spent most of his waking hours surrounded by dewy young women with pert bodies and enthusiasms to match couldn't have been easy. And Julian's manner with women wouldn't have helped matters. I could understand suspicions. I could even understand arguments. I could not understand throwing over an entire career.

"Did she have reason to be?"

He sat across the table staring at me. He wasn't smiling now. "I don't know why I'm telling you all this."

I sat absolutely still, waiting for him to go on.

"Once." He held up his index finger in illustration, in case I'd missed the point. "Only once. I figured if I was going to be accused of sinning, I might as well sin. Hell, I'm not excusing myself. It was a dumb thing to do. Anyway, that's when I decided I had to get out. I don't know, maybe I'm being too easy on myself. Maybe I didn't leave for Emma's peace of mind, or my own. Maybe I left because I couldn't stand the temptation. You know what I mean. All those eager young things who think you're God, or at least larger than life, just because you know a little more than they do."

I thought back to a history professor who'd made the Franco-German controversy over Alsace-Lorraine throb like a bodice ripper. I knew what he meant.

"Have you ever regretted leaving?"

"Not for a minute. I don't miss teaching. I sure as hell don't miss the petty politics. I don't even miss the nubile young things. Because I learned something from that one incident." He hesitated.

I waited.

"I learned that it wasn't worth it. Emma and the kids mean too much to me. I learned I'd never get mixed up with someone for the hell of it again. If I were going to risk that much, I'd have to really care for someone."

I wasn't sure what I was supposed to say to that, so I didn't say anything.

"The only problem," he went on finally, "is that Emma doesn't believe me. She's convinced that if she found out about that one incident—"

"How did she find out?"

He gave me a shamefaced look. "I told her, of course. Raskolnikov rides again. Part of me knew it was a dumb thing to do. But part of me couldn't resist the impulse. I'd confess, she'd absolve or at least forgive, and we'd start over. Only it doesn't work that way. She's still convinced that if there was one incident I admitted, there must be dozens, hell, hundreds I haven't. And it gets worse rather than better. If I talk to someone at a party, she thinks I'm making an assignation. If I'm a half hour late because I can't get a cab, she has me in bed with another woman. You must have noticed."

I thought about it for a minute. "If you don't mind my saying so, and you probably do, your behavior toward women isn't exactly designed to reassure her."

He started to say something, then stopped. I waited again. "I know," he said finally. "I was going to deny it. I was going to pretend I didn't know what you were talking about, but you're too smart for that. Okay, I admit it. I can't help myself. I like women. I like talking to them. To tell you the truth, I like talking to them more than I like talking to men. And I like looking at them. Maybe that's a sexist statement, but it's true. I even enjoy flirting with them, which, depending on your postfeminist stand, is either a heinous crime or a natural instinct. But for Christ sake, Hallie"—he leaned toward me across the table— "just because I read the menu doesn't mean I eat the food."

Twelve

BABE WAS STANDING beside her car as I came down the steps from the railroad platform. My mother would have been waiting in the car. Babe had got out and was leaning against it. Something about her stance made the drab gray Toyota disappear, and for a moment I saw a white Buick convertible with red leather upholstery in its place.

She was standing with her hands in the pockets of a pair of well-cut gabardine trousers. A cashmere cardigan hung casually over her shoulders. Though her skin showed the signs—not the ravages but the signs—of years on the golf course, and her hair, which she wore pulled back in a knot, was entirely gray, she gave an impression of lean and rangy vitality. As I crossed the pavement to her, I realized something I'd known all my life but had never thought about: Babe was a sexy woman. It had to do with the angles of her body, and the way she held them, and her consciousness of self, which is different from self-consciousness. Even at seventy-four she gave off an aura or at least a memory of sexuality. I could imagine what she'd been like when she'd met her flier, and for years after that. My mother had been prettier, but Babe had had what they'd called sex appeal. It couldn't have been easy for her, in that town, in that era, in her situation.

We hugged, cheek against cheek. Unlike my mother, she

didn't feel fragile. Maybe that was why her request surprised me.

"I have a favor to ask, cookie. I want you to go shopping with me."

"For what?"

"Get ready for a good laugh. Retirement communities."

I didn't laugh. "You're kidding."

"I'm not going to be an ingenue all my life. And when I start putting my bra over my blouse instead of under it, I want someone around to tell me. Besides—and this is the real laugh— there's a waiting list for these places. You have to put your name down years in advance. As if it's an exclusive club. I know I'm imposing on you, but I'd really like someone else's opinion. It could be worse. I could be asking you to help me shop for cemetery plots."

I told her I'd be happy to go shopping with her.

As she started around the car to the driver's side, I asked if she wanted me to drive. My mother would have.

"Are you kidding?" she said. "I've got to get in practice for the wheelchair drag races."

I climbed into the passenger seat, she got behind the wheel, and we swung into traffic. She hadn't been kidding about the drag races. Her driving combined all the recklessness of youth with the delayed reactions of age. My foot kept exerting involuntary pressure on an imaginary brake.

She made a wild and illegal left and started down the main street. The sight of it made me forget her driving for the moment.

Though I'd gone back regularly while my parents were alive and still came out to see Babe, the changes in the town always caught me off guard. Signs in the windows of the formerly pricey specialty shops—there were no boutiques in those days— where my mother used to shop when she wasn't up to taking the train into New York screamed that I could have anything in the

store for ninety-nine cents. The luncheonette where we'd gone
for Cokes and pound cake in high school was a substance abuse
center. Two of the movie theaters were boarded up, but a third
was papered with posters of naked women sporting black
squares and rectangles and X's like salacious bikinis. Billboards
and signs sold me things I didn't want in languages I didn't
understand. Babe and her contemporaries clung to the few sur-
viving upscale residential pockets of the city and mourned that
downtown was dead. It wasn't dead, merely different.

We passed my old friend Nancy's house, which sat on a
large corner plot on the fringe of what used to be the best neighborhood in town. Babe took her eyes from the road, though she
didn't slow the car.

"They finally sold the Gold place," she said, glancing at the
fake Tudor facade with its pattern of leaded windows. "They're
going to make it into a funeral parlor." She turned back to the
road just in time to avoid a parked car. We sped through town
and out into the suburban sprawl.

I was relieved when we pulled into the driveway of a large
ugly red-brick building. Then I looked more closely. It could
have been an upscale motel or a hospital. There was a little
grass, some pavement, and too many ramps and electronic sliding doors.

We parked the car and made our way up a ramp and
through a set of sliding doors into the lobby. It was like walking
into a mass of cotton candy. Everything was pink and gossamer.

Babe got it before I did. "You know why it's decorated like
this?" she asked.

"Bad taste?"

"Bad taste and all women." She straightened the sweater
around her shoulders with a sharp tug.

The comment surprised me. When I was growing up, Babe
had been the only woman I knew well who wasn't going

through life as someone's wife. Though the achievement hadn't been entirely her choice, she'd carried it off with panache. She had a thrilling, at least to me, irreverence born of independence. She also seemed to have more fun than the other women. And though she was the only one of their group without a husband, at least a husband on site, she seemed to take a more genuine pleasure in the company of men. That last was a sad irony or maybe, I thought as I followed her across the lobby, merely a case of cause and effect.

From behind a white desk scrolled with pink, a security guard eyed us as if we intended to make off with the tall pink urns filled with pink and white feathers. This was a home for aging women done up like a bordello specializing in underaged girls. But something more than the decor was bothering me. The place was cheap, but it wasn't inexpensive. I didn't know how Babe was going to afford it, but then I didn't know much about Babe's finances. She'd never worked, unless you called helping her friends redecorate their houses work. I'd never understood why, once her flier was no longer on the scene, she hadn't got a job, but that said more about me than about Babe. She'd had a small inheritance from her family and some benefits from her flier, but neither of those would have kept her in greens fees. Even my mother, who'd known more about Babe than anyone, hadn't known how she did it. Mainly my mother chalked it up to Babe's resourcefulness and my father's good advice on investments.

Babe told the security guard she had an appointment with Mr. Damon. Only faintly reassured, the guard picked up the phone and grumbled into it. A moment later a portly man with rosy skin that seemed too tight for his body and the solicitous air of an undertaker came striding across the pink marble floor. He took Babe's hand, told her he was so glad to meet her, and said he knew she was going to be happy at The Towers. Then he repeated the ceremony with me. I couldn't decide whether he was being polite to her or insulting to me.

He rubbed his hands together and asked if we were ready for the grand tour. Babe said she'd like to see the facilities. He led us up and down halls and through common rooms, past women in groups and women with walkers and women in wheelchairs and one man with a cane. He showed us the library, which had a few shelves of books and a large television that took up one wall, and the solarium, which had a round skylight and pots of pink and white artificial flowers, and the exercise room, which had nothing except pink mats stacked against one wall. He led us past a door that said "Doctor's Office" and another that read "Beauty Shoppe" and into a dining room where gray- and white- and blue-haired heads bent and bobbed and trembled over pink tablecloths. Several of the heads looked up as we passed. I saw eyes narrow behind glasses. I watched women taking in Babe. I noticed Babe quickening her step.

Mr. Damon took us to his office and indicated two pink upholstered chairs across from his desk. I took one. Babe sat on the edge of the other.

He told us about care plans and floor plans, meals per day and costs per month, trays to the room and outings to the big city, the rate of turnover and the length of the waiting list. "Of course," he said, "we never know when we're going to have a vacancy." He paused for a moment, like a mourner paying tribute over a grave.

Babe stood. Mr. Damon looked startled. Clearly he wasn't accustomed to being interrupted in the middle of his spiel. She shook his hand, thanked him, and started for the door.

"Your floor plans." He picked up the brochures from his desk and held them out to her.

She kept going. I took the brochures from Mr. Damon and followed her out of the office.

She was walking quickly now, moving down the overdone halls and across the garish lobby and through the sliding doors with her familiar athletic stride. By the time we reached the car, her breath was short. This time I didn't offer to drive.

"I think," Babe said as she turned the key in the ignition with an angry twist, "I'd rather be caught walking Broad Street with my bra outside my blouse. Come on, I'll take you to the club for lunch."

I usually hated to go to the club for lunch, but after what we'd just seen, the prospect of eating overcooked, under-seasoned food in an anachronistic setting didn't seem so terrible.

I hadn't been to Rolling Hills Country Club, which lay on a pancake-flat parcel of land beneath one of the flight paths to the airport, in years, but the minute we pulled up in front of the fake colonial clubhouse with the out-of-proportion pillars—it had been built in the fifties during the first major revival of *Gone With the Wind*—it all came back. Even the clean-cut, conventionally barbered, earringless kid who took the car from Babe could have stepped out of my adolescence.

On the grounds groups of men, turned out like paunchy Popsicles in raspberry and lemon and lime golf clothes, were getting ready to tee off. In the clubhouse women waited their turns. That hadn't changed either. The patience of Babe's contemporaries, older women who still called themselves girls, though these days they were living off tales of the successful women who were their daughters, didn't surprise me, but who were these contemporaries of mine who waited docilely until the men had had their hour in the sun, or at least time on the green?

We went into the dining room. The steward greeted Babe effusively. He was as smarmy as the director of the retirement home, but not so offensive. It took me a moment to realize why.

He treated Babe like the woman he remembered she'd been rather than the burden he was expecting her to become.

He led us to a table in a far corner. Over it hung a plaque listing the winners of the annual mixed foursome tournament. Close to the top Babe's name and my father's were carved in bronze. I used to wonder how my mother felt eating in the shadow of that plaque, but as she'd always been the first to admit, she wasn't athletic, and as she'd never dared say, Babe was a much better woman's player than my father was a man's. In other words, he never could have made it to that plaque without Babe.

Babe didn't mention the retirement community during lunch or even on the ride back to the station, but as she pulled the car up in front of the steps leading to the eastbound platform later that afternoon, she came as close to complaining as she ever did.

"Sometimes I think Henry and Adelaide were lucky," she said. "They lived full lives and went quickly. While they still had their wits about them."

"Within eighteen months of each other," I added. When her head swiveled to me sharply, I wished I hadn't.

On the way back to town I thought about my parents' quick and connected—at least in my mind—deaths and Babe's life. She'd outlived her flier by several decades. She could easily live for another ten or fifteen or even twenty years. First she wouldn't be able to grip a golf club, then she'd have to stop driving, and finally she'd begin forgetting things or remembering them so often that she'd tell me the same stories again and again in the same conversation. But she'd never check herself into that retirement home. Any more than she'd married any of those men that my mother had begun turning up after Babe's flier was finally and completely out of the picture. She'd go out with them for a while, and my mother would get her hopes up, and my father would warn her not to, and suddenly it would be over, and my mother would tell Babe she was a fool, and Babe would say no, she guessed she was just a one-man woman. Then my mother, the happily married woman, the devoted wife, the incomplete half of a perfect married whole, would shake her head and say that Babe was even more of a fool than she'd thought.

Thirteen

EMMA HAD told me when we'd first discussed the article that she'd be away for the third and fourth weeks in June. Her son would be home from Princeton, and her daughter would be out of school, and they were going to take a family vacation in Devon before Becky went off to her summer program in York and Matt headed for his in Aix. At the time I'd told her we'd probably be finished with the interviews by then, but as her departure drew closer, I found I didn't feel finished. There was more I wanted to know, though I couldn't say what. I felt as if I were missing something, that crucial piece about Emma or her life or maybe only my take on Emma and her life that would give the profile a heart or at least a center. My lunch with Julian hadn't helped. He'd answered a couple of questions, but raised a lot more. I set up another meeting with Emma for the week she returned.

In the meantime, there was nothing I could do while she was away except read and reread the transcripts of our conversations, a pastime more likely to produce boredom or panic than insight or inspiration. I suppose the fact that Dexter's itinerary didn't take him near New York for the next several weeks didn't help. I ran off a fresh copy of the proposal for the women of death row and sent it to Kay Meechum, who'd expressed an interest at lunch.

Then two days after Emma left, Dexter called and asked if my passport was in order.

"In order?" I repeated. "It's a garden-variety American passport, not the letters of transport in *Casablanca*."

"What I meant, smart-ass, was, do you have one that hasn't expired? And if you do, would you like to use it to meet me in Italy?"

Would I.

I'm usually a careful, maybe compulsive, packer, but then I've never packed for a week in Italy on forty-eight hours' notice. I know these days that's a shameful admission to make— one of my neighbors has a lawsuit pending against an airline for refusing to enroll her cat, who pays full feline fare, in their frequent flier program—but it's true. At any rate, when I got back from the Alitalia office and The Traveller's Bookstore and the bank and started throwing things into my suitcase, I managed to forget a robe, an extra pair of sunglasses, and my address book, but for some reason in my haste I tossed the profile of Dexter into my briefcase along with an Italian dictionary and the *Blue Guide: Northern Italy* and the *Cadogan Guides: Tuscany, Umbria, & the Marches*. I'm not sure why. I still didn't plan to let him read it before publication. I especially didn't plan to let him read it sitting on an ancient terrace in the shade of an umbrella pine sipping Orvieto during what was supposed to be an Italian tryst. Looking back now, I suspect I packed it for my own reassurance. The closer I got to publication, the more I worried about how he was going to react to it. Or maybe it was only the closer I got to Dexter.

And we did get close that week, closer than I'd ever gotten to anyone before. I said that to one of my long-married friends later, but she insisted vacations didn't count. They were too easy. I didn't agree. I still don't. Maybe a week or two on foreign soil isn't what Auden called for in that line I'd finally tracked down after Julian Weill had quoted it, "a creation of time and will," but that doesn't make it a piece of cake.

Cast adrift from accustomed identities, isolated by language, severed from the familiar, people tend to react intensely. The self becomes more fragile. The other person's influence grows stronger. Circumstances force intimacy the way speed photography in a nature documentary propels a bud into a flower or a harmless larva into a predatory beast. The acceleration takes away perspective as well as breath. At least that was the way it happened to me.

Strengthened emotions obliterated memory. We had no pasts. At least we'd never done any of this before. One afternoon, climbing to a medieval church perched high in a hill town, we stumbled across a street sign. "Via S. Giovanni" stood out in freshly painted white letters against the age-blackened building. "I have to get this," I said as I took the cover off my camera lens. Without a word Dexter crossed the street to the sign and stood beneath it, squinting into the sun behind me and grinning to beat the band, grinning as if he hadn't done this a dozen times in front of a dozen other signs saying St. John this or S. Giovanni that for a dozen other women or at least his former wife.

Suddenly everything was mixed up with Dexter. It wasn't enough to stand on a terrace overlooking a patchwork quilt of ripening fields; I had to call to him to come out on the terrace to see the view. In museums I was always hurrying to catch up with him or slowing down to wait for him. Meals were orgies of moving plates and mutual tastings. I couldn't separate the sound of water splashing into a stone fountain from the cadences of his absurd exaggerated Robert De Niro–Al Pacino Italian; or walk across a cobbled square without hearing the crunch of his shoes beside mine; or, when we awakened from a nap late one afternoon in a big square room with putti cavorting on the carved ceiling and Italian voices dancing beyond the big open window, distinguish Dex from the landscape of my life as he loomed over me, his shoulders as brown as the Umbrian earth against a mauve sky, his mouth open in a silent scream like one of Maitani's damned souls in the bas-relief of the Duomo.

Another night I awakened disoriented, lost, listening to the pounding of my own heart and thinking of death, which suddenly seemed appallingly imminent. Then without thought, without hesitation, I turned on my side, wound myself around him, and hung on for dear life, because I finally knew, with a shock of comprehension, about love, which was nothing more and nothing less than a beating back of death. Or so it seemed in the three-o'clock-in-the-morning darkness.

Miraculously we seemed to want to do the same things at the same time. That surprised me. For one thing, my occasional travels with men had led me to expect idiosyncrasies, if not downright peculiarities. The political writer's idea of getting to know a city was sitting in on municipal hearings. Before that I'd been mixed up with a naturalist who'd insisted on spending one of our three days in Paris at the zoo observing the social order of the primates and watching the lions fornicate. For another, I'd grown up with two parents whose perfect marital compatibility had been marred only by the fact that they'd shared few interests. My mother had a profound, if promiscuous, passion for the theater, which she nourished in New York but loved to satiate in London. My father always complained that the applause at the end of a play wakened him. My mother, as I've said, was an inveterate shopper. My father, once he'd reached a point in life where he could pay for my mother's shopping, took up golf with a vengeance. They joked about taking separate vacations. Of course, everyone knew it was only a joke. Now and then they took Babe along instead. Babe might be a one-man woman, but she was eclectic in her interests. She was also a good sport. When my father needed a surrogate wife to make up a mixed foursome, Babe was available. If my mother wanted company while searching for the best buys on shoes in Florence or perfume in Paris, Babe was game. Babe was also no fool. She knew that as a third wheel she was along on the Caribbean jaunt or the European tour on sufferance.

One afternoon, as I stood on the terrace of an old manor house outside Orvieto, I found myself remembering the disparity of interests that my parents seemed to notice only on vacation. The manor house was part of a working farm, and at dinner the night before Dex had joked about the way the wife stood over the huge wood-burning stove, her face shiny with perspiration, her hands constantly in motion, her eyes tracking the team of local girls who carried the heavy platters of pasta and poultry and meat to the dining room, while her husband, a lithe northern Italian blond who oozed charm the way his wife did sweat and looked ten years her junior, sat at the head of the long farm table entertaining Milanese businessmen and Roman journalists and American tourists. Some joke, I said to Dexter.

I stood on the terrace in the late afternoon thinking about my parents and the manager and his wife and watching the men who'd come in from the fields and were leaning against the buildings, some standing, others hunched down with elbows resting on bent knees, each with a cigarette dangling from his mouth. As I stood watching, I saw Dex, who was coming back from the pool carved into the side of the hill below the manor house, start across the courtyard. The manager called to him, and he answered in his excessive but still-musical Italian. The manager said something else, Dex stopped, crossed to the men, and, as they stood talking, eased his shoulders against the wall in line with them, one of the group. The only difference was that Dex had a towel around his neck and didn't have a cigarette dangling from his mouth.

Nothing happened for a while, except the occasional comment I couldn't understand and the languid inhaling and exhaling of carcinogens in the syrupy warmth of the late-afternoon sun. Then one of the young women who worked in the kitchen came out of a building and started across the courtyard toward the manor house. The men went on leaning and smoking. No one moved, but I sensed a shift, as if they'd drawn together. One or two of them said something to her—nothing hostile, I knew from the tone, but something easy and good-natured—and as she made her way past them, she answered in the same vein. She wasn't especially beautiful, but she was ripe. She was the kind of young woman at the stage of life when men and other women, ungenerous women, point out that in five or seven or ten years she'll have put on weight, and lost her looks, and become that shameful thing, a prematurely old woman. Maybe that's what the men were joking about as she moved out of hearing and disappeared into the house, because one of the laborers said something else, and the manager answered him, and a ripple of laughter ran through the group. The laughter wasn't mean, but it wasn't as good-natured as the comments to her had been, and as I stood listening to the sound, I heard, mingling with it, imitating it just as his accent imitated theirs, the familiar deep roll of Dexter's laughter. It crept across the sunny courtyard as relentlessly as the shadows of the ancient walls and crenellated battlements fell across the perfect clarity of the Renaissance squares every afternoon, and it carried the same chill. Suddenly I realized that what I'd mistaken for intimacy was merely proximity. I thought of another quote about marriage. This time I couldn't recall who'd said it, but I knew the words exactly. "If you fear loneliness, never marry."

Dexter pulled himself up and away from the wall and moved off from the other men. A few minutes later he came out onto the terrace talking about how tobacco was one of the last of the capitalist and colonialist scourges. By the time the dusk had crept up the valley and onto the terrace, I could barely remember the line about marriage, let alone who'd said it.

* * *

Two days later we said good-bye in a chilly, crowded marble and plastic airport arcade. Dexter was flying east. I was flying west. We kissed, then picked up our carry-ons and stood looking at each other for another moment.

"You know," he said finally, "I could get used to this."

It occurred to me as I sat waiting for my plane to board that I already had.

The panic struck somewhere over the Atlantic, an hour or two into the flight. I told myself it had to do with my old terror of being suspended several thousand feet in the air where surely no man, or woman, was meant to go. I told myself it was the emptiness beside me where Dex had been for the last week, or rather the intrusive presence of the suit in the next seat, who was putting away prodigious amounts of diet soda while he chuckled and snorted and guffawed at Steve Martin on the screen a few rows ahead of us. I stopped the steward and told him I'd like another split of wine. But the wine didn't help, and finally I pulled my briefcase out from beneath the seat in front of me, where I'd stowed it in keeping with airline regulations, opened it, and took out the draft of Dexter's profile.

I was halfway through the first page and feeling marginally reassured when the steward came by and told me I'd have to lower my window shade because other people wanted to enjoy the in-flight movie even if I didn't. I lowered the window shade. A shadow fell across the manuscript. I turned on the overhead light. It wasn't as brilliant as the blinding sunshine outside the window, but it was bright enough to read by.

The comment from Dexter's colleague appeared on the next to the last page. I read it once, then a second time, though I'd already read it so many times I knew it by heart. But now I saw it in a different light. And now I knew I'd been fooling myself. It was no good telling myself that it could have been worse. I could have used the entire quote. Dexter wasn't likely to see it that way. And he wasn't likely to forgive me for it either.

Fourteen

HE STEPPED into the plastic bubble that was supposed to shut out the noise of the airport and punched in the phone number. He knew it was a mistake. It never worked when he called from hotels or airports halfway around the world. When she was younger, she'd always wanted to know when he was coming home. Try to explain four days or two weeks to a three- or five- or seven-year-old. Now she didn't even bother to ask.

He put his hand against his free ear as he listened to the phone ringing. He hoped Nan wouldn't answer. They were on good terms. A civilized divorce, she told everyone. She even made a point of inviting him to Thanksgiving and Christmas dinners. So Sophie wouldn't have to choose between parents, she said. He wondered what she'd do if he ever accepted.

He recognized Nan's voice, though Sophie was sounding more like her every day.

"Hi," he said. "It's me. Dexter." He waited for what he knew was coming. What she couldn't resist saying.

"Where is it this time? The North Pole or just Timbuktu?" She was civilized only if you didn't know the timbre of her voice or hadn't spent nine years listening to her digs.

"Italy," he answered as if she'd asked the question out of interest rather than vindictiveness. "Rome airport."

"The airport. That means your flight was delayed."

"Is Sophie there?"

"She's here. Hang on."

He waited. He could tell from the sweep of the second hand on his watch that no one was hurrying at the other end of the line. Then Sophie was on the phone with that awful flat, bored voice that made him wish he were back to explaining how long four days or two weeks were.

"How're you doing, sport?"

"Okay."

There was a silence while he waited for more, though he knew he wasn't going to get any more. He tried to think of another gambit. He didn't want to ask about school. The question made him feel like a stranger and her angry.

"How's the tennis going?"

"Okay."

"What about that new serve you were working on?"

A disembodied voice announced first in Italian, then in English that his flight was still delayed.

"I didn't hear you," he said.

"Okay," she repeated.

"You know, Soph, I really admire your ability to carry on a conversation with a bare minimum of vocabulary."

"Where are you?" she said, and he thought he could hear a slight relenting in her voice.

"Rome. Leonardo da Vinci Airport."

"Is your plane delayed again?"

She was her mother's daughter all right.

"Delayed? Alitalia never heard of the word. It's merely the national flair for living in the moment and savoring life. I thought I'd catch you before you left for school."

"School's over for the summer. I got out last week."

He winced.

"Listen"—she went on—"I have to go now. Mom says we'll be late."

"Take care of yourself."

"Sure."

"I miss you."

"Sure."

It could have been Nan speaking. The edge of irony was that sharp.

"I'll be home in a week and a half."

"Listen, Dad, I really have to go."

"Sure."

There was a moment's pause, as if she'd heard the echo of her own skepticism.

"See you," she said. And then, out of nowhere: "Buy me something nice in Italy."

Her laugh was childish and greedy and genuine, and it went through him like a shot of whiskey, relaxing every muscle.

"I already have," he said, but he couldn't tell if she'd heard him before the connection had gone dead.

He hung up the phone and stood for a moment inside the plastic bubble. She'd sounded all right at the end. And at least Nan hadn't got back on the phone to talk to him. Lately she'd taken to getting back on the line to discuss what she called Sophie's problems.

"She has trouble with men," she'd said a month or so ago.

"Men. Christ, Nan, she's fifteen."

"All right, boys. But she has problems, and I hate to have to tell you this, but it's your fault."

He bet she hated to have to tell him that.

"What problems?"

"She's inordinately needy."

"What does that mean, Nan?"

"It means that she wants boys to give her the affection her father never did."

"I give her affection."

"When you're around. It also means she gets mixed up with unavailable men. Boys."

"What's an unavailable fifteen-year-old? A kid who cares more about basketball than marriage and children?"

"I'm not going to talk to you about this if you can't be serious."

"I'm being serious, but I think you're exaggerating."

"If you lived with her, you'd understand. She develops these wild crushes on older boys who won't give her the time of day."

"That's adolescence, not psychosis."

"I knew you'd say that. Tell me, if she were suffering from a vitamin deficiency rather than an emotional deprivation, would you pay attention then?"

"I'm paying attention now. Just what is it you want me to do?"

But of course, what she wanted him to do was to undo the nine years they'd spent together, or at least the last five of them, which she insisted they hadn't spent together at all, and he had to admit she had a point about that. What she wanted him to do was take an hour of prime time on all four networks and CNN to announce that it was his fault. He was a selfish bastard and an insensitive lout who'd ruined her life and was now going to work on Sophie's. And maybe she was right. At least about Sophie.

He picked up his briefcase and his carry-on and stepped out of the plastic bubble.

Maybe he hadn't been around enough. Maybe he was, as she said, as she'd never tired of saying toward the end, distant and unavailable and too busy playing God to bother being a father, but Christ, it couldn't all be his fault. You had to factor in Nan, who had her own problems with men, as she liked to phrase it, and genes and temperament and, as he'd told Nan, plain old adolescence, which would pass. You couldn't blame it all on him. But she did. And he wasn't sure she wasn't right.

Fifteen

EMMA SAT in the oversize club chair redolent of new leather, aged tobacco, and other Savile Row shop pretensions, and wondered how men had managed to keep the secret for so long.

The tailor's hands, lightning quick as a magician's, smoothed the buttery fabric over Julian's shoulders.

She wondered how they managed to go on keeping the secret, because most women still didn't have a clue. Even the ones who'd won all the other male perks hadn't caught on. She knew dozens of women who waved the flag and spouted the credos and brought the lawsuits, but just let a waiter approach with the check, and they launched into their best imitations of Phyllis Schlafly. She'd pointed out the inconsistency to her friend Greta, who, perhaps because she was ten years younger, had no qualms about asking a man to dinner but would rather eat Chinese takeout food alone in front of television reruns than take a man to dinner. "When women's salaries catch up with men's," Greta had countered, "then I'll begin picking up the check." The argument would have been more convincing if Greta weren't pulling down a hefty six figures a year in a white-shoe Wall Street law firm.

The tailor's magical hands gave a little tug to the back vent; then, as miraculously as if he were pulling a rabbit from a hat, a small chalk mark appeared at the soft tweed base of Julian's spine.

What Greta and the rest of them missed was the thrill of magnanimity. The feeling wasn't as heady as achievement or as heated as sex, but it was related to both. That was what men had always known. That was why they ran around buying women diamond bracelets and mink coats. They did it to show off, and they did it in exchange for sex, but they did it for the sheer palpable pleasure of it too.

The salesman stood solemnly at the ready to help Julian off with one jacket and on with the next.

It wasn't power. She'd never dream of telling Julian he couldn't buy something or even make him ask for anything, though God knows she knew enough men in her position who would. She remembered the women who used to come into her mother's store. When business was busy, she'd had to pitch in and ring up and wrap their purchases. "Take the price tag off," some of the women would whisper, their voices rustling like the peach tissue paper, "so he won't know how much it cost." Then there were the others, the ones who'd married generous men. She could still see them standing at the desk signing their names in bold, flourishing scripts. Their wrists circled imperiously as they wrote; their chins rode at a stately angle. When it came to courage and pride of signature, the Founding Fathers had nothing on those women. They too were making a declaration, a statement that they existed and were to be reckoned with. Only Emma had known even then that they didn't and weren't, because the names those women had signed had belonged to their husbands, and the only claim they'd had to them had been the pathetic attenuated "Mrs." they'd written in front. That was evident on the occasions when those same women came back a day or two later, clutching their purchases, some shamefaced, some on the offensive because they knew the items were nonreturnable, making a variety of excuses for the simple fact that the man who paid the bills had said no or at least not this time. Then for one delicious moment her mother, to whom they all condescended because she no longer had a full man's name to call her own, got her own back. Almost.

The American Express bill that Julian had signed the week before when he'd ordered the clothes was in his own name, of course, so neither the salesman nor the tailor could have guessed. But she and Julian knew the truth. It was their secret, not dirty exactly, but faintly erotic.

The salesman asked Julian if he'd care to step into the fitting room to try on the suit, asked as if Julian would be doing him a great favor, and Julian disappeared behind a heavy oak door and reappeared a few moments later looking like something out of a Noël Coward comedy or at least a *GQ* spread. The tailor guided him back to the three-way mirror. Emma watched as Julian faced off with an audience of his own images. She saw his eyes narrow as he took them in and his mouth widen into a devastating smile, and for the first time in a long time she felt the charge of that smile. In some sane corner of her mind she knew the whole ceremony was absurd—the unconscionably priced clothes he didn't need, the narcissism she shouldn't encourage, the pride she didn't want to feel—but the kick was still there. It was thrilling to be able to do this for him.

She came out of the oversize hotel bathroom into the overdone hotel bedroom and stood beside the bed looking down at him. He was lying on his back, his eyes closed, his mouth slightly open to emit a peaceful rasp as he inhaled and exhaled. She hated to wake him.

She sat on the side of the bed. His lashes fluttered. She put a hand on his chest. His eyes opened.

"The shower's all yours."

He closed his eyes again. "Five more minutes."

"We'll be late."

"All your fault," he murmured with his eyes still closed. "First you drag me up and down Savile Row like some born-again Pygmalion, then you bring me back to the hotel and have your way with me." He opened his eyes. "And now you expect me to go out and play Prince Philip to your Queen Elizabeth."

She stood and pulled the covers off him. "Albert to my Victoria, sweetheart. Theirs was a real love match. Now get moving. And wear your new gray suit."

He swung his legs over the side of the bed and stood. His eyes were unfocused, but his hand went automatically to his penis, as if he were checking to make sure it was still there. Though her sexual experience was limited, she knew from other women's stories and from her own son that it was a universal male reflex. Sometimes it drove her crazy. Now it struck her as innocent and childlike, more like Matt when he was a toddler than drunken bag men wandering the streets or sexual deviates exposing themselves and molesting others. Now it made her feel protective or at least indulgent.

As he padded into the bathroom, she crossed the room to the fake Georgian armoire, took out his new gray suit, and hung it on the front of the door. Then she went to the matching chest of drawers, opened the top one, and took out shorts and a pair of dark socks. That was when she noticed the brown paper bag beneath them. She didn't remember buying anything in a flat brown paper bag. She put the underwear down, picked up the bag, and took out the two sheets of paper inside. They were prints of London. He must have bought them when she'd left him alone for an hour this morning while she'd gone to see her British agent. She wondered why he hadn't shown them to her. There was no reason he should have, really, except that he was usually eager to show her the old books and prints he picked up at secondhand shops and stalls. That was part of the pleasure. He was always so proud of his finds. She didn't understand the collecting instinct herself. Her acquisitiveness ran along other lines. But she always managed to work up some enthusiasm for his.

She looked at the prints again. They were scenes of Fleet Street. That was why he hadn't shown them to her. Because he'd bought them for her. The last time they'd been in London he'd found some illustrations from an early edition of *Alice in Wonderland* and had them framed for her birthday. "Carroll created Alice, but you went him eight better," he'd written on the card and listed the names of the heroines in her nine books. She'd hung the illustrations over her desk, and sometimes, when things were going badly, it helped to look at them. Sometimes, the worst times, she'd compare them with the gifts some of her friends received from their husbands for birthdays and anniversaries and Christmas: clothes they'd never wear, jewelry they'd practically had to draw sketches of, and gift certificates. One of her old friends from college received blank signed checks from her husband on all three occasions. Emma had thought that was the worst until the Christmas the same friend's husband had given her a two-week trip to a fat farm.

She looked at the prints again. The Fleet Street connection was a bit of a stretch, unless you counted all the press about her, but it was still sweet. It was so sweet she wanted to go into the bathroom right now and tell him how much she liked them, only she didn't because she knew how much he enjoyed surprising her.

She slipped the prints back into the bag and put the bag back in the drawer beneath a pair of socks. Then she carried his underwear and one of the shirts they'd ordered a week ago and the tie they'd bought that afternoon to go with the new suit to the rumpled bed and laid them out for him.

* * *

The entire A-team had assembled by the time they arrived at the restaurant. Seated around a large circular table were her British publisher, her editor, the directors of advertising and publicity, the London saleswoman, and the Australian salesman, who just happened to be in town and, according to the publisher's introduction, had begged for a chance to meet Emma Weill and tell her how much she was loved Down Under. They stood as one at Emma's approach. She wasn't surprised. All her books, including *Happily Ever After,* were still in print in the U.K. The publisher held the chair between him and the editor for her. Julian slid into the empty chair between the director of publicity and the young woman in charge of advertising. The publisher asked Emma what she wanted to drink. The entire table waited while she told him. It was absurd, Emma knew, but it was nice.

Except for the Australian salesman and the advertising woman, who was new and looked barely old enough to drink the wine that was already flowing the way Pellegrino did at American publishing dinners, they were all old friends. At least that was the way several years of heartwarming royalty statements made it seem. The publisher asked after Matt and Becky. Emma wondered if there was a file card in his office with her children's names on it or if he just had a good memory. She asked after his children, though she couldn't remember their names or even their genders. They talked about the editor's new baby, then moved on to the problems of traveling with small children as opposed to the ordeal of touring with teenagers. It was one of those business dinners where no one would be crass enough to mention business. The closest anyone would come would be a polite inquiry over coffee about what Emma was working on now.

It wasn't until the waiters had taken away the first courses and were bringing the entrées that Emma noticed what was happening. Julian's body was turned to one side and his head was bent close to the advertising woman's, and the woman, who was young, but still old enough to know better, was listing toward him like a ship about to go down.

Emma went on talking about the RSC production they'd seen the night before, and the publisher and the editor went on hanging on her every word, but the editor must have noticed something because a moment later she called across the table to ask the advertising woman, who'd seen the production too, what she'd thought of it. The only problem was that she had to ask twice, because Julian was saying something to the woman, no, he was whispering something to the woman, and she was looking into his eyes and listening as if whatever he was telling her were the goddamn revealed word. By that time the publisher and the publicity director and the London saleswoman and Australian salesman had picked up on what was going on. Emma knew because suddenly they all began to talk. They talked at her and at Julian and at one another. They talked as if they were creating a goddamn diversionary tactic.

The advertising woman turned back to the group, though she didn't meet anyone's eyes, and Julian looked at one after another of them and flashed his take-no-prisoners smile. Then the publisher launched into an anecdote about publishing the royals, and Emma heard the relief in his voice and saw it on the faces of the others. Relief and something else. Pity. Within minutes she'd gone from being a woman to be reckoned with to a figure to be pitied.

She looked across the table at Julian. He was leaning back with his legs crossed and one hand on the back of the advertising woman's chair so that the jacket of the beautiful bespoke suit she'd bought him hung open to reveal the custom-tailored shirt and expensive silk tie she'd paid for. His clothes were perfect and his smile was assured and he gave off a stench of smug pleasure so thick she wanted to slap him.

Sixteen

HE FELT the mattress shift beneath Emma's movement and held his breath. If she gave some sign—her hand on his back, a whispered "Are you up?"—things were all right. It shifted again as she stood. No sign, no word. Things were not all right.

The bathroom door opened, then clicked closed. A lock turned. Things were definitely not all right.

He never should have spent all that time talking to that advertising girl last night. She didn't even have that good a body. One of those horsey English types that look as if they've checked their riding crops and corgis at the door. He hadn't meant to, but he'd had to do something to amuse himself while everyone else danced attendance on Emma. Especially that Oxbridge asshole of a publisher who kept pontificating on the current state of publishing, and the future of a united Europe, and the decline of the whole fucking post–cold war world. Sitting there oozing that insufferable Brit superiority, while he anglicized every French word he could get his hands on, and sucked up to Emma as if she were a Nobel laureate instead of the author of a couple of racy kids' books, and threw him, Julian, an occasional asinine question as a sop. The prick hadn't even bothered to wait for the answers before he'd turned back to Emma. The whole thing had been stomach-turning.

He heard the muffled roar of a toilet flushing, then the pounding of water as she turned on the shower.

It wasn't fair. All he'd done was talk to the girl. Of course, that was all he'd had to do. He'd had her practically coming just sitting there listening to him. That had been the funny part. She'd kept staring up at him with those big faded eyes that looked as if the color had been washed out of them by too many generations of too-careful breeding, and as he'd pretended to look back at her, he'd seen his own reflection, dark and smooth and silky in the new suit, better, certainly, than that beefy prick of a publisher in that cheesy, wrinkled Marks and Spencer off-the-rack number. Christ, the bastard hadn't shut up for a minute. So who could blame Julian for entertaining himself a little?

But Emma hadn't seen it that way. She'd been furious. All that carrying on in the taxi on the way home about humiliating her in front of her publisher. *Her* publisher. As if she owned the little turd. He didn't know which of them he'd hated more, her or that pompous prick.

The problem was she was still angry this morning. He was willing to let it go, why couldn't she? Especially since he hadn't done anything. But he knew from the way she'd got out of bed and disappeared into the bathroom that she wasn't going to let it go. She was going to make him pay. Damn it, it really wasn't fair.

The water was still running in the shower. She'd stay in there for a long time. And when she finally came out, she wouldn't look at him. He hated it when she did that. It made him sick to his stomach. Especially at times like this, when he didn't deserve it.

He had to find a way around it. There was always a way around it.

He picked up the phone and dialed the concierge. It was lucky she was brooding in the shower because he'd need a little time for this.

He was just hanging up the phone as she came out of the bathroom. She'd wound one towel around her body like a sarong and another around her head like a turban. Sure enough, she didn't look at him as she crossed the room to the dresser.

"Don't you want to know whom I was talking to?" he asked in a careful voice, not too cheery, but not apologetic either. After all, he had nothing to apologize for.

She didn't answer.

"I was making travel arrangements."

She closed the drawer and started back to the bathroom with a fistful of lingerie. She was going to get dressed in the bathroom. It was worse than he'd thought.

"For Paris," he said.

She stopped halfway across the room. Now she was looking at him.

"Yeah." He smiled. "I thought we could hop over for a few days."

"We're flying home tomorrow afternoon."

He calibrated her voice. Anger shifting to begrudgment.

"The concierge is taking care of that right now. And don't worry. It's not going to cost that much to change flights. I checked before I told him to go ahead."

"I wasn't worried about the money."

Who was she kidding? But he wasn't about to say that. Not when he'd finally got her talking.

"Then what?" he asked, though he knew the answer. He saw it on her face. She wanted to go home. To her work. To her own life. To other people. To a world where she existed, no, thrived, without him. He couldn't let that happen. "Don't you want to go?" he asked, because he knew the one thing she wouldn't do was come out and say she didn't.

"Without any plans? Without reservations?"

"The concierge is taking care of all that. I told him to get us a room at L'Abbaye. Remember that armoire with all the mirrored doors in the room we had last time?'' He winked at her.

She went on standing in the middle of the room, wound up in all those towels and her anger. He decided not to notice the anger. It was the only way to get her to go. And she had to go. Now that he'd started making the arrangements, he was really high on the idea. They hadn't been to Paris in a couple of years. It would be fun. It would be romantic.

"I thought you'd be pleased. You're the one who's always talking about Paris."

"I am pleased."

"You could've fooled me."

"It's just that . . ."

"What?"

"I don't know. I guess I just need a little time to get used to the idea."

"Look, if you don't want to go, we won't go."

"No, I want to go. It'll be fun."

"Don't do it just to please me."

"I'm not. You know I'm not. I'm the one who's always talking about Paris."

"You're sure?"

"Of course, I'm sure."

"I don't want to force you into anything."

"You're not. It's a great idea. We'll have a wonderful time."

She knew before they even checked into the hotel that he'd been right. Now that they were here. In the little hotel that used to be a convent where they always stayed when they were in Paris. Listening to the sound of French rising and falling around them like the fountains of the city. Mapping out walks together so they could hit this museum at the right time and that shop before it closed and end up at the stalls along the river late in the afternoon so that Julian could buy his books and prints. Sitting in the courtyard of the hotel with aperitifs, debating which restaurants to go to, weighing the two-star meal they'd had at one against a bistro where French publishers dined and they'd sat next to Clint Eastwood last time they'd been there.

Even as they were doing all those things, she knew the four days in Paris were one of the good times that she'd carry around with her from then on. The only thing that kept them from being perfect was her anger at herself for being so small-minded, so recalcitrant, so unfair to Julian that she'd almost missed them.

Seventeen

THE MORNING AFTER I returned from Italy, I was sitting at my desk, thinking about the profile of Dexter and debating whether to call Kay Meechum to make one last stab at changing it, when Kay called me.

I tried to figure out the best way to approach the issue while we exchanged clichés about Italian art and scenery and food and men. Then suddenly Kay got down to business before I had a chance to.

"About the women of death row," she began, "I'm running into some opposition."

Years on the job have made me a good listener. I noticed the way she stumbled over the word *some*. She had more trouble with it than the Italian we'd just been tossing around.

"How much is some?"

"Think brick wall. Face it, Hallie, the thought of women maiming, mutilating, and murdering their nearest and dearest makes women uneasy and scares the living daylights out of men. Even gay men."

"Exactly! It strikes chords. That's why it's such a good idea."

"Maybe, but not for us. Listen, I'm sure you'll place it somewhere."

I recognized the professional kiss of death. Whenever an editor tells you that you're bound to place a piece somewhere, you can be sure there isn't a magazine in the English-speaking world that will buy it.

"What about the other ideas we discussed at lunch? Write up a couple of proposals and send them down to me. Better yet, fax them. I wasn't kidding about the response to the Dexter St.John profile. Your name is still golden around here. Let's not lose the momentum."

I hadn't even known I'd had momentum. Now I felt it running out of me like sand out of a timer. I decided not to ask her about changing Dexter's profile.

The housekeeper who let me in told me Mrs. Weill was in her study and wanted me to go right up. "The fourth floor," she said, and pointed me in the direction of the stairs.

Though I'd been in the garden and the living room and downstairs study of the house, I'd never been upstairs. I started up the first flight. It was a journalist's dream, and a child's. All those empty rooms filled with secrets.

The first door on the second floor was open. As I went past, I glanced inside. I wasn't going to stop and snoop, but I didn't want to overlook background material. Posters of people I didn't recognize hung on the walls. Electronic equipment I wouldn't know how to operate filled the corners. It was the room of an adolescent, and though there was nothing as sexist as the canopied bed and mirrored dressing table I'd grown up with, the worn stuffed animals and dolls on the window seat gave it away as Emma's daughter's room. As I went past, I wondered if it would be any easier growing up with a mother who spoke the language of adolescence, spoke it straight from the heart to millions of other teenagers. Somehow I doubted it.

The door just beyond it was closed. Though there was nothing mysterious about that—logic told me the room probably belonged to Emma's son—I felt the old journalistic itch to open the door and peek inside.

I climbed to the next floor and made my way past a den. I'd written enough breathless appreciations for home design magazines to take it all in at a glance. There were two oversize club chairs, a couch you could drown in, three walls of books, and a fourth fitted with what men's magazines and real estate brokers call an entertainment center. The coffee table was bigger than my dining table. A cashmere throw that experience in the field told me ran to the low four figures was tossed artfully over the back of the sofa. It was the kind of room where two people could read companionably in front of a fire or let down their hair over shitake mushroom pizza and an old Ingmar Bergman movie. I thought of the time Dexter had got sick and we'd had dinner off trays in my bed. The arrangement seemed, by comparison, improvised and fly-by-night. It seemed like Dexter and me. The thought didn't bother me nearly so much as it should have.

I made my way past the room and kept going toward the next open door, which logic told me had to be the master bedroom. I didn't exactly stop, but I did slow my pace. There was a handsome sleigh bed dressed in a lot of embroidered white linen, another fireplace with a Queen Anne chair in front of it, and an armoire with another television inside. There was also, glimpsed through an inner door, a narrow room lined with mirrored doors and furnished with a slipper chair and a valet. Like the closed door downstairs, the room took me back to my childhood. My best friend Nancy's mother had had a similar dressing room where Nancy was always dragging me to show off something she was hoping her mother would let her wear someplace. One day when we were fourteen or fifteen, she put aside a cashmere sweater set and led me into the bathroom that opened off the dressing room.

"You're not going to believe what I found," she whispered.

"What?" I answered in a whisper instinctively.

She opened the medicine cabinet, took out what looked like a powder compact, and held it out to me. I didn't take it from her but stood looking down at it in surprise. My mother and Babe carried silver compacts. I would have expected Nancy's mother to carry something similar, but the one Nancy was holding was a cheap blue plastic number you could pick up at any drugstore or, worse yet, Woolworth's.

Nancy stared at me over the compact with narrowed gimlet eyes. Whenever she looked at me that way, I knew I was going to start to dislike her.

"I bet you don't know what this is," she hissed.

"A powder compact, dummy."

"Shows how much you know, dummy."

Still holding the compact between our chests, mine flat and tight with anticipation, hers rounded and heaving with excitement, she pressed the soft pad of her thumb against the catch. The top popped up. Inside lay a small rubber disk. It was dusty with powder, as I'd expected, but I'd never seen a rubber powder puff, though I'd read in fashion magazines about makeup sponges. Mostly it reminded me of a miniature trampoline.

"What is it?" I asked, though I hated to give her the satisfaction.

"God! Don't you know anything? It's a diaphragm."

"A what?"

"Diaphragm, dummy. For sex." She drew the word out as if she were slurping up a soda. "You know, so you don't get pregnant."

I suppose I did know, because my mother was scrupulous about making sure I knew the things girls were supposed to know, though the bulk of them seemed to have to do with setting tables and writing thank-you notes and turning garments inside out to check for sloppy workmanship, but at that moment the only diaphragm I could think of was the one the music teacher was always carrying on about in glee club.

"What's your mother doing with it?" I asked finally.

Nancy stared at me for a moment, then snapped the compact closed. "I guess they still do it," she mumbled, and turned away from me to put it back in the medicine cabinet.

It was my first experience with the power of the unintentional insult. My question had been genuine. Pregnancy was something that happened to tough girls who wore nylons instead of knee socks to school and the occasional cheerleader. It wasn't something someone's mother had to worry about.

As I started up the last flight of stairs to Emma's study, I remembered another incident that had occurred a few months or maybe even a year or two after that. My mother and father and I had gone to Babe's for dinner, as my mother condescended to do only occasionally—it was more logical, she always argued, for Babe to come to the mountain or at least the family with a full-size house and full-time help than for us to go to her—and though I liked Babe, I didn't like being stuck in her apartment with a bunch of grown-ups. Just in case they'd missed the fact, I'd gone into one of those adolescent sulks I'd perfected to an art by that time and was wandering around the apartment looking at Babe's things, which, despite Babe's slimmer financial straits, weren't terribly different from my mother's things, wondering if I'd die of boredom, and spoiling for trouble. I went into the bathroom and stooged around, sniffing the boxes of Babe's dusting powder and sampling the bottles of her lotion and examining the pink electric razor she kept on a shelf. After I'd exhausted the exposed possibilities, I opened the medicine cabinet. There on the second shelf between a jar of Vaseline and another of cold cream was a blue plastic compact exactly like Nancy's mother's. I stood staring at it for a moment. It looked like Nancy's mother's compact, but it couldn't be like it, because if it was bad enough for Nancy's mother, it was inconceivable for Babe. I knew that kids did it without being married —the tough girls again and some of the cheerleaders again—but I never dreamed that old people might. I remembered the last man my mother had introduced Babe to. His belt had ridden high over his small round belly, and when he'd sat on the end of our sofa, the lamp on the side table had polished the top of his head to a burnished glow. I locked the bathroom door, took the compact from the medicine cabinet, and opened it. Inside was another dusty miniature trampoline. I couldn't believe it. Not Babe. I thought of the balding man with the paunch again. I thought it was lucky I was in the bathroom because I was definitely going to be sick. Gingerly, using only my forefinger, I prodded the trampoline. It gave off a small puff of powder. Or maybe it was dust. That was it! The thing was a memento of Babe's marriage, like the framed wedding picture of her in a short-skirted, big-shouldered suit standing next to a boy whose face was barely visible in the shadow of his peaked officer's cap. Except that I knew it wasn't, because the blue plastic case was new and shiny, and the powder smelled sweet rather than musty, and even then I knew if you were going to keep something as a memento you'd put it in a drawer under a bunch of handkerchiefs or a silk nightgown, not on a shelf in the medicine cabinet, where you'd have to see it every time you went for an aspirin or even brushed your teeth. I put the compact away and went back to the living room, where my father was telling one of his jokes and my mother and Babe were laughing as if they hadn't heard it before.

I never told my mother what I'd found in Babe's medicine cabinet, though several years later when I was living a life that frequently led my mother to ruminate about how things weren't the way they used to be, once or twice I came close.

I reached the fourth floor. The door at the top of the landing was closed. That had to be Julian Weill's study. I glanced down the short hall and saw, through the open door, Emma sitting at her desk. She was holding a phone to her ear with one hand and motioning me in with the other. The gesture was familiar and easy, as if I were a friend and her life an open book.

I spent several hours with Emma that afternoon. They were pleasant but not especially productive. Most of the things we talked about were variations on things we'd talked about before. I told myself, as I went down the stairs past all the open and closed doors that it was time to start writing, though we'd made another appointment for the day after next. More than time. Sugar hadn't commissioned a definitive biography. She wasn't even looking for dirt. All she wanted was a flattering profile to make the women of America salivate over Emma's life, and one or two warts to convince them they were really better off with their own.

I came out of the house into a colorless afternoon that felt more like March than June, but at least the rain had stopped. I put my umbrella back in my briefcase, and as I stood on the sidewalk debating whether to walk or take a cab, I heard the heavy front door of the house open and close behind me. I turned to see Julian Weill coming down the steps. When he got to the bottom, he looked at me, then up at the sky, then back at me and gave me one of those killer smiles. "Might as well be back in England." He lifted his arm to flag down the cab coming toward us. "Come on, I'll give you a lift and bore you with stories of our travels. Everything short of slides."

I thanked him but said I was going to walk. The words were out before I'd thought about them, and I didn't understand why. All I knew was that I felt suddenly uncomfortable with him. Maybe it was the fact that I hadn't seen him since that confessional lunch at the Princeton Club. Or maybe it was the more recent memory of peering into his bedroom and dressing room.

He stood looking down at me for a moment with another

smile. The man had a trunkload of them. I pegged this one as faint amusement. "Then I'll walk too," he said. He motioned the driver on. The driver suggested in an accent that was thick but not thick enough to disguise the words that Julian Weill and I go fuck ourselves.

"Has it occurred to you," Julian asked as the driver gunned his motor and sped off, "that the quality of life in this city isn't what it used to be?"

I started east. He fell in step beside me. "You sound like my mother."

"Obviously a woman of some discernment. Does she live in town?"

"My mother died three years ago. But I was just remembering the way she used to complain . . ." I hesitated. "She used to deliver these . . . not diatribes exactly . . . more like plaints really . . . about how things weren't the way they used to be . . . which, of course, they never were." I finished lamely because I realized where the conversation was taking me and, worse still, where it had come from, and I couldn't very well tell him how a glimpse of his dressing room, which I hadn't been invited into in the first place, had made me remember my first encounters with adult sex, both licit and illicit. So I asked him about England, and he told me for a while.

"I brought something for you," he said.

I was so surprised that I stopped walking. "For me!"

"Keep calm. It isn't much."

"I can't take anything from you. You know that."

He'd stopped walking too and stood looking down at me with the amused smile. I was beginning to dislike it seriously.

"I told you, Hallie, we're not talking crown jewels here. Just a couple of prints I found in a secondhand store, which set me back all of about two pounds. Do you think your professional scruples can handle that?" He took a brown paper bag from the outside pocket of his briefcase and handed it to me. "The damn things aren't even framed or gift-wrapped. If I were trying to bribe you or seduce you or whatever the hell you want to call it into writing something wonderful about Emma, I'd at least frame the damn things and have them gift-wrapped. Go ahead and look at them before I begin to feel stupid."

I slipped the prints out of the bag. They were scenes of turn-of-the-century London. The script in the lower left hand corner read "Fleet Street." I liked them a lot. I also had the feeling they cost more than a pound apiece, but then I'm the woman who splurged on a pair of vintage art deco earrings only to find out they'd been made in Korea circa 1995.

"They're terrific, but I really can't."

He shook his head slowly back and forth. "Come on, Hallie. I've known reporters who've gone to jail rather than reveal a source and writers who've quit when Murdoch took over. Even I have turned down the occasional scurrilous assignment. But I've never known anyone who thought a couple of secondhand prints would compromise her professional ethics. A couple of prints of Fleet Street that were probably clipped from an old magazine in the first place. Let's get real here."

Now I felt stupid as well as compromised. I looked from him to the prints, then back at him.

"Besides," he said, and put his hand on my elbow to start me walking again, "you're writing a piece on Emma, not me, and this has nothing to do with her. Except that she's the one who gave me the articles."

"What articles?"

"The ones you gave her when she said she wanted to see some of your work. I read them on the plane to London, and I was impressed."

"By a weekend at Canyon Ranch?"

"Okay, so that one didn't exactly push the envelope of investigative reporting. But the others were good. Really good. You do the thing I can never pull off. You stay out of the piece.

The things read as if they wrote themselves. That's good stuff. Good journalism, if you'll excuse the expression." He stopped and turned to me. "That's why when I saw the prints of Fleet Street, I thought, hey, I know someone who'll get a boot out of these."

"They're nice . . . they're terrific . . . but really, I can't."

"Come on, Hallie, colleague to colleague. Besides, I wanted to say thank you."

"For what?"

"For listening. That day at the Princeton Club. I don't usually run off at the mouth that way."

"You didn't run off at the mouth."

"The hell I didn't. I was practically foaming. I guess it had just been building up for too long." He glanced at his watch, muttered something about being late, and stepped into the street to hail a cab.

I stood looking after him. "Thanks," I said above the noise of the traffic.

"*De nada,*" he answered as the cab pulled up. He opened the door, then turned back to me. "I mean that literally. They don't mean anything."

I stood on the sidewalk watching the cab pull away. I was angry at myself for accepting the prints, but I'd felt churlish when I'd tried to refuse them. No, not churlish, foolish and self-important. My refusal had implied that the prints meant something. That was why he'd gone out of his way as he was getting into the cab to tell me they didn't.

As the taxi turned west on Seventy-ninth Street, I caught a last glimpse of Julian Weill lounging back in the cab and smiling to himself. That was when I remembered another piece of advice Pat O'Dougherty had given me when I was starting out. "Trust your instincts," she'd told me after she'd compared an article I'd written with the notes I'd given her for the fact checkers. I thought of my first meeting with Julian Weill at the reception when Emma had presented an award. I looked down at the prints in my hand. They didn't mean nothing. No matter what he said.

Eighteen

JULIAN LEANED FORWARD and gave his own address to the driver. As the cab turned west, he got a glimpse of her standing on the sidewalk looking surprised. She hadn't expected him to pick up and leave so suddenly. After that business with the prints she'd been sure he'd try to press his advantage. And she'd been gearing up for it. If he'd offered to walk her home or suggested coming up, she'd have protested. She thought of herself as high-minded. He'd bet, right here and now, that at some point in the next couple of weeks she'd invoke Emma's name and use the word *sisterhood*.

God, he loved women. They were so much damn fun. And so eager. At least in the beginning. It was only later that the eagerness became something else. That obscene hunger. Talk to me. Pay attention to me. Fill me up. That disgusting possessiveness. Where were you? Whom were you with? When am I going to see you again? It was funny how they all turned out to be the same, because in the beginning they were all different or at least new, and the challenge was figuring out how to play them.

Like that business with the prints. The minute he'd seen those prints, she'd popped into his head. That was funny because he hadn't given her a thought after they'd left New York. He'd been too busy with the kids and Emma. It had been a good vacation. Except for that night in London when they'd gone to dinner with Emma's prick of a publisher. And he'd managed to snatch victory from the jaws of defeat on that one. But the minute he'd seen those prints he'd thought of her and known right off she'd like them. It was a gift he had. A gift for giving. Every woman he'd ever given anything said so. Even his mother used to say so. Other kids had bought their mothers crap jewelry from Woolworth's. He'd given his sheet music she could play on the piano and, later, records. She used to like to dance with him to the records. He just couldn't help choosing the right thing. Sometimes, like at Christmas when he saw all those poor schmucks stooging around lingerie departments looking as if they wished the floor would open up and swallow them or wandering around jewelry stores shelling out bundles because they couldn't think of anything else to do, he had to feel sorry for them. Just pay attention, he wanted to tell them. Just listen to her for a minute and think a little. It was so easy he didn't understand why they didn't catch on. But they didn't, fortunately, because that made him a prince among men.

It also meant all the shrinks, and the card-carrying feminists, and Emma when she was on one of her tears were wrong. He'd read the books, and he knew the arguments: Compulsive womanizers didn't love women; they hated them. Well, to begin with, he wasn't a compulsive anything. He just loved women. If he didn't, how would he know so much about how to get around them?

Like the business of convincing her to accept the prints. He'd known when he'd bought them that she'd refuse them at first. As if two lousy prints would compromise her precious professional integrity. As if someone who wrote about weekends at fat farms and life after the Betty Ford Clinic had any integrity to compromise. He wasn't blaming her. In this business you wrote what you had to so you could occasionally write what you wanted to. He hadn't even been lying, at least not entirely. She was pretty good at what she did. Maybe not as good as he'd made her sound, but not bad. The point was he'd known which buttons to press. Even with Emma he knew. Though he really did love Emma.

But he loved women too. God, he really did! It was like that old French saw. *Plus ça change* and all that. She never would have bought a compliment about her, but talk about her work, tell her she was the greatest thing in print since H. L. Mencken and I. F. Stone, and she began to melt like butter on a hot grill. Because that was all they really wanted, for some man to make them feel good about themselves. At least that was all they wanted in the beginning. And that was why he loved them. At least in the beginning. He really did. He didn't care what anybody said. He was crazy about women. He wished he could fuck each and every one of them.

Nineteen

WHEN I GOT BACK to my apartment, there was a message from Dexter. He was calling from another place I had to look up on a map to say he'd be back in New York the following Thursday. As I stood listening to his voice, I made up my mind. Maybe it was guilt about breaking another of Pat O'Dougherty's rules by accepting the prints. Or maybe it was just that I'm an impatient woman, even for disaster. I was going to give him the profile to read.

Dexter's plane was due in at eight-twenty that Thursday night. With luck he'd get to my apartment by nine or nine-thirty. By ten o'clock he'd have read the profile. I figured by ten-fifteen it would all be over, one way or another.

I began looking at my watch at a little after four. The gesture was so powerfully familiar it was almost a flashback. And it had less to do with the expectation of disaster than the anticipation of Dexter's arrival. I grabbed my bag and left the apartment.

As I came out onto the street, Pasha, the doorman, asked if I wanted a cab. I told him I was going to walk.

"Nice day for it," he said. "Have a good one, Mrs. Fields."

Now there was a subject for an *Era* article. To New York doormen all women past a certain age are Mrs.

When I reached the corner, I hesitated. I could go east and walk along the river, but it was too early for the evening joggers. The path would be deserted except for the occasional fisherman and odd mugger. I turned west and started across Seventy-ninth Street. I was walking rapidly, as if I had a purpose or at least a destination.

At that clip I reached the Metropolitan Museum in no time. Tourists were spilling out of the building down the wide stone steps. The sounds of Japanese and French and German clashed like cymbals in the late-afternoon air. Vendors hawked cheap jewelry and stale pretzels and original works of art painted on velvet. A teenage boy and girl tried to push each other into one of the fountains. I told myself, again, that I really ought to do a piece on New York street life and sat on one of the benches in the shadow of the building. It occurred to me that in all the years I'd been roaming the area, in all the time I'd been frequenting the museum, I'd never sat on one of the benches in front of it. I saw myself suddenly as I must look to the tourists and vendors and young mothers and nannies walking strollers. A woman without purpose, killing time. Then I saw my mother.

My father had been an easygoing but orderly man. He was always telling my mother and me that punctuality was the politeness of kings. Each morning at eight-fifteen he left for the law office he maintained across from the courthouse in that insulated community where Emma and I had grown up. Each evening he returned home at seven-thirty. My mother usually began looking at her watch around five. Even before I learned to tell time, I knew when the day was drawing toward evening by the quickening of my mother's expectations, which ticked through the rooms of the house as loudly as an old grandfather clock. At five-thirty she'd go into the kitchen to make sure Mary or Norma or Gloria had begun scrubbing potatoes or shelling peas or stuffing chicken. At six she'd turn her attention to me, at least when I was small and still helpless. By seven the aroma of roasting food hung in the house like bunting; I'd been bathed and combed and curried; and my mother, her clothes bandbox perfect, her makeup glistening, would be sitting, in the living room if it were winter, the screened-in porch in summer, with a magazine in her lap and an expression of such desperate readiness on her face that it scared me. As I grew older and could no longer be groomed like a dog or horse, I came to see these weren't domestic preparations but religious rituals based on cause-and-effect observations. My mother might as well have been sacrificing two rams and a chicken for rain or a virgin for good crops. Though she was not a devout woman, some atavistic strain told her that if she didn't adhere to the strictures, if the house and the child and the wife didn't look like something out of a magazine ad, if they didn't measure up, my father might not show up.

Sometimes when she was ready especially early, she'd call Babe to kill time until my father got home, but Babe never wanted to talk at that hour. Babe had her own evening ritual, which involved a single martini, drunk from one of a set of cocktail glasses with miniature horses and riders encased in bubbled stems, the essence of sophistication as far as I was concerned, and the local evening newspaper. My mother always said she didn't see why Babe couldn't have her drink while talking on the phone, especially since there was nothing in the newspaper except malfeasance, injustice, scandal, and an occasional wedding announcement or obituary they already knew about, but Babe was adamant. Occasionally when Babe was especially abrupt and my mother's feelings were particularly hurt, she'd get off the phone muttering that it wasn't her fault Babe had no one coming home to her every night, because God knows she'd done her best to produce someone. Once she even added that if Babe had any sense, she'd grab one of those eligible divorcés or widowers soon because she wasn't getting any younger. It was the only time I ever heard my mother speak unkindly about Babe. I'm not talking about innuendo; I'm referring to the spoken cruelty.

The memory of my mother sitting that way had always infuriated me, but now I felt a sudden irrational flash of fear, like the fright you get from the sight of an intruder who turns out to be your own image in a darkened window or mirror.

I looked at my watch again, though I hated myself for doing it, and tried to calculate the timing. I wanted to pick up a few things for breakfast on the way home, though I had no reason to assume Dexter would be there in the morning if he read the profile tonight. Then there was the time required for showering and drying my hair and getting dressed. The timing was crucial. If I got ready too early, I'd end up like my mother, sitting nervously with an unopened magazine in my lap and a desperate look on my face. On the other hand, if Dexter's plane was early, he'd find me with dripping hair and a rattled psyche. And I was rattled enough as it was.

I pulled myself up short. I wasn't my mother. Neither was I staging Operation Desert Storm. I was merely getting ready for an ordinary evening. Maybe it would be an ordinary evening. Maybe Dexter would read the profile, say, "Nice job," and let it go at that. It wasn't likely, but it was possible. I stood and started east.

At that hour the small market near my building was crowded with women and the occasional man on the way home from work picking up fresh produce and last-minute ingredients for dinner. I took a container of orange juice from the refrigerator case and a loaf of neo-Tuscan bread from the bread basket and got in the checkout line. That was when I noticed the buckets of flowers near the door. I got out of line and took a bunch of red tulips from one of them. Then, because they looked so cheerful, I took another bunch of red and one of white. I got back in line and looked at the bunches of tulips I was holding. I remembered my mother fussing over bowls of flowers on the dining room table. She hadn't been good with flowers. Whenever she had a dinner party, Babe used to come over to arrange the flowers. I'd inherited my mother's shortcoming. Besides, I didn't want Dexter to think I'd spent the week or even the day preparing for his return. More important, I didn't want to think it myself.

I got out of line and put two of the bunches back in the bucket. Then I got back in line, paid for my purchases, and walked home through the lengthening shadows of the late afternoon.

"Nice tulips, Miss Fields," Pasha said as I went past him into the lobby of the building. On the way up in the elevator, I cursed myself for not buying more.

I let myself into the apartment and, without stopping to put down the flowers and juice and bread, without even thinking about it, went through the living room and into the bedroom. It was no longer a task; it was a reflex. So was the feeling of apprehension as I approached the answering machine and saw the small red number 1 glowing on the dial. I suppose there are people who could look at that number without trepidation. Dexter, for one. But those of us who are only a few generations from ancestors to whom a knock at the door meant marauding Cossacks or threatening mafiosi or the heartless agents of absentee British landowners expect the worst. No, that's not true. As I stood there staring at the machine, I thought of Emma, whose heritage was much like my own but whose life was so different. A woman whose work was always in demand, whose income was reliable, and whose husband didn't even have to turn up like clockwork every night, as my father had, because he was already there wouldn't approach her answering machine as if it were a mysterious package that could as easily hold an ingeniously wired arrangement of plastic, or whatever terrorists were using for bombs these days, as a piece of good news.

I pressed the play button and waited through the series of clicks that meant the tape was rewinding. Then Dexter's voice filled the room. He was talking about a canceled flight and a lack of planes, not to mention the rubber bands and paper clips that held them together, and the astonishing level of surliness, bureaucracy, and sheer incompetence in emerging nations. It was a droll message delivered with a stiff upper lip, which presumably I was to emulate, because to tell the truth, he said, it didn't look as if he was going to get out of there in the foreseeable future. He promised further bulletins would be forthcoming, and the machine clicked off. I stood there for a moment thinking about what Dexter had said and what he hadn't bothered to say, such as that he was crestfallen or at least disappointed, or words to that effect, and wondering if perhaps he'd somehow got hold of the profile and decided to break things off. I told myself I was paranoid. If the magazine wasn't on the stands here, it certainly hadn't found its way into emerging-nation airports or *International Herald Tribune* excerpts. Besides, I knew enough about Dexter's behavior, with other people, if not with me, to know he didn't lie.

I carried my purchases into the kitchen, put the juice and bread away, and took down a bowl for the tulips. I tried to see it as a stay of execution. Obviously the research on the women of death row was getting to me. I stood back and looked at the bowl of flowers. It wasn't going to win any awards in Tokyo, but even my mother's daughter couldn't do too much damage to a bunch of tulips.

I carried the bowl into the living room, put it on a table, and stood looking out the window at the river. For the first time I understood what had driven my mother on those nights. And I hated myself for the understanding.

*　*　*

Five days later Dexter called to say he'd be in the evening after next. "Hell or high water," he swore. "I hope," he added.

I'd learned my lesson. This time there'd be no anguished preparations and no unseemly counting of minutes. Just to make sure I set up an interview with a woman from the NOW Legal Defense and Education Fund for the afternoon of the day he was due in. I was still determined to write a piece on the women of death row, despite Kay Meechum's kiss of death.

I'd also decided not to show Dexter the profile. Babe was the one who'd changed my mind. "Why're you rushing at disaster?" she asked me one night on the phone when I mentioned my fears about how he was going to take the article.

I thought of the stories about her and her flier. She'd gambled on a single weekend leave with him, two at the most, and ended up with several years after the war, years she always swore she wouldn't swap for anything, despite what finally happened.

I decided Babe was right. There was no hurry to show Dexter the profile. I'd let him read it on his own, in his own good time.

The interview with the lawyer for NOW Legal Defense went well. She, at least, thought the article was a terrific idea. She quoted statistics. She presented legal strategies and cited legal precedents. She explained the difficulties of convincing a jury that a woman had acted in the heat of passion when the man had been turning up the heat for five or ten or fifteen years, and the woman had waited until he was dozing defenselessly in front of the television or for the proper amount of time to elapse so she could purchase the gun legally. "You see," the lawyer explained to me, "battered women rarely strike back in the heat of an attack, when according to male prosecutors, the danger is greatest. Maybe it's simple self-defense. They know that fighting back will only arouse the men more. But unlike the prosecutors, battered women know there are no safe times. They're always in danger. So they act not at the moment that other people perceive as the most perilous but at the point when their strength and alternatives and hope, especially hope, run out."

The more I listened, the more certain I was that Sugar and Kay were way off base. This was a story crying to be written. And the lawyer must have thought I was the woman to write it, because she kept talking, and referring me to cases, and giving me files to go through, and by the time I left her office there was a good chance Dexter was going to get to my building before I did. I wasn't too worried about that. For one thing, I'd just spent a couple of hours listening to stories of man's inhumanity to woman. I'm not suggesting I held Dexter responsible for any of that, but my consciousness was scaling some dangerous peaks. For another, surely a man who could find his way around emerging African nations and former Soviet spheres of interest could survive on the Upper East Side until I arrived.

It took me a while to get a taxi, and then, of course, at that time of day the traffic going uptown was impossible. As Pasha helped me out of the cab in front of my building, he told me there was a man waiting for me in the lobby. I asked how long he'd been there. "A while," Pasha said.

Dexter was sitting in the fake Elizabethan throne chair beside the nonworking fireplace reading a magazine. The first thing I noticed was the expression on his face as he read. It struck me as excessive. All I'd done was keep him waiting for a few minutes. He'd stood me up for a week. The second was the magazine he was reading. I was surprised. I was sure it wouldn't be on the stands for several days.

I stopped a foot or two away from him. He looked up from the magazine and saw me. He managed to ratchet the Old Testament fury in his face down to ordinary WASP annoyance, but he was too late. I'd seen it, and suddenly I knew, I suppose I'd known all along, that the quote from his colleague wasn't only provocative but insightful.

"Well?"

He opened his mouth. I waited to be damned forever or at least cast out of the fold. "It's clever," he said.

"I wasn't trying to be clever. I was trying to be honest."

Something close to a tic pulled at the side of his mouth. It did nothing to soften the stern set of those thin lips. His eyes moved to a point beyond me. I realized Pasha was hovering.

"Could we go upstairs?" Dexter said.

"Sure. If you still want to."

He gave me another Old Testament look, then stood and picked up his briefcase and carry-on bag. I started to say something. "Upstairs, Hallie." It wasn't a suggestion; it was a commandment.

I crossed the lobby and stepped into the elevator. He followed me. We stood in silence, staring at the dial above the door as if neither of us had ever seen one before. The indicator crept from one to two to three. The door opened. He followed me off the elevator and stood with his briefcase in one hand and his carry-on in the other as I opened my bag for my key. I knew what he was thinking. Why hadn't I taken out my key in the elevator? Why had I just stood there stupidly watching the floor indicator, then acted as if the door to my apartment had come as a surprise? Nothing turns endearing quirks into infuriating character flaws faster than an argument about something else.

I usually keep my keys in the small inside pockets of my handbags. Of course, that day I'd just dropped them into the main compartment. It took me only a few seconds to fish them out. I knew it was only that because I was counting them. Like the device that triggers a time bomb.

He went on watching in silence as I unlocked the door, then followed me in and put his bags down in the front hall. I stood waiting for the explosion. He walked past me into the living room.

"I really was trying to write an honest piece," I said again.

"Do you think I could have a drink?" he asked without looking at me.

I went into the kitchen to make drinks. He didn't follow me. When I came out, he was standing in front of the window staring out at the East River. Can the wrinkles in a Brooks Brothers polo shirt show fury? As I came up beside him, I saw he was watching an empty tanker make its way out to sea.

I handed him one of the two drinks I was carrying. He didn't thank me.

"A balanced piece," I added. "You knew that when you agreed to it."

He still didn't say anything.

"At least you should have."

He went on watching the fleeing freighter.

"Can we talk about it, or are you just going to stand there like some Old Testament prophet—"

He was looking at me now.

"I'm sorry. I didn't mean that."

"Sure you did. You meant it in the profile, and you meant it now."

"It was one opinion. One quote."

"The one you chose to use."

"I told you, I was writing a profile. Not a puff piece. Not a PR release. A serious portrait. That means criticism as well as praise. Detractors as well as admirers. You knew that when you agreed to it."

"I expected it to be balanced. I didn't expect it to be snide."

"I wasn't being snide! I wasn't even being critical."

"I know, you were just quoting someone else."

"That's not what I meant!" My voice sounded desperate in

my own ears. It probably sounded hysterical in his. "I meant I was trying to show the tough reality behind the heroic pose."

" 'The heroic pose'? Quit while you're behind, Hallie."

"You know what I mean. That in your position you have to make hard choices, and you have the courage to make them."

"You showed that, all right. What did you call it? 'The awful godlike power.' I'm sorry if I'm mangling your deathless prose, but I only had a chance to skim the piece."

"Can we leave my prose out of this?"

"No, I don't think so. I don't think we can. Because it wasn't just the quote; it was the goddamn picture of me playing God. I have to hand it to you there. I mean, you've never even been near Mozambique, but that didn't stop you from knowing what it was like. Even down to the smells. And those poor, suffering children. Some people might think the children were gratuitous or at least overkill, but not you. You got them on wires, all right, with the distended bellies and festering sores and dead eyes. You got them, and you got me. Hell, the only things missing are the flowing white robes and long white beard. Strutting through the camp that way, deciding who gets medical treatment and who doesn't, who gets food and who's left to starve to death. I come off looking like goddamn Charlton Heston playing God, all right, or at least Moses. Thanks to you, the fucking Cecil B. De Mille of the printed word."

"I wasn't trying to make you look like God."

"No? Then why did you use that quote from Rapaport? The picture you painted was bad enough, but you had to make sure you got the point across. You had to quote one of the biggest horse's asses who ever worked for the fund."

"I told you, I was trying for a balanced profile."

"Balanced!" He began to say something, then stopped and started toward the front hall. For a moment I thought he was walking out, but he took the magazine from his briefcase, came back to the window seat, and began flipping through the pages angrily. "Where the hell is it?"

I didn't answer him. I knew where it was. And I knew exactly how it went. I didn't need to hear it again. I especially didn't need to hear it again from him.

He found the page and started to read. " ' "St.John isn't afraid to make the hard decisions," Rapaport, who worked with him in Africa for four years, said. "And he never lets emotion get in the way. It could be his own child there in the camp being weighed for optimum chance of survival, and he still wouldn't let emotion get in the way. You might not like him for it, but you have to respect him for it. The man isn't afraid to play God." ' "

He tossed the magazine aside. "That presents a balanced picture of me, all right. The man who'd let his own kid starve to death to feed his ego."

"Nobody said anything about ego."

"Tell me what else 'isn't afraid to play God' means."

"Those are his words."

"Quoted by you."

"At least I cut them."

"What?"

I didn't say anything because I knew I'd already said too much.

"You mean there was more?"

"Nothing, really. Nothing responsible. Or even substantial."

"He, and you, accuse me of playing God and Abraham at the same time. Now let's see, what could be less responsible, less substantial than that? Josef Mengele? Is that it, God, Abraham, and Josef Mengele?"

"It wasn't that bad."

His eyes widened. "Christ! I was kidding."

"He didn't compare you to Josef Mengele."

"Then who? Come on, Hallie, don't stop now. Who'd he compare me to? Hitler? Stalin? Jeffrey Dahmer?"

"He didn't compare you to anyone."

"But he said something. What was it?"

"Nothing."

"What was it, Hallie?"

"He just said that sometimes he had the feeling . . ."

"Yes?"

"He said, sometimes . . . watching you work . . . he couldn't help thinking . . . it isn't anyone specific . . ."

"He couldn't help thinking . . . go on."

"He's an idiot."

"I know that, but you seem to think he's the voice of truth and wisdom. He couldn't help thinking . . ."

"He couldn't help thinking of that classic character in all the movies and books . . ."

"Go on."

"It was nothing."

"All what movies and books?"

"About the Holocaust."

"Christ!"

"That's what I mean. It was stupid. That's why I cut it."

"Cut what? The comparison between me and Josef Mengele?"

"He didn't compare you to Mengele."

"Then who? Come on, Hallie. At this point anyone short of Mengele's going to be a goddamn compliment."

"He said he couldn't help thinking of the Nazi officer who stands on the railroad siding . . . the one who . . ."

"Yes?"

". . . sorts the Jews. . . ." My voice trailed off.

He sat staring at me.

"I didn't say it. He did."

He was still staring at me.

"That's why I didn't use it. It was such a vicious thing to say, such an obviously wrongheaded—"

He stood. "You're right. It is vicious. And I think it's wrongheaded."

"That's why I didn't use it."

He was still standing there staring down at me. "Thank you," he said, and the way he said it frightened me, because I knew there was more. "Thank you for not using the rest of the quote. But there's one thing I don't understand." He hesitated.

I waited.

"This idiot." He went on. "This purveyor of wrongheaded, vicious lies . . ." He hesitated again.

"Yes?"

"Why did you quote him at all?"

I had no answer for that, or at least none I was willing to give him.

"Because it made good copy."

This time it wasn't a question. This time it was a zinger. And after he delivered it, he picked up his things and left.

Twenty

AFTER DEXTER walked out, I went on sitting in the window seat for a long time. And as I sat there staring out at the river that had turned black in the gathering dusk, I couldn't help thinking that Pat O'Dougherty and my mother had been right after all. My mother had been right in more ways than one.

Though my parents had not been religiously observant, a day never went by without their being aware of, and defensive about, the fact that they were Jews. Like many defenses, that one frequently took on an offensive edge. They still referred to Great-aunt Bridget, who'd been married to Great-uncle Isaac for more than thirty years, as the *shiksa*. They talked of the family across the street that had changed its name from Wichansky to Winchell with alternating disapproval and envy. And they never tired of pointing out the dangers of intermarriage. The dangers of a less binding and more compromising union were too terrifying to contemplate. "The first time you have a fight," my mother warned, "he'll turn on you with a racial epithet." My mother was not a woman to whom the words *racial epithet* came easily, which just went to show how carefully she'd rehearsed that particular warning.

I'd never believed my mother. I still didn't. But that night, in the wake of Dexter's departure, in the intrusive noisy absence of

Dexter, I couldn't stop thinking that I'd been the one to cast the first epithet.

When I opened my eyes the next morning, things didn't look much better. In fact, in the glaze of summer sunshine that poured through the windows like honey, they looked worse. I'd done something shameful and irreparable.

I know there are women, some of them my friends, who would have stayed in bed grieving over Dexter that morning. Most of them are the same women who would have stayed in bed celebrating with Dexter if he'd asked them to. But I have always believed in the therapeutic value as well as the inviolable nature of work. In the face of personal disaster, I tend to go into professional overdrive. I was early for my lunch date with Emma.

And I had an agenda. I was going to tell her about the prints Julian had given me. I'd intended to last time we'd seen each other, but somehow I hadn't gotten around to it. Now I wanted to make sure she knew about them. I was trying to cover myself. I was also trying to find out about them. If Emma was the possessive harridan Julian had described at lunch, surely she'd give herself away when I told her about the prints. On the other hand, if she wasn't paranoid, merely realistic, she still wouldn't take them too well. Either way, I'd have the missing piece that was holding me back from writing the profile. I don't mean I'd say or even imply that Emma Weill was a crazed wife or Julian Weill a philandering husband, and I certainly wasn't going to speculate in print about why the woman who had it all settled for so little, but as Hemingway—not exactly my role model of choice—said about fiction, you have to know a lot more about characters than you ever put on the page. If I didn't understand Emma's feelings about her husband, I didn't have the first clue to who she was. I knew what that meant for the profile. The most I could hope for was a big yawn from Sugar, the least a kill fee. In either case, there'd be no further assignments for *Era*. I thought of Kay Meechum's comment about losing momentum. Clearly my career was not going in the direction I'd hoped. On the other hand, the profile of Dexter was a success, and look where that had got me.

Emma didn't miss a beat when I mentioned the prints. She didn't ask me what prints I was talking about. She didn't even look surprised.

"The ones of Fleet Street, you mean?"

I nodded.

"I told Julian you'd like them."

The most I can say in my defense is that I was thoroughly ashamed of the disappointment I felt.

Twenty-one

EMMA STOOD on the sidewalk in front of the restaurant trying to hang on. She'd lost her gravity, or the world had. Suddenly everything was spinning away: Hallie's smiling face looming in front of her like a great mocking billboard; the smug, uncaring people who rushed past on the way to their own lives; the afternoon traffic swerving and screeching and honking down the avenue. She felt as if she were looking at the world through the wrong end of a telescope. Everything was too small and too far away. It was a familiar feeling. Alcoholics managed to function with hangovers. Smokers grew used to coughs. She'd learned to live with this floating feeling that kept her on the edge of nausea just as morning sickness had so many years ago. Only this time there was no end in sight. She wondered how many days she'd drifted through in this empty, alienated haze, facing the children with a stupid smile painted on her numb face, talking to people through a scrim, even forcing herself to put one meaningless word after another on a piece of paper that felt so far away she didn't know how her hands held it, and all the while feeling as if she were about to float off somewhere, float farther and farther away like the helium balloons that had escaped from Matt's and Becky's small fists when they were children. Eventually she'd disappear the way those balloons had because there was nothing inside to ground her and nothing outside to catch on to.

She heard herself saying good-bye to Hallie, saw Hallie turn and start to walk in the other direction, felt herself turn away. She saw it all through the wrong end of that telescope.

She started walking. The buildings passed her as gray and brown smudges. If only she could focus, she could reason things out. She slowed her step and tried to concentrate. They were only a couple of inexpensive secondhand prints. They didn't mean anything. Only she knew they did, and what they meant was worse than sexual betrayal. Or perhaps she'd merely become inured to that. Perhaps she'd begun to buy his story. "Don't you see?" he'd plead when he was caught. "The sex doesn't mean anything."

"Then why do you do it?" she used to scream. "If it means so little to you, why the fuck do you keep doing it?"

Sometimes he was abject and apologetic. "I don't know," he'd say, his voice weak with defeat, a whipped-dog expression on his face. But other times he'd explode in a rage so violent it snuffed out her own.

"Why do I do it?" he'd shout back at her. "Don't you think if I understood why, I'd stop? Do you think I'm an idiot? Or just a degenerate?" He'd pause and look at her hard, through narrowed eyes, as if he were sizing her up. "Now I get it. Now I see what you really think of me. You think I enjoy making you miserable. You think I actually go out of my way to hurt you and the kids. That's the kind of man you think I am. Oh, you talk a good game. 'Your work is ten times more important than mine,'" he'd go on in a high, mincing tone that was supposed to be an imitation of hers. "'You don't care about success. All you care about is saving the world.'" His voice would drop a register, but it wouldn't grow any kinder. "Nice try, sweetheart, but now your real feelings come out. You think I'm scum."

"What I think," she'd say in a tone that walked a tightrope of control because at times like that she was afraid of him; she knew he wouldn't hit her, but she was still afraid, "is that if you really wanted to stop, you would."

"Perfect!" He'd turn a venomous smile on her. "Absolutely perfect. If I were an alcoholic, you'd probably blame it on a weak character rather than a genetic disposition, which in case you haven't read anything except those adolescent magazines you subscribe to—the only woman on the verge of menopause who still gets *Seventeen*—happens to be the current medical thinking on the problem."

"So you're telling me this is genetic. You've got some bent DNA or something that makes you have to fuck every woman you come in contact with."

"What I'm telling you," he went on in a suddenly dejected tone—he could do that, he could turn on a dime—"is that the sex is just sex, the way alcohol is just alcohol. There's no love. Christ, there isn't even any feeling. Except maybe self-hatred." His voice cracked on the last word.

Part of her had come to believe him, not because of the humiliation that racked his voice and made him unable to meet her eyes—at least not only because of that—but because she herself didn't attach that much significance to sex. If she did, she'd have to rank her marriage as one of the top ten in the country. They made love more often than the various studies said they were supposed to—Julian saw to that—and, she was sure, more expertly—he saw to that too. Sex was important. When things were going well, it could open secret doors to strange dark rooms. When things were going badly, it was a source of pride in the face of other people's pity. But it wasn't enough. It wasn't what held people together or, if they had any sense, drove them apart in the long haul.

"If I were impotent," he'd argued once, "would you hound me about it like this? If I'd been wounded in Vietnam—"

"You weren't in Vietnam!"

"You know what I mean. If I were maimed in some way. If

I'd had an accident in the Peace Corps, you wouldn't have left me. Sex isn't that critical. Not compared to everything else we have. So if you could live with that, why can't you live with this?"

And she'd learned to, more or less. They still fought about it. It could still drive her crazy when it happened or at least when she found out it had happened. But in the long run it was only sex. She wouldn't leave him because of it. He'd never leave her for it.

A horn pierced the bubble of air around her. She jumped back on the curb. The cabdriver shouted something in an unintelligible language as he swerved by. A woman on the sidewalk put her face in Emma's. She saw the woman's mouth moving. The words rained down on her, but she couldn't make out their meaning any more than she could understand the cabdriver's language. She saw the traffic lights change as if they were in another galaxy. She willed herself to start across the street.

The problem was that this time it wasn't sex. At least not yet. She was almost sure of it. But that only made it worse, because now when the sex did come, it wouldn't be an inexplicable itch or a bent gene. It would be an act of will, an expression of sentiment and sympathy and desire.

She stopped in the middle of the sidewalk. A man crashed into her back, then cursed as he pushed his way around her. The sounds came from far away.

She should have seen it coming. She had seen it coming. Little by little, in inevitable steps. That first night at dinner Julian had made a joke about the genius of a woman who could write, not to mention think, like a prepubescent, and Hallie had laughed appreciatively, and Emma, watching the sparks of complicity crackle between them in the quiet restaurant, had felt like a child gaping at fireworks exploding in a black summer sky. First there'd been the insider gossip about the world they both knew, the world, he'd said once as if it were a joke, only it wasn't, of grown-up writing. Then there'd been the articles, which she'd been stupid enough to leave lying around and he'd picked up. And finally there were the prints. This wasn't an opportunistic grope with a graduate student behind the locked door of his office or a winy lunch-and-fuck with some junior editor in her studio apartment. This was a progression, a course of action, set in motion by her but now beyond her control, an affair with all its terrifying cataclysmic potential.

She felt herself spinning out again, hailed a cab, and flung herself into it.

The driver mumbled something in another foreign accent. It took her a moment to make sense of the words. He wanted to know where she was going. She was due at a meeting of a sub-committee on gender stereotyping in juvenile and young adult books. Fuck the subcommittee. And fuck the little girls who were going to get stereotyped too. Let them learn the hard way. The way she'd learned. She was going home. She was going home to have this out with Julian. She gave the driver her ad-dress. It came out as a shout. She was still compensating for the distance between her and the rest of the world.

This time she'd throw him out. She swore she would. The kids would survive. Matt wasn't even living at home. And Becky was old enough to handle it. This time she meant it. No matter what he said. Or how he pleaded. She'd change the goddamn locks if she had to.

Except she'd already done that. The memory closed around her, sucking the breath from her body, and all that shining new hope.

It had been the first summer after they'd bought the town house. She remembered it was summer because the children had been away at camp. She never would have had the nerve to do it if they'd been home.

She couldn't even remember what the fight had been about.

That ought to tell her something. But she remembered the rest of the night. She'd surprised herself that night, but Julian had surprised her more. She'd come to expect the worst from him, but she hadn't expected that.

He'd slammed out of the house. Her first reaction had been terror. She'd sat on the side of the bed, their bed, wondering what she was going to do and how she and the children would survive. For some reason she'd kept thinking about wine. She'd never know which wines to order without him. But gradually, as she'd sat there telling herself that was ridiculous, any idiot could learn about wine, she'd noticed something. She didn't feel awful. She was scared. She had that hollow sensation. But she didn't feel bad.

She'd gone up to her study and taken out the Yellow Pages. There were twenty-three pages of locksmiths. She'd dialed one called Protect Yourself Incorporated.

It had been close to dawn when Julian had come home. She was still wandering the house, hollow and disconnected and scared, but euphoric too. Of course, that might have had something to do with the wine. She'd opened a bottle almost as a challenge.

When she heard the sound of his key scratching against the new lock, she went into the hall and stood listening. Metal scraped against metal as he tried to force the key. A breath of curses crept under the door. Silence followed, then the scratch of metal again.

"Fuck." The word came long and slow, a sigh of amazement. He'd realized what she'd done.

The front buzzer sizzled through the house. It jolted her like an electric current.

"Fuck!" he said again. There was no wonder now. It was a sudden violent hit. Then the thud of the heavy brass knocker, once, a second time, a third. The blows went on and on. She stood hugging her arms to herself, hunched over as if she were protecting herself against the onslaught. She was terrified—and thrilled.

The thuds were duller now, the sound of human fists on wood. The door shuddered faintly with each blow. She slid to the floor and sat with her back against the wall, watching the trembling door, and hugging her knees, and shivering, though the night was hot and muggy and she was sticky with sweat. Finally he stopped banging. She sat listening to the sound of a car cruising down the street and her own breathing.

She heard another thud, saw the door shudder again, and knew he'd slumped to the floor too. She sat, her muscles tensed, her body hunched for protection, and listened to the silence. Another car, a siren, wind through the leaves, her own jagged breathing. He must have heard the last too or maybe only sensed it. Maybe they were that connected.

"Emma," he said tentatively.

She hugged herself more closely.

"Em," he begged.

Another car passed, then silence. She heard the squeak of a brass hinge as he lifted the mail slot. A thin ray of light from the streetlamp spilled into the dark hall. The words started again. He was pushing them through the opening in the door. It would have been ludicrous if it weren't so awful. Please, he said. And sorry. And anything. Anything you say. They fell through the slot, one after another, and lay there like junk mail.

"Em," he said. "Emma." It was a racked sob.

She was trembling again.

"Em," he pleaded, "what's going to happen to me?"

She clenched her jaw.

"What will I do?"

She listened to him waiting.

"How will I live?" The question slid through the slot and hung in the suffocating night air. "Please, Em, please."

She leaned toward the door and put her mouth against the

mail slot. "I'll give you a settlement," she whispered. "I'll divide everything in half."

The sobs were so deep and pain-racked that she could barely make out what he was saying. "That's . . . not what . . . I . . . meant. . . . What will . . . I . . . do . . . without . . . you? How can I live . . . without you?"

He was still crying when she opened the door.

The cab pulled up in front of the house.

That was then and this was now. She wasn't going to back down this time. No matter what he said, no matter how he pleaded.

She paid the driver, got out of the cab, and slammed the door.

"Hey, lady," he shouted, "watch it!" She could understand his accent now.

"I don't believe this," Julian said. "After everything we've been through. Okay, I admit it, after everything I've put you through, you're telling me this is it. This is the proverbial last straw. A couple of prints! A couple of lousy prints, which weren't exactly a secret since I gave them to her in front of you—"

"You didn't give them to her in front of me. She told me about them."

He shrugged and sat on the side of the bed. He was still holding the tie he'd been taking off when she'd heard him on the stairs and raced down to the bedroom. "Exactly! I wasn't trying to keep them a secret. Neither was she, obviously. Come on, Emma, think about it. I found a couple of secondhand prints I liked, which happened to be so dirt cheap even I could even afford them. That might not sound like much to you, but for those of us whose annual incomes aren't in the six figures— who're we kidding, are barely in the five figures—it's a real boot. Then, after I bought them, it occurred to me it would be a smart move to give them to this so-called journalist. Smart for you, sweetheart, not me, because I'm not the one who's been trying to seduce the bitch for the last month."

"Seduce! All I did was grant her a couple of interviews."

"Grant her a couple of interviews!" he shouted to the ceiling. "God I wish I had that on tape. Pols fight for Larry King, the president goes on MTV, but my wife *grants* interviews."

"Fuck you!"

"Now why can't I ever think of snappy rejoinders like that?"

"Maybe because you think with your cock and not your brain."

"Another one! You ought to go into comedy writing, sweetheart. I mean, it's a crime to waste a wit like that. And just for the record, I thought the problem was that I was using my brain this time. Isn't that what you're screaming about? Not that I fucked her but that I talked to her. I actually carried on a conversation with another woman. Have I no shame? We traded a couple of quips. Nothing as clever as your one-liners, but enough to actually make us smile. At each other. Together. At the same time. Let's face it, sweetheart, coming together's nice, but smiling together . . . Wow, I'm getting a hard-on just thinking about it."

If only she could hit him. Wipe that filthy superiority from his face with force.

But he was too quick for her. Suddenly, without warning, his smile shriveled to a small, sad crescent. He shook his head slowly back and forth.

"Listen, Em, I don't blame you for trying to seduce her." He held up his hand before she could interrupt. "You want her to write a flattering piece. So do I. That's why I gave her those prints. And while we're at it, I also bought a coffee mug with the queen's picture on it for Carol. Are you going to accuse me of having it off with her too?"

"That's different." She was trying to keep her voice calm, but she was no match for him.

He stood and started toward the dressing room. "The only difference is that my researcher is about a hundred and three years old." He patted her behind as he passed. "Better watch it or the politically correct vigilantes will get you on ageism."

"I'm glad you think it's such a joke."

He stopped, turned around, and came back into the bedroom. "I don't think it's a joke. I think it's pathetic. I made a couple of mistakes—how long ago now? Ten years?"

"What about—"

"I'm talking about what I've done, not what you've been accusing me of doing all these years. Sins of commission, sweetheart, not sins of thought. In this case the dirty little thoughts of your small, suspicious brain, not mine. I made a gesture toward a woman who's doing a profile of you, not me. If that's a fucking crime, I'm sorry. I'll never do it again. Better than that, I'll call her right now and tell her I'm sorry if she misinterpreted two secondhand prints as a come-on. I'll tell her they weren't meant that way, and if she has any idea they were, she's wrong." He crossed the room to the night table on her side of the bed and picked up the phone. "What's her number?"

"Stop grandstanding."

He looked across the bed at her. "I'm not the one who's grandstanding. I'm not the one who came tearing in here screaming divorce. And I'm not the one who's out of control."

He was still holding the phone. "If you need help, hang up and dial your operator . . . if you need help . . ."

She stood on the other side of the bed staring back at him. Something had happened to his face. The tense set of the jaw had eased. His brow was furrowed as if he were worrying about something.

He put the receiver back in the cradle gently, the way he used to put the babies into the crib, then turned back to her. "You've got to stop this, Em. Before you ruin both our lives. Ours and the kids. You know what Matt said to me when we were in England? The first day we were there, for Christ sake. We were picking up the car, and a group of kids passed. Three or four girls in jeans with backpacks. He told me not to look at them. I said just because I was his father didn't mean I was over the hill. 'That's not what I meant,' he said. 'It's Mom. It drives her crazy.' "

Liar, she wanted to scream, only she didn't, because she knew this was one thing he wasn't lying about.

"And what did you tell him? That his mother was a possessive, paranoid bitch and you'd look as much as you liked?"

He went on staring at her for a moment. "I thanked him for pointing it out to me and said I'd try to watch it."

"Give me a break," she said, but she'd begun to cry before the words were even out.

He asked her if she wanted to go out to dinner. He made it sound as if they had something to celebrate. She couldn't imagine what. She'd given up the idea of changing locks, but she wasn't sure that was a cause for celebration. A reason for relief maybe, but not exactly an occasion for shouting from the rooftops or dancing in the streets. The most she could say was that she no longer felt as if she were floating like that untethered balloon, free and weightless and liable to disappear. She felt a heaviness again.

She said she supposed they might as well go out to dinner. "Great," he said. "Terrific," he added. "Where do you feel like going?" he asked, and began listing restaurants like a goddamn Zagat's. There it was again, that idea that a shared meal could heal anything.

They'd promised her nothing would change. They'd both go on loving her, they'd said. She'd see her father every weekend. Sometimes during the week too. She and her mother would go on living in the house. Nothing would change. Except everything did. Suddenly she and her father had to do things together. Before they'd just been together. He took her to restaurants, where people stared at the middle-aged man who talked incessantly and the sullen girl who sat pushing food around her plate. He took her ice skating, which he was no good at; and to baseball games, which she found endless; and on occasional excursions with another divorced father and his daughter, where by some grim process of mitosis two miserable people were suddenly four. Later he simply took her to his new house with his new wife, but by then she no longer cared. At least that was what she told herself.

The outings with her father were awful, but they were outings, aberrations from real life, unpleasant but bearable because she knew they'd be over in six or four or two hours. Her life with her mother was another story. There was no escaping from that. It was her real life, grown small and mean and miserable.

If her father was always doing something with her, her mother refused to do anything at all. She wouldn't go to the movies. Why bother when they could stay home and watch television without having other people pity them for having to sit alone without a husband and father? She wouldn't go out to dinner. People would stare at two women alone in a restaurant, and they'd probably get bad service anyway. Meals at home shrank to a motley assortment of canned and frozen convenience foods and comfortless leftovers consumed in the cramped breakfast nook. When Emma asked why they weren't eating in the dining room, as they always had, her mother said she no longer had help. After a few weeks Emma offered to set the table in the dining room. "Why bother?" her mother asked. "Just for the two of us."

It had gone on that way, with life growing more meager and colorless until Emma had thought she'd fade away completely or become just like her mother, which was the same thing. Then one night she'd caught a glimpse of her old life. She'd become editor in chief of the school paper by then, one more way to keep from going home each afternoon, and she'd had to stop at the house of a girl who hadn't been able to turn in an article on the Thanksgiving Turkey Drive because she'd been home with a cold.

It was dark when Emma got to Nancy Gold's house, and as she cut across the front lawn, the last leaves of her last autumn at home crunching under her loafers and the windows glowing like candles in the darkness made her ache with longing, though she couldn't have said whether the longing was for something she'd lost or something she had yet to find. When Mrs. Gold opened the door, a wave of warm air reached out and grabbed her in an embrace.

Mrs. Gold drew her into the front hall, and while Emma stood waiting for Nancy and answering the inane questions other people's parents asked when they were trying to be friendly, her eyes kept swerving beyond Mrs. Gold to the dining room. The table was set for dinner. It wasn't exactly an impressive sight. Five plain white plates, each bracketed by a knife, a fork, and a spoon, sat on five straw place mats. The napkins folded beside each plate were even paper. But Emma stood waiting for Nancy, and answering Mrs. Gold's questions, and staring at the dining table set for the Golds' dinner as if it were a movie set. It struck her as that romantic.

The image followed her home. It hung before her eyes in 3-D Technicolor and hammered in her head like stereophonic sound. She was still thinking about it as she came up the back steps and opened the door to the kitchen. Her mother, wearing an old blue flannel bathrobe and pink kid scuffs, was standing at the counter with her back to the door. When Matilda Bliss got home from a long day on her feet selling lacy negligees and satin nightgowns, the first thing she did was get out of her suit and high heels and into something comfortable. Emma stood in the doorway staring at her mother's back. The feather trim on the scuffs was going bald in places. The narrow shoulders shivered inside the thin flannel robe.

"Close the door, Em. You're letting out the heat."

Emma closed the door behind her.

"Thanks," her mother said as she began opening one of those half-size cans of food she'd begun buying lately. You'd think she was cooking for a bunch of Lilliputians.

"How was school?"

Emma made a sound. If something in a saucepan hadn't been bubbling, her mother might almost have heard it. She moved to the alcove next to the stairs, put her books on the bottom step, and hung her coat on the rack on the wall.

"Am I getting the silent treatment again tonight?" her mother asked. "I'm not complaining. I just want to know in advance. That way I won't waste breath trying to talk to you."

Emma stood staring at her mother's back and feeling the hatred rising in her. She didn't want to feel that way, she didn't mean to, but she couldn't help herself. She crossed the kitchen to the silverware drawer and began taking out knives and forks and spoons.

Her mother raised her eyes to the ceiling. "She's a good daughter, Your Honor. She really is. Sets the table without being asked. Does her homework without being told. Gets straight A's. She just doesn't like to talk."

"Mom," she groaned, and took two dinner plates from the cabinet.

Her mother dropped her eyes from the ceiling and stirred whatever was in the saucepan. "Ah, she has vocal cords." She put down the spoon and began opening another half-size can. "I was beginning to worry."

"The paper," Emma mumbled.

"If you were much later, I was going to call school."

That was all she needed.

"I had to pick up an article from Nancy Gold. She was home sick."

Emma carried the plates and silverware to the table in the cramped breakfast nook, then stood for a moment hugging the plates to her and feeling her mother's eyes on her back.

"Don't put the plates on the table," her mother said. "I'll serve them over here. That way we'll have less to wash. We'll pretend we're in a restaurant."

Restaurant! When was the last time you were in a restaurant? And we have a goddamn dishwasher! Emma turned and walked into the dining room.

"What are you doing?" her mother called after her.

She switched on the light, opened the sideboard drawer where her mother kept the everyday linens, what used to be the everyday linens, and took out two place mats and two cloth napkins.

Out of the corner of her eye she saw her mother appear in the doorway between the kitchen and dining room.

"What are you doing?" her mother asked again, though any cretin could see what she was doing.

She put the plates and cutlery down, arranged the two place mats at right angles, and began setting the table.

"What's the occasion?"

She folded a napkin and put it beside one of the plates. She could feel her mother watching her and hear the unspoken message. That's all I need, to come home from the store at night and have to start ironing linen napkins. Or maybe you expect me to pay twenty-five cents apiece to have the hand laundry do them. On what your father sends a month, don't make me laugh.

Emma opened another drawer in the breakfront, took out a silver trivet, and carried it to the table.

"Who're we expecting? Cary Grant? Or maybe Liz and Dick."

"For Christ sake!" The words exploded from Emma's mouth. "All I'm doing is setting the table. You complain when I don't, and you complain when I do."

"I wasn't complaining."

" 'Who're we expecting? Cary Grant?' " she mimicked. "I'm just trying to make it nice. I'm just trying to make it—" Her mouth clamped shut again. She dropped her eyes and went back to arranging the silverware.

"Go ahead, say it. You're just trying to make it the way it used to be. Well, maybe you better talk to your father about that, because I wasn't the one who changed things. I wasn't the one who picked up and left."

"I was going to say"—Emma went on in a tight voice—"that I was just trying to make it normal. Like other people."

"Normal." Her mother stood with her arms folded across her chest. "Like other people. What other people? Your friends' parents? The people on this street? Or maybe the women who come into the store? Because I could tell you all about those other people. Those normal people."

Emma went back into the kitchen. Her mother turned and followed her.

"I could tell you how normal and nice and respectable they are. All those people who are always so busy feeling sorry for me. Did you ever get a whiff of the ginger ale Mrs. Shaw next door drinks all day? Or how about the Golds, where you just had to go this afternoon so you didn't get home till all hours? You think she walks around in a mink coat and he drives a Cadillac on what he makes from that candy store? Well, take a look at the ticker tape in the back room of the candy store and think again. And as for the women who come into the store, I could give you a mouthful about them. With their good intentions and high-and-mighty ways. You'd think we were one of the Hundred Neediest Cases the way they carry on every time they buy so much as a pair of stockings. Like that Adelaide Fields and her friend Babe Wertheimer. Friend! With friends like Babe Wertheimer, you don't need enemies."

Emma turned back from the cabinets with two glasses in her hands. "What do you mean?"

Her mother looked at her, then shook her head and walked to the stove. "Nothing." She picked up a spoon and began stirring pots and peering into pans. You'd think she was whipping up a feast for a bunch of gourmets instead of opening a couple of cans for Lilliputians.

"Nothing," her mother said again. "Finish setting the table. In the dining room."

Emma dragged herself back from that hot, unhappy kitchen to the restaurant. Julian was telling her about some statistics he'd unearthed that afternoon, working himself up to a heady indignation at a kindergarten in California that was located too close to a high-voltage wire, thereby placing innocent children and their well-meaning teachers in jeopardy.

They'd had dinner in the dining room that night, but it hadn't made any difference. She'd sat hunched over her plate, sullen, furious, miserable in her inability to change things. There was nothing she could do, except grow up and get out and make her own life. She felt the same impotence now. Only now she was grown up, and the life she had was the one she'd made. She felt the flames of the old, unwilling hatred of her mother licking at her feet.

Twenty-two

AT FIRST Dexter thought the bells were an alarm clock. Then he felt the light searing his eyelids, and heard the shuffle of feet and the babble of voices around him, and knew he was in a public place. This was a different kind of alarm.

He opened his eyes. The harsh lights and garish signs and close-faced strangers came into focus. He was in an airport. He just didn't know which airport. He blinked against the glare. The signs were in English. The bells had stopped, and there was a voice coming over the loudspeaker. The accent was Brit. Gatwick. Or was it Heathrow? He tried to remember.

Whichever it was, the Brit voice was telling him to evacuate the area immediately. The words were clear, but all around him people were milling about asking one another what to do. Only the girls who worked in the duty-free shops, all those good-looking girls in their Hermès scarfs and Cartier watches and Chanel perfume, knew what to do. The grates were coming down on the shops, and the girls were complaining and giggling among themselves and herding the passengers down a ramp and through a door that said "Authorized Personnel Only." Then they were in another waiting room, waiting. The adventure of international travel.

He found a seat, rubbed his eyes, and tasted the foul taste of his own saliva. He hated layovers, though God knew by now he ought to be used to them. They were such a waste of time. Still, he'd been lucky to get the flight out of New York and the connection here.

He wasn't running away. He just hadn't seen any point in hanging around town for more than a day when there was work to be done somewhere else. He glanced out the big plate glass windows. Beyond the planes and machinery crouching in the predawn gloom, a faint stain of crimson seeped over the horizon like blood. He sat staring at the violent dawn. God and Abraham and a Nazi guard. Jesus, she made Nan look like a goddamn fan. When they turned, they really turned.

The Brit voice on the PA system told him he could return to the area he'd just left. No explanation, just orders. Move here, move there. As if it would violate security to say simply what had happened. As if everyone didn't know it was another bomb threat. He picked up his hand luggage and trucked back up the ramp, one of the herd, following mindlessly.

He had to go through security again. He put his carry-on and briefcase on the moving belt and passed through the metal detector. A strange woman stared at the X-rayed contents of his life without interest. He picked up his briefcase and bag on the other side.

The gratings were going up on the duty-free shops again. How early did they open anyway, or didn't they ever close? He'd never thought about it before. He never even noticed the shops anymore, except to notice the girls who worked in them. He never could figure out why all those girls with good bodies and great legs wanted to spend their lives smiling at strangers in airports. It couldn't be just for the discount.

He made his way back through the garish terminal, past the neon-lit McDonald's, reeking of stale cooking grease and industrial-strength disinfectant, past the gloomy plastic pub, where travelers sat numbing themselves for the journeys ahead, past more snack bars and souvenir shops and bookstores.

He went into one of the bookstores and headed for the magazine section in the back. It was empty except for a man in a blue pin-striped suit with a pasty, arrogant face. He was standing with an umbrella hooked over one arm studying a center spread in a sex magazine. Dexter made his way past him to the general-interest section. Just to see if it was there. Just out of curiosity. He sure as hell wasn't going to buy another copy of it. God and Abraham and Nazi guards. Fuck! But fuck what? That was the question.

There were hundreds of magazines but not that one. On his way out he accidentally bumped into the man with the umbrella. He murmured an apology. The man didn't lift his face from the blur of close-up body parts and pink and white flesh tones.

He made his way back to the area where he'd been dozing before the bomb scare. It was filled with men with luggage and women with babies and kids with backpacks. The press of people made him irrationally angry, first at them, then at himself. When had he become that absurd cliché, the man who loves humanity and hates his fellowman, and woman?

He made his way past the area, looking for a quiet corner. A popular song from his youth played by too many strings in a tempo that could only be called peppy kept pace with him. A recorded announcement admonished him at maddeningly regular intervals not to leave his luggage unattended and warned that if he did, it would be confiscated within three minutes.

He took a plastic molded chair in a line of attached plastic molded chairs near the window and put his hand luggage between his feet. He told himself to buy a newspaper or take out some work or do something, but he sat there staring into space like the people he always pitied. No demanding work, no pressing interests, nothing to kill the time.

As he sat staring into space, men and women passed back and forth through his line of vision like figures in a video game.

This was his universe, a world of constantly moving icons. The walking dead. Who else could put up with the tawdry sights and sickening smells and sounds so banal they'd send any sentient human being on a murderous rampage? He wondered, if you added it up, how many years he'd passed this way. How much work had he done in airport lounges, how many hours had he slept on planes, how many meals had he eaten on the run? In how many public rest rooms had he taken care of his private functions, like Louis XIV without the grandeur? How much of his private life had he conducted from public telephones? The only thing he didn't do in this bright unreal world of muffled despair was fuck, and that was only a matter of choice. He knew men who picked up other men in public rest rooms or screwed women in cramped airplane bathrooms. Or was it only a matter of time? Was that why he kept noticing the duty-free girls?

This was crazy. All because of a stupid article in a mindless popular magazine. All because of a quote from that horse's ass Rapaport. Or maybe all because she'd chosen to use the quote.

He stood and started toward one of the snack bars. A thin woman was standing behind the counter biting her nails. She asked him what he'd have. He looked at her. Her eyes had a slight bulge. Her neck was faintly swollen. Her nails had been chewed to the quick in a continuing orgy of nervousness. Without meaning to, he added up the symptoms and made the diagnosis. Goiter.

The diagnosis said as much about his condition as the woman's. He couldn't stop, and he couldn't change. He told the woman he'd have a large black coffee.

He carried the coffee to another chair. People didn't change. They gave up smoking and took up exercise and traded one mate for another, but they didn't change anything that mattered. The smokers became addicted to candy. And he wished the fund had a dollar for every Tunturi exercycle and Nordic-

Track machine gathering dust in American basements. As for changing mates, every divorced man he knew had married the same woman, only younger, or the exact opposite of his first wife, which was the same thing. He was no exception. He'd gone from a woman who used to stand in the window watching the street for his cab when he came home from a trip to a woman who'd gone out of her way not to be there when he was due in. That was okay. That had been part of her attraction. But it wasn't a change in him.

People didn't change. If he had any doubt, all he had to do was remember Hezron. The name floated to the surface of his consciousness like a bloated and lifeless body. But that was okay. He could think about Hezron. He could think about the fund. He just didn't want to think about that damn article. He didn't want to think about himself. If there was one thing he hated, it was people who shrank the world to their own tiny spheres of interest. If there was one thing he hated, it was people who conducted their lives as if they were living proofs of solipsism.

They were about forty minutes into the flight when he noticed it. He'd looked up from the report he was reading and glanced out the window. Houses and yards and roads made a pattern below. He shouldn't be able to make them out this long into the flight. He checked his watch. They should have climbed to a higher altitude by now. He wasn't worried, merely curious.

When he glanced up again a few minutes later, he noticed two stewardesses bending to look out of one of the windows. They seemed to be staring at the wing. As one of them came back down the aisle, he stopped her and asked if anything was wrong. Her smile snapped into place. She reassured him that everything was fine and asked if she could get him anything. He looked out the window again. He could still make out houses and yards and roads.

Now a steward had joined the two stewardesses staring out the window at the wing. A man two rows in front of Dexter stood, walked up the aisle, and said something to them. They nodded and smiled brightly. A moment later the announcement came.

Dexter listened to the pilot's guttural speech and tried to get the meaning. He couldn't even distinguish words, let alone translate them into English. He cursed himself for not keeping up his premed German. An English translation followed a moment later, though it seemed to take longer than that. They were experiencing some mechanical difficulties, and the plane was returning to London. The attendant repeated the message, presumably it was the message, in Arabic.

Around him several dozen voices asked and pleaded and demanded to know what was wrong. The attendants worked the aisles, repeating the sentence. The plane was returning to London because of mechanical difficulties. They smiled and nodded their way among the passengers as if they were delivering wonderful news.

"What kind of mechanical difficulties?" a man shouted.

"Don't panic," another man yelled at him. "The worst thing to do in a situation like this is panic."

The woman in the seat next to Dexter took out a set of rosary beads and began working them between her fingers as she murmured to herself. He glanced out the window again. They weren't flying any higher, but they weren't flying any lower.

For the next half hour the pilot continued to make regular announcements without giving away any information, and an attendant continued to translate his statements into English and Arabic, and the flight crew continued to work their way up and down the aisles, assuring passengers there was nothing to worry about.

The woman next to Dexter was still saying her rosary, and another woman across the aisle was dabbing at the mascara that was running down her cheeks. A man behind him was threatening to sue the airline. Another man in a natty blue blazer and bow tie had gotten out of his seat and was going up and down the plane telling people he was an oncologist and saw people die every day and therefore there was nothing to worry about. It was a crowd, Dexter knew, on the verge of hysteria.

The pilot came over the loudspeaker in German again. Dexter tried to make out the words. All he understood was "Gatwick" and the number *zehn*. He heard a sigh of guarded relief go through the plane. The pilot went on. The woman with the streaking mascara let out a sob. The attendant translated. They would be landing at Gatwick in approximately ten minutes. Another murmur of guarded relief. At that time they would be asked to assume protective positions, which the attendants would demonstrate.

A stewardess came and said something in German to the woman next to Dexter. He couldn't make any sense of the words. She nodded her head yes, unhooked her seat belt, and followed the stewardess forward. A moment later the attendant was back.

"Would you like us to find you an English-speaking passenger?" she asked.

"What?"

"A passenger who speaks English, sir? Studies have found that most passengers prefer to have someone to be with. Someone who speaks the same language. So we try to find someone for passengers who have no one."

"Thank you," Dexter said. "I'm fine."

"Are you sure, sir?"

"I'm sure," he told the stewardess. "I don't need anyone."

And for the next ten minutes, while a baby shrieked, and the woman across the aisle sobbed, and the man behind him cursed; while passengers hunched forward, and placed their arms over their heads, and made whatever bargains with God or peace with themselves they could; while the lights suddenly went out and the plane dropped and the ground bounced up to meet it so roughly that several people screamed; while he felt the wind go out of his lungs as his body hurled forward against the seat belt, and, after a moment of dazed silence, the crowd around him burst into applause and cheers, those four absurd words kept running through his head.

The terminal was still bright and ugly and mindlessly busy, but now he barely noticed it. He made his way to a bank of phones. His hand was steady as he punched in the numbers. That was funny because he didn't feel steady. He was still sweating.

It took several seconds before the ringing began at the other end. He counted one, two, a third. If the machine answered, he'd hang up. He had no idea what he was going to say, but whatever it was, he wasn't going to say it to an answering machine.

She picked up on the fourth ring and said hello. He opened his mouth, but no sound came out. "Hello," she repeated. Her tone was querulous now, as if she suspected a crank caller at the other end of the line.

"This is the camp commandant," he said finally.

"I never said—"

"It was a joke, Hallie."

"It's not funny."

"I know, but maybe we ought to pretend it is." He hesitated. "It's one way to get around it."

The silence seeped across the wire again. He tried to figure out how to go on. He hadn't expected it to play like a telephone commercial or a flowers-by-wire ad, but he hadn't thought it would be this hard.

"Where are you?" she asked finally.

He told her, and the rest of it too, the mechanical difficulties, and the crew that kept insisting everything was fine, and the woman who said her rosary all the way back, and the oncologist with the wildly illogical reassurances, and the stewardess who wanted to find him an English-speaking seatmate.

"Did she?"

"I told her I didn't need anyone."

She didn't say anything to that.

"An apt phrase, don't you think? There are some who might say it's my motto."

He stopped and waited.

"People don't change, Hallie. Not about anything that matters."

There was another silence. This wasn't getting any easier. She wasn't making it any easier.

"Did I ever tell you about Hezron?"

"About what?"

"Not what, who. Hezron. He used to work for the fund. Did I ever tell you about him?"

"I don't think so."

"He was terrific. Guide, translator, facilitator, the man could do it all." The words were coming now. This was something he knew about. "Without Hezron, and there are dozens of Hezrons, we couldn't get anything done."

"You mean he oiled wheels. Saw to it that medical supplies could be unloaded or food distributed—for a price."

"No, Hezron was a good guy. High-minded. Dedicated. Spent his spare time studying. He knew more about sanitation and water supplies than you do."

"I don't know much about sanitation and water supplies."
Her voice was flat.

"You know what I mean. He was the real hope of the fund."

There was another silence. "And?" she asked finally.

"His daughter died."

"I'm sorry."

"It was a couple of years ago."

"I don't understand."

"She died from a botched circumcision."

"Oh!"

"With all Hezron knew, with all his reading, all his so-called enlightenment, he went ahead and had his daughter circumcised. He said if he hadn't, he never could have married her off."

"That's disgusting."

"I know, but that's the point. People don't change."

She didn't say anything.

"I was thinking about Hezron on the plane. Even before I got on the plane. This morning in the airport." He stopped.

"Yes?"

"Look, maybe this sounds like a walking proof of solipsism or something—"

"You? Never. I'm sorry." She went on quickly. "That was a cheap shot."

"The point is, if they don't even try, there's no damn hope at all." He stopped again. He could hear his own breathing. He wondered if she could too.

"Are we talking about Hezron or you?" she asked after a while.

"We're talking about me. That's what solipsism means."

"Thanks for the explanation. Now I won't have to get out my dictionary." It was a smart-ass answer, but she didn't deliver it in a smart-ass tone.

They talked for a while longer, though later neither of them would be able to remember what they said. Then, just as they were about to hang up, something occurred to him.

"Listen," he said, "if you think about it, we're starting out ahead of the game."

"What do you mean?"

"I mean, we already know the worst about each other."

Twenty-three

I DIDN'T TELL anyone about Dexter's call from London. I learned a long time ago that trying to explain what went on with a man to another woman was a little like selling old jewelry. There was no way you were going to get full value from the transaction.

The romantics among my well-meaning friends would find Dexter unromantic. The psychologically attuned would diagnose him as withholding. I didn't agree with either judgment. But then I've never trusted the sweet-tongued Cyranos of this world, "golden-mouthed men bearing gifts of verbal jewelry," and I'm almost as wary of their smarmy brothers who trade in semiprecious trinkets like "commitment" and "communication" and "sharing." They all seem to be reading from someone else's script. But a man who wraps his feelings around a failing in the human condition and then apologizes for his solipsism, a man who can't find anything better to whisper in your ear than the reassurance that you already know the worst about each other, that's a man who's speaking from the heart.

A week later Dexter returned, as promised. He was about the only one who did. It was one of those July weekends when every self-respecting New Yorker is on his way out of town by four in the afternoon. By seven the city had slipped back into an earlier, more civilized version of itself. Taxis cruised politely eager for fares, pedestrians strolled unmolested and unafraid, and a warm breeze rustled through the park and whispered down the side streets. I felt as if we were living in the pages of an old *Life* magazine. On Friday night the sun poured down the Palisades like purple lava and disappeared in the Hudson. The next morning it spilled across the East River and through the windows of my apartment, searing our sex-sealed eyes. The traffic on the FDR Drive was so light we could leave the windows open and listen to the murmur of boat engines on the river, and the slap of their wakes against the bulkheads, and, in the silences between, our own astonished sighs. My phone didn't ring once. Dex never even bothered to call his machine. We were as alone as two people can be only in a desert, or on an island, or, despite the city's misleading ambiance, in an urban center in the last fearful, alienated years of the twentieth century.

I don't mean to make it sound like an idyll. It wasn't. We were like the old joke about two porcupines mating. We were being very careful. Both of us were old enough, and scarred enough, to know that love didn't conquer all, or even much. Both of us were seasoned enough not to be surprised when the volatile intimacy of sex evaporated, fast as sweat, leaving an acrid residue of loneliness. And both of us were smart enough never to ask the other what he was thinking. But somehow, despite the sudden distances and occasional silences, despite the nagging habit of wariness and the stab of loneliness-with-someone, which is so much sharper than the pain of merely being alone, we were easing into something.

Dexter left on Sunday evening. On Sunday night I had the dream for the first time. My dreams tend to be embarrassingly obvious. If I have to give a speech, I dream I'm standing in front of a group naked. When I turn in an article to be edited, that night knife-wielding strangers pursue me in my sleep. Not exactly the stuff of which subtle psychological interpretations or even personal epiphanies are made. The night Dexter left promising that he'd do his damnedest to get back in two weeks I dreamed I was standing safe and warm in the house where I'd grown up. The only problem was that all the windows and doors were closed and locked, and I couldn't get out of that safe, cosseting house.

It wasn't exactly what you'd call a nightmare.

Twenty-four

"YOU WHAT!" Julian's hand stopped writing. His head snapped up from the newspaper. Emma glanced from his face to the crossword puzzle. There were only a few blank spaces. He'd been expecting a good day. She looked back at his face. She could see her reflection in his dark glasses and, behind her, the lawn sloping down to the water glittering in the unrelenting glare of the sun.

"I invited her for the weekend," she repeated.

He went on staring at her. A Sunfish sailed a calm, steady course across the surface of his glasses. "I don't believe it," he said finally. "I just don't believe it. A week ago you were accusing me of screwing her or at least being well on the way to it. A week ago you couldn't wait to move out here and get me away from her. Now you tell me you invited her for the weekend. Do me a favor, sweetheart. Let me know when you make up your mind." He shook his head. The seascape reflected in his glasses glided back and forth. He went back to his puzzle, scribbled in a few letters, then tossed the paper to the white-painted rocker and glanced at his watch. A look of satisfaction, hard and unforgiving as the morning sunlight, flickered across his face. He was still expecting a good day.

"It was the only polite thing to do," she said, and hated the way her voice pleaded for justification. "When she said she wanted to come out for one last meeting. And see the house."

"That should take a couple of hours. Which warrants some iced tea. Maybe a gin and tonic. Lunch at the outside. Not a whole fucking weekend of sun and fun."

"It's too long a trip for one day. With the ferry rides and all."

"Day-trippers do it all the time. Besides, it's her job. *She*'s interviewing *you*."

"That reporter from *Parade* came for the weekend a couple of years ago. You didn't complain then."

"I'm not complaining now. Invite whomever you want. It's your house."

"It's—"

"I know, I know, in both our names, but you and I know the truth, sweetheart. All I'm saying is I don't understand why you invited her. One week you're screaming she's grounds for divorce; the next she's your best friend."

"We did grow up together."

He slid his dark glasses down his nose and squinted at her over the rims. "Come on, sweetheart, this is me, the man who watched you burn your high school yearbook in the fireplace of our first apartment. So don't try to tell me this is a trip down memory lane. The question is"—he pushed his glasses back up to the bridge of his nose—"what is it? What would make you invite a woman you accuse me of wanting to screw to stay with us for the weekend?"

Emma thought about it. She'd been thinking about it ever since she'd blurted out the invitation. It wasn't just that Hallie was involved with someone else. It was more than that. It was more ludicrous than that. She'd invited Hallie for the weekend because of a look she'd seen in Hallie's eyes, the same look she'd seen in the eyes of those women who used to strut around her mother's store showing off their figures and their superiority and their generosity. The women had looked at her mother that way because she didn't have a husband. Hallie had looked at her that way because of the husband she had.

They'd been talking about a husband and wife production team that had optioned one of Emma's books for an after-school special. She'd said it must be nice to work together, and Hallie had laughed, a terrible, knowing laugh, and said it wasn't entirely an artistic decision. "From what I hear—and I know someone who wrote a script for them—he's an equal-opportunity womanizer. Old, young, fat, thin, gorgeous, plain, smart, dumb, white, or, as we say these days, of color. No wonder she won't let him out of her sight."

Maybe it was the expression on Emma's face, but Hallie had stopped abruptly. She'd glanced away, then back, and that was when Emma had seen the look.

"When you come out to the beach," she'd said, "why don't you stay for the weekend? Julian and I would love to have you."

She stood, pushed her chair back from the table, and began putting mugs and plates on the tray to carry them into the house. "You won't have to entertain her. I'll tell her you're working or that there's a tennis tournament or something. The most you'll see of her is dinner Friday and Saturday night."

"No, thanks."

She stood holding the tray. "What do you mean?"

He looked up at her from behind the dark glasses. "I mean, sweetheart, I have no intention of holing up in the study or hiding out on somebody's court for an entire weekend. So when you catch me in the act of saying good morning or do you want a drink or would you mind passing the fucking salt, do me a favor. Don't make a scene. Don't threaten divorce. And don't accuse me of having it off with her. Because you're the one who invited her for the weekend, and all I'm doing is being polite."

*　*　*

She sat staring at the screen of her laptop. She was getting too old to be writing about not making the team and being ashamed of your parents and losing your virginity, even if these days when you didn't make the team, you sued for gender discrimination, and the reason you were ashamed of your parents was that every time you turned on the television there were Mom and Mom on some talk show screaming about gay rights, and irresponsible sex was more likely to lead to death than disgrace.

She swiveled to the window. A dozen small sails glittered immaculately against the dark blue surface of the bay. The junior division of the yacht club was out. She sat watching them for a moment. The breeze was so light they were barely moving. She told herself she was just having a slow day. The characters would come to life tomorrow. The story would take off next week. The important thing was to keep working. Without her work she was nothing, or at least a lot less.

She heard the creak of rubber soles on old wood but didn't turn around, though her eyes were beginning to ache from the glare of the sun on the surface of the water. She could feel him standing behind her. She didn't need this now. She didn't need another argument, not while the new book lay like a dead animal on her desk. She could cope with a dry day or she could cope with him, but she couldn't cope with both together. Not anymore. It was like the adolescent subject matter. She'd been through it too many times. She was too old and jaded and exhausted.

"Em."

She recognized the tone of soft, sad apology, abject mea culpas, self-pitying promises of renewal. Not now, thanks, not today. I've used up my quota of feeling for today.

She dragged her eyes away from the starchy white sails and turned to the door.

"I didn't mean to interrupt you," he said.

Then why the fuck are you standing there in the door to my study?

"You're not interrupting me. There's nothing to interrupt today."

"I'm sorry."

She shrugged. "It'll come again. At least that's what I keep telling myself."

"That isn't what I meant."

He put his hands in the pockets of his khaki shorts and leaned his shoulder against the doorjamb. The seductive ease of the stance struck her, not with desire but with its memory, which was infinitely more painful. The sudden urge to cry surprised her. She clutched the arms of the chair and sat waiting for it to pass.

"I meant I was sorry for what I said before. About inviting her for the weekend."

She felt herself tense. She wasn't going to let him blindside her again.

"It's just that . . ." He hesitated.

"I know. It's just that you don't get it. It's just that you're sick and tired of my fevered imagination, my rich fantasy life, my paranoia."

He sank deeper into the slouch. "It's just that I was looking forward to having the weekend alone. No houseguests. No plans. Just the two of us." He pulled himself up and away from the doorjamb. "That's why I overreacted."

That was her cue. She was supposed to tell him he hadn't overreacted. And she was the one who was sorry. And everything was all right. Then they'd go down the hall to the bedroom and he'd administer first aid, again. He'd pull her up from the abyss hand over hand, and give her mouth-to-mouth resuscitation, and lick her wounds, again. Except he couldn't, not this time, because she was too far away and the wounds were too deep and there was no life left in her. She wanted to tell him that. She even heard the words forming in her head. But before she could get them out, he smiled at her, the old lock-up-your-daughters smile, only this time she couldn't even remember the desire; all she could remember was the habit of what they always did, the knowledge of what he expected her to do. She felt another wave of exhaustion.

Still smiling, he tilted his head in the direction of the bedroom. She didn't move. She couldn't. Her shoulders were weighed down and her bones ached and her muscles throbbed.

He lifted his eyebrows and inclined his head another fraction of an inch. She forced herself to straighten her shoulders. Then numbly, woodenly, like a puppet controlled by the strings he pulled, she stood and started moving in that direction.

He talked about it later. He liked to do that sometimes, like a reviewer critiquing a performance. She won raves that morning, for fire and passion and technique. And all the time he talked, she kept thinking it was the first time she'd ever thought he was stupid. She'd thought he was selfish and cruel and pathetic, but never stupid. It was a harsh judgment, but she didn't know what else to call a man who couldn't recognize hatred when he came up against it, face to face, skin to skin, heart to heart.

She waited until he left the house to call Hallie, though there was no reason to. She wasn't doing this for revenge. She wasn't even doing it for self-protection. She was doing it because it was the logical, the obvious, the only gracious thing to do. The only thing she wondered was why she hadn't thought to do it before.

Twenty-five

I WASN'T SURPRISED when Emma called to suggest that I bring Dexter along for the weekend. I hadn't told her about the call from the airport, but I had mentioned his existence, and Emma was a woman who subscribed to the Noah's Ark school of travel. It would be nice to have me for the weekend. It would be better to have both Dexter and me for the weekend.

I passed the invitation on to Dexter. "You don't have to go if you don't want to," I added.

He said he'd be happy to go.

"I mean, I won't exactly be working, but it is work, and I don't know how much time I'll be able to spend with you."

He said he was perfectly capable of taking care of himself.

"I don't want to force you into anything."

"You're not forcing me."

A cloud of vague apprehension drifted across the weekend horizon. It wasn't that I didn't want Dexter along, only that I didn't want the responsibility. I was worried that he'd be bored. I was afraid that Emma would be overbearing. And then there was Julian. It was entirely possible Dexter and Julian would get along; it was more likely they'd detest each other. Whatever happened, it would be my fault.

I told Emma that Dexter and I would love to come for the weekend.

A few days later Dexter announced a change in plans. He'd been monitoring the situation in Sudan for some time. There was war. There was famine. There was a disease called kala-azar. And there was a formerly hostile government—so hostile that the last time Dexter had been there he'd been shot at—that had suddenly decided to let the fund send aid. It took Dexter seventy-two hours to arrange for the airlift. I watched some of it firsthand while he made calls to pharmaceutical companies and food purveyors and cargo airlines from my apartment. I heard about the rest of it when I turned on my television one morning to find him staring out at me in living color. I got the final details when he stopped by to say good-bye on his way to the airport. I'd never been more in love with him than that afternoon I sent him off to Africa.

Twenty-six

AN ISLAND, even an island that's only a stone's throw from a mainland and boasts all the amenities, including continuous ferry service, two liquor stores, and three antique shops, is an outpost of humanity. As long as it can be isolated by fog, or cut off by storm, or blockaded by man, it's exotic terrain that reeks of adventure and danger and primitive possibilities.

The fact that those were the thoughts going through my mind as I made the six-minute crossing from Greenport to Shelter Island on Friday afternoon shows what kind of mood I was in. I kept thinking of Dexter in Sudan. And of me here. Now that I knew he wasn't coming along, I realized how much I wanted him along.

Of course, the fact that we were starting the second week of a summer meltdown that had already caused one Con Ed brownout and driven weather forecasters to issuing air-quality warnings as if they were jeremiads probably had something to do with my unhinged state. In town air conditioners coughed and wheezed and dripped, and tempers flared, and the homicide rate soared. At the eastern end of Long Island conditions were marginally better.

There was a breeze on the ferry, but it came from our momentum rather than the forces of nature. I stood on the deck feeling the hot metal vibrating through the thin rubber soles of my Top-siders and rubbing sweaty elbows with regular commuters and other weekend guests. There were couples that traveled light with a single duffel and twin briefcases; and families laden down with small children and large dogs and enormous coolers full of food and soft drinks; and solitary men in wrinkled cotton suits and ties draped like casual nooses, who wore secretive expressions because they'd been alone all week, or maybe because they hadn't. The solitary men made me think of Dexter, but then these days everything was making me think of Dexter. I looked at one of the cars filled with kids and coolers and animals and tried to imagine Dex and me in the front seat. The image had about as much reality as a picture I remembered from my mother's old albums. It was one of those corny trick shots with her head and my father's peeking through the holes in a cardboard reproduction of Grant Wood's *American Gothic*.

As the ferry nudged and bumped its way into the slip, the breeze died, and the sun, which had already slid halfway down the cloudless white-hot sky, pressed like a heavy helmet on my head. Around me on the deck people were climbing into their cars and starting their engines. Acrid fumes rose in an inferno of anticipation.

Two young men with white-blond hair and impressively defined muscles secured the lines, a third man wearing a T-shirt that said "Viet Vets Do It in the Bush" swung open the gates, and passengers bent and hoisted their duffels and began streaming off the boat. I picked up my own duffel and fell in with them.

As I stepped from the metal ramp onto the island, the hot tarmac felt soft and squishy beneath my feet. In the glare of the parking lot, children chased each other, and women called after them to calm down, and the occasional man lounged stoically against a car. Tanned to the expensive shades of antique luggage and dressed in perfectly aged and faded sportswear, the waiting hosts had a certain sameness to them, but their vehicles made more individual statements. There were flashy sports cars of the Jaguar and BMW and Mercedes persuasions, and Rovers and Jeeps that told how serious their owners were about carefree living, and old heaps people left on the island so they wouldn't have to wait in the car line for the ferry. There were also sleeker antiques from earlier, supposedly more romantic summers. I noticed a racing green roadster that looked like something out of Scott Fitzgerald, or at least John O'Hara, and a flame red Corvette from my own adolescence, and a luscious white Buick with red upholstery. The white Buick gave me pause because it was the same model that I'd imagined Babe leaning against that afternoon I'd taken the train out to New Jersey to help her look at retirement communities. It occurred to me, as I stood there squinting into my past through dark glasses, that it was odd that I associated the car with Babe because before my father had come cruising up the driveway tooting the horn of a brand-new baby blue Cadillac to the tune of "Happy Birthday," the Buick had belonged to my mother. My mother's first thought, after she'd finished oohing and ahhing over the new Cadillac, was that now they could sell her old Buick to Babe, but my generous father, generous to a fault, my mother always insisted, went her one better and said they might as well give it to Babe. Maybe I thought of the car as Babe's because she'd driven it for longer than my mother had, and of course, by then I was older, but I think the real reason was that it suited Babe better than it had my mother. My mother belonged in that baby blue Cadillac sedan that, despite the extravagant tail fins, was a dowager of a car. Even the color reminded me of a dowager's overtinted hair. The racy convertible with the blazing red upholstery fitted Babe as if it had been designed or at least bought for her.

I was so busy remembering that car that at first I didn't even notice the man lounging against its creamy haunch. Then he waved, and I recognized the killer smile, dazzlingly white now in his deeply tanned face. Julian Weill pulled himself up and away from the fender and started toward me. He was wearing khaki shorts and a pink polo shirt that was faded almost white, and he looked like one of those ads that try to sell you a product by promising you a way of life. The fact that I knew there was probably no truth in this particular advertising didn't make it any less attractive. It occurred to me that a lot of women in this world will forgive a tall, lanky man with a swivel-hipped walk practically anything. It also occurred to me that since I had the perspicacity to recognize the fact, I was not one of them. I thought of Dexter's walk, which had an athletic purposefulness to it.

I began moving toward Julian. When we met in the middle of the parking lot, he bent and kissed me on the cheek.

"Welcome to the Weill Fresh Air Fund. Last summer it was drug-endangered kids from the South Bronx. This year it's sweaty journalists from the Upper East Side."

My hand went to my upper lip. I cursed myself for the reflex, and the thin film of perspiration that sat there like a damp mustache.

"You know the old Orson Welles line," I said.

"Miss Hayworth does not sweat. Miss Hayworth does not perspire. Miss Hayworth glistens."

"You got it," I said, and surreptitiously mopped my upper lip again.

He took my duffel and put a hand on my shoulder, my sweaty shoulder, to steer me toward the Buick. As we reached it, he slowed his pace. "I know," he said. "It's a gas guzzler. An air polluter. An egregious example of America's love affair with built-in obsolescence. It's the embodiment of everything I'm against. But I can't help it." He swung my duffel into the backseat and opened the door on the passenger side for me. "I love the damn thing."

I climbed in and sank into the blazing red upholstery. It was a hotbed of memories. The dashboard practically made me cry.

The only thing missing was Babe's lipstick-kissed cigarette butts in the ashtray. I remembered the time she'd let me have one of my own. My mother had predicted it would make me sick. "Then she'll stop driving me crazy for drags," Babe had said. It hadn't made me sick. It had made me even more crazy about her.

"So do I," I said.

"I had a feeling you would." He climbed into the driver's side. "Emma hates it." He turned to me with a startled expression. "Jesus, I didn't mean that the way it sounded."

I didn't know what to say to that, so I sat watching as he put the key in the ignition and stretched a long tan leg toward the gas pedal. Then he seemed to change his mind. Instead of starting the car, he turned to me, put his arm along the back of the front seat, and took off his dark glasses and rubbed his eyes with the thumb and forefinger of his other hand. If he'd been sitting over a desk or in front of a computer screen, I wouldn't have thought anything of the gesture, but sitting in a vintage car on the eve of a holiday weekend, I didn't trust it for a minute. I don't know what I expected, but I expected something.

"Maybe I shouldn't say this," he said, "but I'm really glad you're here."

Or maybe I had known what I expected because suddenly my mind fast-forwarded through the entire weekend. I saw the meaningful glances, the secret messages veiled in general conversation, the accidental brushing of hands and glancing of bodies. I heard the suggestion of lunch or a drink back in town or, worse yet, the sound of footsteps creeping down the hall in the dead of night. In that moment I knew the whole disastrous episode as completely as if it had already happened, and I knew one other thing as well: This was a game I wasn't going to play.

"I'm really glad to be here," I answered in a voice as sweet and brittle as hard candy.

He sat staring at me for a moment, then shook his head.

"I'm sorry. I didn't mean that the way it sounded either. It's just that we need new blood in the house."

"Here I am, the human sacrifice."

"Don't worry, it won't be that bad. Though it hasn't exactly been a barrel of laughs. Emma's been working her tail off. And, unfortunately, getting nowhere. It happens every time she starts a new book. I keep telling her it will come. It just takes a while." His fist hit the steering wheel. "Christ, you'd think by now she'd know that. But when it comes to her books, my wife's a virgin every time out of the box. She—" He stopped. "My God, it's the Princeton Club all over again. What is it about you that makes me run off at the mouth this way? Mea culpa, mea culpa. I'm sorry."

"There's nothing to be sorry for."

"No, I should keep my mouth shut."

He was right. He should keep his mouth shut. I was another woman. I was also a journalist writing a profile of his wife. I should have told him that.

"It's just that . . . well, I can't help it. I'm worried about her."

"What do you mean?" So much for telling him to keep his mouth shut.

"Nothing really, except . . . I don't know . . . sometimes I get the feeling . . . sometimes, like the other night—" He stopped and shook his head. "Good God, there I go again. Forget it. Forget I said anything." He took his arm from the back of the seat, faced forward, and turned the key in the ignition. "All I meant was that Emma needs a diversion."

"Well, I'm here to divert," I said in that same bright, hard-candy voice, and forced myself not to look at his long, tapering fingers as they embraced the steering wheel and caressed it into a turn.

Twenty-seven

EMMA TWISTED her wrist to see the face of her watch, but the knitted cuff of her canvas glove still covered it. That was all right. She didn't need a watch to know that Julian had been gone far too long. She could tell by the sun. She could tell by her inner clock, for God's sake. He'd left the house more than an hour ago. Much more than an hour ago. The train to Greenport wouldn't be this late. And there was never any wait for a ferry if you didn't have a car with you. What in hell were they doing?

A rivulet of sweat ran down her side, irritating as an insect. What was she doing gardening in this heat? Just because she was too tense to work didn't mean she had to weed the goddamn tomato plants. Julian's goddamn tomato plants. At least they were supposed to be Julian's. What was this obsession of middle-aged men with gardening? As if now that they'd scorched the earth in pursuit of money and power and sex, they were determined to replenish it. Half her friends' husbands seemed to be doing some sort of horticultural penance. And Julian was one of them; only she couldn't help feeling that Julian was up to more, or less, than penance. She could see him urging Hallie to try one of his tomatoes now. The sensitive man in tune with his feminine nurturing side meets Albert Finney as Tom Jones. She flung the gardening tools in the basket, stood, and started for the house.

In the front hall she caught a glimpse of herself in the mirror. The big straw hat with the flowered ribbon sat ludicrously on her head. Talk about Albert Finney. Who in hell did she think she was? Greer Garson? She took off the hat. Her hair was slicked to her head with perspiration. A ribbon of red irritation ran across her forehead.

She hung the hat on one of the wooden pegs alongside Julian's straw boater with the orange and black band, and the various Knicks and Yankees and Giants caps, and her own collection of rain hats and sun hats and garden party hats. Everyone always complimented her on that wall. It was so colorful, people always exclaimed. It said so much about her and Julian and their interests. The only thing it said was that their life was one long pretense. Kitsch masquerading as taste.

She turned away from the wall and started up the stairs. She had to stop thinking this way. She especially had to stop thinking this way before Hallie got here. She was going to wash her hands and face, and brush her hair, and put on fresh lipstick. Then she'd go out on the porch—there might even be a whisper of a breeze on the porch—and read. And that was the way they'd find her when they arrived. She'd be sitting in one of the painted white rockers, reading a set of galleys a publisher had sent her for a quote, absorbed and unruffled.

"What the fuck were you doing?"

The words hit his back like bullets from a gun with a silencer. She was whispering so her voice wouldn't carry from the porch to the guest room, but she was out to kill.

He wiped the sweat from his forehead with the back of his forearm and went on mixing drinks at the wicker tea trolley in silence.

"It takes ten minutes to get to the ferry," she hissed at his back. "Ten to get back. She said her train wasn't late. So what the fuck were you doing for two fucking hours?"

He took a wedge of lime and ran it around the rim of one of the glasses, then repeated the gesture with the second glass and the third. When he'd dropped the last lime in the last glass, he turned and held it out to her. For a minute he thought she was going to knock it out of his hand, but he went on standing there with the glass stretched out to her like a peace offering, and finally she reached out and took it from him. He picked up another glass and carried it to one of the rockers.

"I mean it, Julian. You wouldn't do that to a stranger." Her voice had started to rise. She fought it back to a whisper. "But you don't give a damn about keeping me waiting for two fucking hours."

He took a sip of his drink, leaned back in the chair, and shook his head slowly from side to side. "I give up." His voice was as quiet as hers, and much calmer. "I really do."

"You give up! You weren't the one who was—"

"Do you remember what you said as I left?"

"Keep your voice down."

"Do you remember why you asked me to pick her up in the first place?"

"I asked you to pick her up because I was working. I didn't ask you to spend two hours driving around the goddamn island with her."

"You asked me to pick her up at the ferry because you were finally having a good day, after a long run of bad days. And God knows we've heard enough about those. Do you think Dr. Seuss used to get blocked? Anyway, you said it was finally beginning to come and you didn't want to stop, so would I mind picking her up at the ferry."

"I didn't say I didn't want to stop. I said I just wanted to finish that page."

"Ah, yes, well, you see, sweetheart, those of us who write

for grown-ups sometimes spend hours on a page, days even, if you can imagine that. So, hard as this may be for you to believe, I thought I was doing you a favor by taking her on a tour of the island. I sure as hell wasn't driving around to the local tourist spots in this heat and humidity for my pleasure. I mean I've only seen the ospreys in the Mashomack Preserve a couple of hundred times in the last month. Not to mention the Quaker Martyrs' Memorial. Now there was a thrill and a half."

"You could have told me you planned to take her on a tour. If you were so damn considerate, you could have—" She heard Hallie's footsteps on the old wood of the staircase and stopped.

They stared at each other across the expanse of late-afternoon air that shimmered with heat and tension. There was something sheepish and shameful in their glances. They were relieved. Now they could stop without giving in.

Twenty-eight

I KNEW before I came out on the porch that they were fighting. I'd heard them from my room. I couldn't make out what they were saying, but I could recognize the tone. People with rocky marriages shouldn't invite other people for the weekend, but of course, people with rocky marriages are the ones who want other people around for the weekend. I wondered what Dex was doing at that moment.

I'd stooged around upstairs for a while, giving them time to work it out, or at least have it out, and freshening up a little, because I hadn't forgotten Julian's comment about sweaty journalists. When I finally came downstairs—I made as much noise as possible because I wanted to give them warning, though it didn't take much on those old floorboards—and out onto the porch, they both turned to me with the smiles of confirmed felons. They knew they were guilty of something.

We all began talking at the same time. Emma said she hoped my room was comfortable, and Julian said he'd made me a drink, and I told them how much I admired their house. It was a square white Victorian with beautifully restored gingerbread and a wide porch that wrapped all the way around it like a decorative ribbon. It was the kind of house you wished your grandmother had owned. The kind of place, come to think of it,

Dexter's grandmother probably had. Anyway, I told them it was a terrific house and they'd done a great job with it.

Emma said she hadn't done much with the house at all and explained that they'd bought it before real estate values on the island had skyrocketed.

"My wife is modest," Julian said. "And guilt-ridden. She doesn't think she deserves all this. I, on the other hand, who did absolutely nothing to earn it, enjoy it to the hilt."

Emma stood and said she was going to get some hors d'oeuvres. I offered to help.

"There's nothing to do," she assured me. "I picked some stuff from the garden, and there's a dip in the fridge."

"Are you sure?"

"She's sure," Julian said. "The author as superhostess. She's probably got food for the entire weekend arranged alphabetically out there. You'd just screw it up."

"It's not that," Emma said as she opened the screen door and went into the house. "There just isn't anything to do."

After she left, he stood, moved to the porch railing, and stretched out with his back against one of the pillars and his legs extended along the balustrade. A male odalisque. A male odalisque with impressive balance.

"I suppose you heard us fighting."

I didn't say anything. Later I told myself that at least I hadn't encouraged him.

"I don't know how much longer I can take it. I can live with her jealousy, and I can try to reassure her about her work, but I can't hack it when she comes at me with both at the same time."

I still didn't encourage him, unless you call creating a silence for him to fill encouragement.

"First she asks me to pick you up at the ferry because she wants the rest of the day to work. Because the world is going to come to an end if she doesn't put in another hour or two of work. Then she flies into a jealous rage because I do it."

"Are you sure you're not exaggerating? I wouldn't call what just went on here a jealous rage."

"What went on in front of you, of course not. She's terrific at putting up a front. You must know that by now. But you should have heard what went on before you came down. You probably did hear it."

Before I could decide whether to admit that I had or pretend that I hadn't, I heard Emma's footsteps coming back down the hall toward the porch. The house was beautiful, but it was also noisy. It gave off a lot of warnings. It occurred to me later that we should have paid attention to them.

They took me to a dinner party that night. It was such a typical upscale summer-resort dinner party that I could have written about it before I arrived, and probably had for some assignment in my past. Most of the guests were dressed as if they expected the evening to end in a climb up Everest or a single-handed sail across the Atlantic. The only man wearing a tie was wearing it looped through the belt hooks of his Bermuda shorts. The woman hired to do the serving was decked out in the duck-printed wrap skirt, flower-printed headband, and embroidered espadrilles of a fugitive from a Connecticut car pool. She passed cunning no-fat hors d'oeuvres on a deck with a view of the sunset over the bay that proved that while the best things in life might be free, a front-row seat for them doesn't come cheap. The level of wit was high. The levy of insider savvy was astronomical. Nobody was so crude as to drop a name, but most of the guests were careful to substantiate the sources of their anecdotes. And their seriousness of purpose was impressive. The young hostess, who bore an uncanny resemblance to her husband's daughter from his first marriage, though the daughter looked a few years older, had started a foundation to preserve the weaving techniques of Peruvian women. If Julian had made fun of the group at the literary reception where I'd first met him, I knew he'd have a heyday with this crowd.

He did. Every time I turned around he was at my shoulder delivering a one-liner about one of the guests. At least when he wasn't at the shoulder of the young hostess, or her stepdaughter, or one of the other women. I noticed something about Julian that night, something I'd suspected when I'd watched him in the lobby of the Princeton Club the day we'd had lunch. Julian Weill knew his way around women, but he couldn't handle himself with other men. Once that evening, and only once as far as I knew, he ended up in a group of men. His smile seemed suddenly forced. His voice, usually deep and soothing as a massage, grew too hearty. And when the car pool fugitive came through with a tray of hors d'oeuvres and the group shifted and reformed, leaving him facing a wall of broad collegial backs, he had the tremulous, teary look of the boy who never gets to play or, if he does, always has to be "it." If Emma hadn't detached herself from another guest to join him, I would have gone to the rescue myself.

By the time we drove home in the old Buick, Julian had slipped back into character. He was mildly vicious and fairly funny, and both Emma, beside him in the front seat, and I, who had to lean forward from the backseat in order to hear him because the top was down, kept telling him he was terrible. But neither of us wanted him to stop. His words spun around us in the darkness like a silvery lasso, separating us from the dull and the foolish, the fatuous and the phonies, from all the other guests who didn't have our style and wit and verve, our high moral tone and deep human compassion, corralling us together in safety. The fact that I knew what he was up to didn't make it any more resistible.

He pulled the car into the driveway and stopped but didn't cut the engine. Instead he climbed out, walked the few feet to the garage, opened the latch on the big wooden doors, and dragged first one, then the other across the dirt driveway. He came back to the car, got behind the wheel, and drove us into a barn cluttered with bikes and oars and fishing rods and a Sunfish tiller and dagger board and a variety of other toys. We had to pick our way among them to come out into the night. Emma and I stood waiting while he dragged first one heavy door, then the other back into place and closed the latch. I was surprised. Emma had said they didn't even lock the doors to the house overnight.

"I thought there was no crime on the island," I said.

"Deer," Julian answered as we started toward the house.

"Excuse me?"

"Deer," he repeated. "And raccoons." His teeth flashed white in the darkness as he smiled. He knew I'd heard "dear," and he wanted me to know he knew. I suppose I should have known then that the weekend couldn't possibly turn out well, but I was still remembering how he'd looked when that group of men had closed him out.

"They wander in if we leave the garage doors open," Emma explained.

We said good night in the square hall at the top of the stairs. I went into my room and closed the door behind me. Across the hall their door clicked shut. When I came out of my room a few minutes later on the way to the bathroom, the house was quiet, although on the way back to my room I heard the sound of voices talking softly on the other side of their closed door. It didn't sound as if they were arguing now. In fact, Emma's voice sounded as reassuring as a lullaby.

I opened the door to my bedroom. The chintz curtains danced toward me in the breeze. I closed the door behind me. The curtains fell back against the window frames limply. It was going to be a hot night.

I turned the cotton patchwork quilt back and got into bed. The sheets were crisp and unwrinkled. They felt somehow different from the sheets on my bed at home. At first I thought it was just being in a strange bed in a strange house. Then it came to me. My sheets, high in polyester, went straight from the dryer in the laundry room of my building to my bed. Emma's sheets, pure cotton with probably a couple of million threads per square inch, made a detour through a pricey hand laundry. I hadn't slept on ironed sheets since I'd left my mother's house.

I'd brought two books and several magazines, but Emma had left the requisite guest reading material on the night table. There was a copy of the *Nation,* and another of *Food and Wine,* and a short-story collection called *American Wives,* and a memoir of turn-of-the-century Shelter Island. I picked up the memoir.

The door across the hall opened and closed softly. I stiffened, though I had no reason to. Emma and Julian had the right to prowl their property at whatever hour they pleased.

Footsteps started down the stairs. I opened the book, but my mind was still on those footfalls. They sounded too heavy for Emma. I wondered what he was up to. He wouldn't be locking up. There was no heat or air-conditioning to turn down, no cat to put out. He might be a middle-of-the-night refrigerator raider, but he looked too lean for that. What in hell was he doing? I told myself it was none of my business and went back to the book or at least its title page.

I heard the steps creaking again and stopped reading. There was a soft knock at my door. Maybe I'd read too many articles about English country house parties, not to mention one I'd written about a woman who, as a college friend of one of the Kennedy sisters, had been a guest in Hyannis in the thirties. All the sisters' friends, the woman had told me, knew to lock their bedroom doors when Joe senior was in residence. But I suddenly knew that my fast-forward view of the weekend hadn't been wrong after all.

I considered pretending to be asleep, but only a narcoleptic could have fallen asleep this quickly. I couldn't very well tell him to go away. Not yet. Not before he'd done something insulting or at least unseemly.

I looked at my lap to make sure my T-shirt was pulled down, and the sheets pulled up and said, "Yes?" It seemed less inviting than "Come in."

The door opened. He was wearing the khakis he'd worn to dinner and no shirt. I was willing to bet he spent a good deal of time on the tennis and squash courts and, I was further willing to bet from the way he slouched against the doorjamb now, not just for the love of the sport.

"It occurred to me that we're lousy hosts. I never asked if you wanted anything when we got home." He lifted the brandy glass in his hand toward me. "You interested in one of these?"

I thanked him and told him I wasn't.

"Wine?"

"No, thanks."

"Milk and cookies?" Another loaded grin.

"I'm fine."

He stood there for a minute staring at me. I don't wear much makeup at any time, but at that moment I was acutely aware that I wasn't wearing any. Or a bra. Not that I particularly need one, but I still wasn't wearing one.

"Okay, but if you change your mind, you know where to find it."

For a moment I thought he meant across the hall in their bedroom. Then I realized he meant the wicker tea trolley downstairs. He really was unhinging me.

"Thanks," I said again.

We wished each other good night two or three or five times, and he finally pulled himself up and away from the doorframe and closed the door. A moment later I heard the one across the hall open and close again.

I went back to the memoir. To judge from the pictures and

text, there was a lot of good clean fun on Shelter Island in the old days. Of course, those pictures of the Kennedy clan always looked like good clean fun too. From across the hall I heard the faint sounds of conversation again. They were so faint that I probably wouldn't have noticed if I'd been listening less attentively. I tried to summon a picture of Dexter, but the background was murky. I hadn't done my research on Sudan.

What came next was even more disturbing, and not merely because of my current state of mind. If you're a woman of a certain age and particular proclivities, you don't have to be halfway around the world from a lover or obsessing about the sexual practices of American political dynasties to find disturbing the experience of sitting alone in bed, listening to the sound of creaking springs, rhythmic creaking springs, across the hall.

For the second time I read through the paragraph about how to make an old-fashioned clambake. I was concentrating on the order in which the potatoes and corn and lobsters and clams went into the pit. Now that I was mixed up with a man with "Saint" in his name and WASP blood in his veins, you never knew what arcane rituals I might have to perform.

The rhythm was picking up a little. I started the paragraph a third time. Maybe if I could find a mnemonic for the sequence.

I'd got as far as *cpr,* though I couldn't find anything for the *r,* when I heard the first moan. I gave up on the clambake and turned the page. A bevy of women, corseted in whalebone, swathed in yards and yards of white muslin, shaded by wide brims of straw, cavorted on a beach. Across the hall Julian and Emma romped on the bed. I knew because I could hear the headboard banging against the wall. But in case I was hearing-impaired, there was another moan.

I sat with my back pressed hard against my own headboard and my fingers hanging on to the open book in my lap. My breath had halted somewhere around my heart. I'm not sure why. I wasn't the one in the throes of passion.

I tried to summon a picture of Dexter again. Julian's voice rattled my door and possibly every window in the house. Then he moaned again, more softly. The rhythmic creaking stopped. The house sank into silence.

I looked down at the book in my lap. I'd left damp marks all over the page.

Twenty-nine

THE BASTARD!

She glanced over at Julian guiltily, as if he might have sensed her thought. He lay on his stomach with his head turned toward her. His eyes were closed; his breathing was deep and steady. One arm hung across her body, dead weight.

No, that wasn't fair. She could blame him for a lot, but not for that. You couldn't blame a man for being carried away by passion.

Then how come he was never carried away by passion when the children were home? How come there were no operatic orgasms when Matt and Becky were across the hall or in the next room? Because he knew the way sound carried in this house, that's why. He knew it so well that sometimes when the kids were home, he put a pillow between the headboard and the wall. But not tonight. Not with an audience. With Hallie across the hall, the sound of the bed groaning and creaking and thumping against the wall hadn't been enough. He'd had to do a play-by-play as well. Why hadn't he just opened the goddamn doors and let her watch? The bastard!

He turned on his side and tightened his arm around her. She pried it off. He whimpered in his sleep. She could just make out his features in the muffled moonlight filtering through the window. The expression of startled distress matched the whimper. She felt another stab of guilt.

Maybe she was imagining it. "You have a rich inner life," he said, teasing her when things were good between them. "You're fucking paranoid," he said when they weren't. And they definitely weren't now. Maybe that was coloring her judgment. Maybe he hadn't been showing off for Hallie but had just got carried away himself. She remembered the way he'd looked standing alone outside that group of men tonight. At that moment she'd known the way the rest of the evening would play. Either he'd turn on her in rage—those sons of bitches were all her fault, and she was just like them—or to her for affirmation. Fortunately he'd done the latter, so why in hell was she angry? What kind of woman got angry with her husband for making too much noise during orgasm? The next thing she knew she'd be using euphemisms, and turning off the lights during sex, and carrying a bottle of Lysol to wash off toilet seats when she traveled. The next thing she knew she'd be turning into her mother.

His arm circled her again. She fought the urge to push it away.

Everybody had faults. What was that proverb about how if you put all the problems in the world in a heap, you'd pick out your own all over again? Nobody's husband was perfect. And the traits, if not the flaws, Julian had were the ones she wanted. He was a good father. Maybe a better father than she was a mother. Sometimes she suspected he was better with the children because he cared less, but that was all right. Whoever said you were doing people a favor by loving them too much? He was smart. And he had a social conscience. She couldn't have stood being married to a man who chased ambulances or sold cigarettes or even thought making money was the most important thing in the world. God knows that was one thing she couldn't accuse him of. But she wasn't going to think about that either. They'd come a long way from the days when he'd decimate the weekly budget buying flowers or champagne to apologize.

She turned her head on the pillow and looked at him again. It wasn't fair. He slept like a goddamn baby, and she lay here arguing with herself. She went on watching him. It really wasn't fair. Even in sleep his face didn't go slack or stupid. Okay, maybe appearance wasn't the most important trait to look for in a husband, but what was wrong with wanting nice eyes and great smiles and lean, lanky bodies for your children? Lindbergh had married for genes. Of course, Lindbergh had also been a Nazi sympathizer who subscribed to social Darwinism and the racial theories of the Third Reich.

This really was crazy. It was after two. Julian slept beside her like a baby, or at least a sexually satiated middle-aged man. Her houseguest slept across the hall in an authentically restored guest room. The whole damn island was probably sleeping, and she was lying here thinking about Charles Lindbergh and deconstructing the sounds her husband made during orgasm. Julian was right, she really was paranoid.

She turned on her side. He didn't loosen his grip. She pried his arm off her again. She wasn't angry anymore. Really she wasn't. It was just the heat. She couldn't stand to have him hanging on to her in this heat.

Thirty

I'D THOUGHT I'd have trouble falling asleep that night, because of
the heat and of everything else, but I must have dozed off as
soon as I turned off the light. That was why the scream, when it
came, was such a shock. It crashed into my unconsciousness,
yanking me awake.

Suddenly I was sitting up in bed gasping for breath and trying to piece together a strange room with windows that opened
into darkness rather than the neon glow of Roosevelt Island and
Queens. It took me a moment to put the darkness and the still-
ness and the chintz curtains together. Then the house and the
weekend and everything fell into place, everything but the
scream that went on splitting the night like a bolt of lightning. It
was coming from outside the house, but not far outside the
house. And it was bloodcurdling.

Footsteps pounded down the stairs outside my door. A better or a braver woman would have flung open the door and
followed, but I'm a coward as well as a journalist. I wanted to
know what was happening, but I didn't want to get involved. I
went to the window facing the front of the house. The scream,
which was still coming, seemed to be coming from there.

Milky moonlight filtered through the cloud cover and
glinted off the porch roof below my window, but beyond it
the grass lay in dark shadows beneath the trees. Gradually I

made out a faint shimmer of white. My first thought was that it looked like a woman in a nightgown. My second was that it looked like the cover of a gothic novel. Then I saw Julian streaking across the lawn toward the figure. I dropped to my knees. I wasn't hiding, I swear; I was just trying to get a better view.

He reached Emma. Of course, it was Emma out there on the lawn screaming. She was wearing a short robe, not a flowing nightgown, I saw now. Julian was in a pair of boxer shorts. I remember thinking at the time that he must have pulled them on before he'd run out of the house. Julian Weill didn't strike me as the kind of man who slept in clothing.

He shook her. Hard, as far as I could tell from this distance. The scream trailed off like a dying siren.

He put his arms around her, and they stood that way for a moment. Of course, I should have turned away, and of course, I didn't. I don't know how many minutes we spent that way, Emma and Julian holding each other in the shadows of those big elms and me crouching at the window of their guest room like a Peeping Tom, but on the inside looking out.

Finally they broke apart, though he kept one arm around her shoulders, and started back to the house. I crept away from the window. By the time I heard their footsteps coming up the stairs, I was back in bed. I could hear the murmur of voices or at least of his voice, but I couldn't make out the words. Then I heard a door close, and the house exhaled into silence.

I lay in bed thinking about Emma and that scream. While I'm not exactly a connoisseur, I haven't lived in one of the noisiest and most dangerous cities in the Western world without picking up a certain degree of expertise. I like to think I can distinguish among a plea for action, as in get-that-sucker-he-just-grabbed-my-handbag, and a Kitty Genovese howl for help, and the playful cries of kids horsing around on the street. But Emma's scream was none of those. She wasn't asking for help, and she wasn't scared, and she certainly wasn't kidding around. Emma's cry was a shriek of rage. She was mad as hell.

I've gone over the events of that weekend again and again, with people who had a legal right to know, and people who had a moral right, and people who had no right at all, but I've never told anyone, not Dexter, not Babe, certainly not the police, about that incident on the lawn. I never even mentioned it to Emma after the weekend. In view of what happened, or what she thought happened, how could I?

Thirty-one

EMMA STEPPED OUT of the shadowy house onto the porch. The air steamed off the bay. The sky pressed down like a tight platinum hood. She glanced down at the tray in her hands. The sliced melon lay like glistening wet smirks on the serving plate. The berries sweated in the hand-painted bowl they'd brought back from Deruta. Martha Fucking Stewart in Hades.

Her head hurt, and her bones ached, and her eyes burned from lack of sleep. Her throat felt sore too. Maybe she was coming down with a summer cold. Or maybe that was from screaming. Julian said she'd been screaming for a long time before he'd shaken her awake. She wondered how long and how loud. Had the whole neighborhood heard, or merely Hallie? She'd asked Julian that too, and he'd told her not to worry about it. Who cares what people think? Who cares what she thinks? What if she'd said the same thing to him last night when those men at the party, the successful, smug, superior men, had shut him out. No, that wasn't fair. He'd been kind to her last night. He'd come out to the lawn to get her, and he'd brought her back to the house, and there in the dark privacy of their bedroom he'd held her and talked to her and reassured her.

She went back into the house. As she moved around the kitchen taking out plates and mugs and cutlery and napkins, she could hear Julian's footsteps above her in the bedroom. She could also hear him humming. As if nothing had happened.

"Don't bring it up," he'd said. "If you don't, she won't."

Maybe Hallie wouldn't bring it up, but she might use it. Emma saw herself as Hallie would paint her, the Lady Macbeth of Shelter Island. The only thing missing was the blood on her hands. So much for the ordinary woman who'd got incredibly lucky.

She heard his footsteps on the stairs. He came into the kitchen and asked how she felt.

"I'm okay. Is she up yet?"

"I heard signs of life in the bathroom." He took the pot from the machine that she'd set the night before to grind and perk the coffee and poured himself a mug.

"She's probably taking her time because she's too embarrassed to come down."

"She probably didn't even hear. She probably slept through the whole thing."

"Not the way you said I was screaming."

"Listen, you sleepwalked. Sleptwalked. It's no big deal. Forget it."

"I have to explain it somehow."

"Why?"

"What will she think?"

"What do you care? You don't have to say anything. Never complain, never explain."

He stood there leaning against the counter, cradling the mug of coffee in his long fingers, well rested, relaxed, at ease in his own skin. Never complain, never explain. That was his motto all right.

Thirty-two

WALKING OUT of the house into that summer morning was like walking into a clothesline of damp laundry. My first thought was that I should have stayed in town. The weather couldn't have been any worse, and the atmosphere might have been better.

Julian glanced up from the paper, said good morning, and went back to filling in the blanks in the crossword puzzle.

Emma asked if I'd slept well and said she hoped there'd been at least a whisper of a breeze in my room.

I said my room had been more than comfortable and I'd slept like a baby.

The moment hung between us in the hot air. I waited for her to say something. I wondered if I should. But before either of us could, Julian slapped the paper down on the table. *"Voilà!* Hundred percent."

I glanced at the puzzle. All the spaces were filled in.

"Oh, God!" Emma said. It was supposed to be a complaint, but I could hear the relief in her voice. "For most people the puzzle is just the puzzle. For Julian it's a sign from the heavens. If he does the daily in a certain amount of time—it varies with the day of the week—he's going to have a good day. If he finishes the Sunday one before noon, he's got the week by the tail."

"Talk about casting the first stone." He turned to me and

cocked his head toward Emma. "This is the woman who used to make revolting spitting sounds every time someone told her her babies were beautiful. To ward off the evil eye."

Emma asked if I'd like eggs, I said I wouldn't, and a bell went off in the kitchen. I asked if there was anything I could do, and she said absolutely nothing and started into the house.

I was sitting with my back to the door, but I heard the screen slam behind me.

Julian took off his dark glasses and raised his eyebrows. "Now you understand what I was talking about," he whispered.

I'd made up my mind. I wasn't going to play conspirator this morning. "What do you mean?"

"Last night. You must have heard. I just wish I knew what to do. I just wish—"

The screen door creaked. Emma came out carrying a straw basket lined with a flowered linen napkin heaping with bread and muffins. "What do you wish?" she asked.

"I wish this goddamn weather would break," he said.

After breakfast I offered to help again, and this time Emma didn't refuse. When we were alone in the kitchen I realized why. She wanted to explain what had happened, but she didn't want to do it in front of Julian.

"About last night." She was putting dishes in the dishwasher. "That business on the lawn."

I waited for her to go on. It wasn't a ploy. I didn't know what to say.

"Don't make too much of it." She straightened and faced me. "I mean, you don't have to worry or anything like that. When I was a kid, I used to sleepwalk all the time. It's a fairly common pediatric problem, you know. I used to worry that Matt and Becky would inherit it, but fortunately they didn't. Anyway, all I wanted to say was that it still happens to me occasionally. It doesn't mean anything." She bent and began putting dishes in the dishwasher again. "Actually, when you think about it, it's kind of kinky." She looked up at me from under her fringe of bangs. "Think of the things I could get away with if I wanted."

When we came back out on the porch, Julian was gone, but across the lawn the heavy wooden doors to the garage stood open.

"He must be getting the beach chairs," Emma said, but a moment later he emerged from the shadowy rectangle of the garage door carrying a wooden centerboard in one hand and a rudder and tiller in the other.

"I thought we were going to the beach," Emma said.

"It'll be cooler on the Sunfish," he answered.

"There's no wind."

"There's a breeze on the water. Not much, but a breeze."

Emma turned to me. "Do you want to go out on the Sunfish?"

"Whatever you two want to do."

"See," Julian said, "Hallie's dying to go for a sail."

Emma looked out at the water, then up at the trees. "There may be a breeze, but there isn't enough of a breeze to drive that thing with three of us on it."

Julian stopped halfway across the lawn and followed her gaze. "You have a point." He looked out over the bay again. "I have an idea. Why don't you two go?"

"Why don't we all just go to the beach?" Emma said.

"Because I promised Hallie a Fresh Air Fund experience, and she's going to have a Fresh Air Fund experience." He turned to me. "Anyone can sit on a beach. I want you to go back to town and tell all your friends in the underclass how you learned to sail."

"I know how to sail. A little."

"Then that settles it. The women's team will take out the Sunfish. That okay with you, Hallie?"

"Fine." At this point I would have agreed to a cruise on the *Titanic.* "Terrific."

"Just be careful," he said to Emma, then turned back to me again. "She has a tendency to put the thing in irons in anything less than a force five wind. Last time I had to swim out to save her."

"Why don't we just forget the whole thing?" she said.

Julian rested the pieces of wood on the ground and stood looking up at the two of us on the porch. "You really don't want to go?"

"I really don't want to go," Emma said.

"Okay, then Hallie and I will go. That all right with both of you?"

Thirty-three

SHE STOOD in the shadows of the screen door watching as he led Hallie down the lawn to the bay. She didn't care. Usually when he pulled something like this, she got angry or jealous or something. Now she just felt numb. Take her out on the Sunfish, Julian. Screw her. Drown yourself. I don't care.

They reached the crescent of beach. He put down the centerboard and rudder, unlashed the sail from the boom, and began to raise it. Even from this distance she could see the force of his movements. You'd think he was raising the main on a twelve-meter. You really are a buffoon, Julian.

She went on watching as he dragged the boat down to the water, walked it out, and locked the tiller and rudder in place. Then he held it with one hand and gestured for Hallie to climb in with the other. After she had, he slid the centerboard half in and, still holding the sheet, used his hands to propel himself into the cockpit. Nice move, Julian. Not exactly City Ballet level, but nice.

He threw the tiller to the right with one hand, tugged the sheet with the other, and caught the breeze. She watched as they sailed off toward the horizon, tan shoulder to tan shoulder, sweaty hip to sweaty hip, salt-slicked thigh to salt-slicked thigh.

She really didn't give a damn. Let him be the Lothario of Shelter Island. The Dennis Conner of the Sunfish set. Though it annoyed her that she had to be totally incompetent by comparison. Like that line about her putting the boat in irons all the time. She'd put the Sunfish in irons once. And she would have gotten it out if he'd given her a chance. But there'd been people on the beach that day, the Coopers and the Rados and the Rados' guest who was recently divorced and wearing a string bikini. He wasn't about to let an opportunity like that slip by. He'd just had to swim out to save her. Save her from what, for Christ sake?

And then there was the time on a chartered sloop when they really had got in trouble because he'd snarled a lobster pot on the rudder and couldn't free it up, so he'd had to hail a passing powerboat. "I wouldn't have bothered," he'd told the men on the other boat. "I would have just jumped over and cut us free, but my wife was scared."

Oh, Julian, you really are a buffoon. And a show-off. And a coward. And a cheat. And a liar. And an A number one prick.

She put her forehead against the screen door. The hot wire pressed into her skin. And what does that make me? The wife of a buffoon and a show-off and a coward and a cheat and a liar and an A number one prick.

She turned away from the door and climbed the stairs to the second floor. Fans whirred like nasty little insects. No air conditioners for them, environmentally enlightened, historically accurate restoration junkies that they were.

She went into the guest room she used as a study and sat at the desk. The plush of the chair scratched at the back of her thighs. She turned on her laptop. Letters and icons sizzled across the screen. She laid her hands on the keyboard. Her fingers stuck to the hot keys. She could barely lift them. Besides, what did she have to say to the young women of the world?

She got up and walked to the window. The sail was a tiny red, white, and blue triangle in the distance. She thought of those legendary men who went out for a loaf of bread or a pack of cigarettes and never came back. Go, Julian, go. Only he never would.

She went back to her desk, sat, and put her hands on the keyboard again. This time it felt hot in a different sense. All the things she could write came racing into her head. Dear Julian, I'm leaving. Dear Sirs: I would like to retain your services in a divorce suit. Dear Matt and Becky, I can no longer go on with a life that has become intolerable. Except she'd already written all that, the ultimatum to Julian, and the letter to the divorce lawyer, and the explanations to her children. Because she was a good girl who always did her homework, and a professional who turned in polished manuscripts, and a perfectionist who had to get it right, she'd not only written them but edited them and even spell-checked them. She'd just never bothered to send them. And sitting in that stifling study with a relentless sun beating against the screen of the open window, and droning fans shoveling the thick air back and forth, and empty rooms throbbing with the ache of her ironically blessed life, she knew she never would.

Thirty-four

"WHO'S THIS GUY Emma tells me about? The one who was supposed to come for the weekend and couldn't. Hang a little to port. You keep creeping up on the wind."

"Sorry."

"Who is he?"

"Just a man."

"Try to contain your enthusiasm."

"Well, what do you want me to say?"

"Ah, it's too intense to talk about. This must be serious. You're creeping up on the wind again."

"You take the tiller."

"Shucks, we've just had our first spat. Don't try to cheat on the wind, and you'll be fine. What does he do? Am I allowed to ask, or is that too intense too?"

"He's the director of an international health fund."

"Good. Good. That's the way the sail should look."

"Something called the Twenty-first Century Health Fund."

"Uh-oh, a professional altruist."

"Look who's talking."

"Yeah, but I'm not successful at it. Now you've got the hang of it.

. . . .

"Hey, do you have sunscreen on?"

"Fifteen."

"Could've fooled me. You better put on some more."

"I didn't bring any."

"Lucky for you one of us thinks ahead. Here."

"Thanks."

. . . .

"Christ. The Gerald Ford of the sailing world. She can't steer and put on sunscreen at the same time. Give me the tiller.

. . . .

"You missed a spot."

"Where?"

"There. And there. Why don't you just let me . . ."

"It's okay. I can . . ."

"Ah, she thinks it's the old slather-the-sunscreen-on ploy."

"I just don't want to capsize."

"Not a chance. I can steer this thing with my toes. Give me the damn stuff and turn around."

"Ouch!"

"Sorry.

. . . .

"Better?"

"Mmmm."

"Okay, that's it."

"Thank you."

"*Nada.* You would have been sizzling in a couple of minutes."

"Thanks."

"You're a babe in the woods, Hallie. You need someone to take care of you."

So there was someone else in the picture. Well, that was okay. That was even better. Safer.

He knew what the shrinks said about that too. The old

homophobia vigilantes. He'd read their journals. He'd listened to their cocktail party erudition. *You want to screw her because you want to get close to him.*

Nope, doc, I want to screw her because I want to screw her. It has nothing to do with him. It has to do with the fact that she's got good legs and the best ass I've ever seen on a white woman. No tits, though. Shame about that. But it has nothing to do with him.

Of course, he wouldn't mind fucking him over while he was at it. Who the hell did he think he was anyway? The Twenty-first Century Health Fund. He'd known guys like that in school. The old-family old-money boys, the JFK-RFK-John Lindsay wannabes, the guys who chanted slogans through locked jaws and then went home to their trust funds and old boys' networks and willowy blond women. The graceful, effortless men at the top of the sexual food chain. Well, fuck him. Or better yet, fuck her. It would serve him right.

Thirty-five

WE FINALLY DID get to the beach that afternoon. It was not a relaxing experience. Emma was working hard at being cheerful. We both were. Julian didn't seem to have to work at it.

When we got back to the house, Emma went up to her study to check the answering machine. "There was a call for you," she said as she came down and handed me a slip of paper with Dexter's New York number on it. I was surprised. He'd said he probably wouldn't be back till the middle of the following week.

"Everything was under control," he explained when I called him back, "so I figured I might as well get out while I could. Besides, I had another one of those airborne epiphanies."

"I'm afraid to ask."

"It occurred to me somewhere over the Atlantic that I'm not the only one who can run the fund. I mean, it's not as if I'm God or anything."

"Can we please not start that again?"

"Are you having a wonderful time?"

"I'll tell you about it when I see you."

"That good?"

"Do you want to come out and see for yourself?"

"By the time I got there it'd be the middle of the night. How early can you get back tomorrow?"

"They've made plans for lunch and tennis around a neighbor's pool."

"Can't you get out of it?"

"I'm the fourth. The neighbor's wife doesn't play tennis."

"In that case I'll call some brokers in the morning and get started."

"On what?"

"Putting our real estate together, of course."

After we got off the phone, I stood thinking about his words. They still wouldn't have endeared him to the romantics among my friends, nor would they have satisfied the self-styled psychologists, but they'd hit me where I lived.

When I came downstairs, Emma said we had time for a nap. "The summer afternoon lie-down," Julian called it.

I didn't tell them that daytime sleep reeks too much of runny noses and raging fevers for me to enjoy it. I was looking forward to an hour or two away from them.

We went upstairs. I stretched out on the bed and opened the turn-of-the-century memoir of the island. I was asleep in minutes. I even dreamed. It was the dream I'd been having off and on lately, the one where I was locked in my parents' house. Only this time the mood was different. This time it felt more like a nightmare. At least that was the impression I had when I awakened sweating, confused, and unreasonably frightened.

There was another party that night. Different actors, same general cast of characters, only more of them. In place of the single car pool fugitive, there was a team of nubile young things in shorts and polo shirts who looked like Olympic medal winners and a professional chef who stood sweating over a huge grill dispensing free-range crab and scallop fritters. There were also several movie people. I knew because every time someone mentioned a book, one of them said he'd read it in treatment. And every time one of them did, Julian caught my eye and rolled his.

It was a large party, and there was a lot of milling around, and since the house was one of those sprawling geometric puzzles I associate with the Hamptons rather than Shelter Island, it wasn't in the least odd that sometime late in the evening I somehow ended up on a small deck off a library at one end of the house alone with Julian. Not really alone, of course. There were people wandering in and out, but somehow we started talking. I mean really talking. He told me about the book he was working on, and if sheer human passion could save the world from the malignant side effects of electromagnetic fields, society was safe. To tell the truth, I'd started listening because I'd felt a little sorry for him after his crack that afternoon when he'd asked about Dexter. The one about not being successful. Then before I knew it, I was telling him about the women of death row. He thought it was a great idea for an article. More than that, he said. It was a great idea for a book. He was making suggestions, and I was running with them, and before I knew what had happened, it had. We might have been sitting upright, side by side in two canvas director's chairs, our four feet braced against the deck railing in a chaste row, narrow white espadrille, narrow white espadrille, big tan boating moccasin, big tan boating moccasin, but our intellectual pretensions were rolling around on that deck like two sweaty animals.

"It's a great idea," he breathed.

"Your suggestions are terrific," I panted.

And on it went for a while. Then something funny happened. We both stopped talking. Suddenly the silence between us was thick and pungent as musk. We were still sitting side by side in those director's chairs, facing out to the bay, and somewhere to our left lightning flashed. It struck me as an extreme and unnecessary bit of symbolism.

A moment later Julian spoke. "It's at times like this that I realize what it could be like."

"What do you mean?"

I know, I know. I should have seen what was coming. Maybe I did.

"Talking to someone who isn't so defensive she turns every word I say into a criticism of her. Talking to someone who isn't watching me every minute to see if I'm looking over her shoulder at someone else. Hell, Hallie, just talking, really talking to someone. I thought I didn't miss it anymore. I do."

I didn't say anything to that. I mean, what could I say? "I forbid you to speak that way." A little Victorian. "I'm in love with another man." Irrelevant, since it hadn't stopped me from all that torrid verbal foreplay. "What about Emma?" And play right into his hand?

"I'm sorry," he said after a while.

"Forget it."

"But that's the problem. I can't."

And then, out of the corner of my eye, I saw him turning toward me. Even as it was happening, I saw it all in that instant-replay deliberately dreamy slow motion. His upper body swiveled around, and his arm came up off the wooden armrest of the director's chair and described a smooth arc through the night air, and his face grew bigger as he leaned toward me. I felt his hand on the back of my neck. I opened my mouth. I was about to say no, or don't, or some negative. I'm sure of it. But before I could, two things happened. The screen door behind us slid open. And Julian pulled back.

The only surprise was that it wasn't Emma who came out on the deck.

I've thought about that moment a lot. Who wouldn't, in view of what finally happened? I don't mean to make too much of it. After all, I'm the woman who carried on a four-year affair with a married man. So an innocent and unconsummated grope on a quiet deck after some pretty heady talk, not to mention the bottle of wine Julian had thoughtfully brought along, wasn't exactly a major transgression or even uncharted territory. But this was different. Before, I'd been an accomplice in someone else's betrayal. Now I was an equal partner. Maybe more than equal. Julian didn't know Dexter. And from what he said, he wasn't exactly happy with Emma. I knew and liked Emma. And I was blissful with Dexter. At least I planned to be as soon as I got back to town and we started putting our real estate together. So what was up? I've never had much patience with people who regard their feelings as a code that has to be broken or a Gordian knot that has to be untied, but the more I thought about it, the less I understood how I'd managed to come so close to committing the unthinkable with the unlikable.

Thirty-six

ALTHOUGH THE STORM that had been threatening Saturday night never came through, by Sunday morning a new front had arrived. I came out of the house onto the porch into air as clear and shiny as Saran Wrap and a sky that looked as if it had just been scrubbed. Emma was leafing through the book review. Julian was doing the puzzle again. She put her section aside when I joined them. He said good morning and went on working on the puzzle.

I'd told Emma the evening before that I'd be leaving as soon as we got back from lunch and tennis at their neighbor's. She asked again if I was absolutely sure I couldn't stay for dinner. It has been my experience, as both a guest and a hostess, that the more vehemently people plead with you to stay, the more eager they are for you to leave. I said I really had to get back to town. We smiled at each other with guilty warmth. Now that we were within hours of getting out from under the weekend, we weren't having such a bad time.

"Genius!" Julian said, and slapped the magazine section down on the table. "Pure genius, if I do say so myself."

I glanced at the puzzle. He'd filled in all the spaces. Do I have to add that he'd filled them in in ink?

"Does this mean we're going to win the lottery this week?" Emma asked.

"To each according to his needs, sweetheart. The lottery for me. A Pulitzer for you."

It was almost four by the time we walked back across the neighbor's yard to Emma's and Julian's. I went up to shower and get my things together. When I came down a little while later with my duffel and found them sitting together on the porch, I knew what was going to happen. He'd offer to drive me to the ferry, she'd say she'd do it, they'd go back and forth that way for a while, each pretending to be thinking only of the other, and finally we'd all drive to the ferry together.

Sure enough, a few minutes later the three of us—Emma in the lead, me following, and Julian bringing up the rear and carrying my duffel—trooped down the stairs from the porch and along the flagstone path to the garage. Julian put my duffel down in the driveway as he went to open the garage doors. Emma told him not to. "It'll get all dusty," she said.

"It's good clean country dust," he answered as he opened the rusty iron latch on the garage door.

She rolled her eyes at me. I smiled and shrugged. Complicity between us against him flared, then died, quick as the flame from a cheap cardboard match.

Julian dragged one of the heavy wooden doors across the dirt driveway, then disappeared into the darkness and emerged, pushing the other door ahead of him. Emma went into the garage. I started to pick up my duffel, but Julian beat me to it. We followed Emma into the gloom.

She opened the car door on the passenger side and pushed the backrest of the front seat forward. I climbed into the backseat. Julian heaved my duffel in beside me. I was feeling better and better. In a few minutes I'd be free of Emma and Julian and their penchant for Virginia Woolfish games, or so it seemed from where I, the guest, was sitting. In a few hours I'd be back in town with Dexter.

Julian got behind the wheel.

"I had a terrific weekend," I said.

"We loved having you," Emma answered.

Julian adjusted the rearview mirror to his line of vision. As he did, I caught a dazzling flash of sunlit lawn and house and sky—Emma's and Julian's world—behind me. He turned the key in the ignition and threw the gears into reverse.

"Watch the spreader," Emma warned.

"I'm watching the spreader," he said as he began backing the car out of the garage.

Emma and I held our breath as he glided past a rusting fertilizer spreader with only inches to spare.

She turned back to me. "He likes to live dangerously."

"I missed it by a mile." He bent his head so he could see over his dark glasses, caught my eye in the rearview mirror, and winked.

We came out of the murky garage into the light. It had taken on a lambency that comes late in the afternoon at the eastern end of Long Island and washes the world in clarity. I've read somewhere that particular luminescence is the result of physical conditions, the bend of the sun's rays or something, but at that moment the light assumed a moral intensity. Everything—the sharp white rectangles of the house and garage, the curving surfaces of the car, Emma, Julian, even I—glowed with goodness.

"Do you want me to get the door?" Emma asked.

"It's too heavy," Julian said.

"I can manage," she insisted.

"I'll do it." He threw the gearshift, opened the door, and got out.

Emma and I sat in the car watching as he walked toward the garage. The afternoon light was still washing us all in its benevolence, and suddenly I knew that despite his behavior on the deck with me, despite Emma's scream on the lawn, Julian was neither so bad as I'd sometimes thought nor so irresistible as I'd occasionally feared, and if he and Emma weren't the happy couple in that book of hers that had gone out of print, they were still a good example of Auden's axiom about marriage and time and will.

He took the handle of one of the garage doors and began dragging it closed. His rear hit the sleek haunch of the Buick. He stopped, turned, and gave the hood, which was obstructing the turning arc of the door, an accusatory look. "Damn," he said.

"He's only been doing this for the past ten years," she muttered.

"Back it up a little," he called to her.

"Leave it. We'll be back in a few minutes."

"A few minutes is all it takes for something to wander in."

"Jesus," she grumbled under her breath.

"Fine. This time I'll let you get a rabid raccoon out of the garage."

"It was years ago," she muttered to herself, or me, or posterity. "And it wasn't rabid."

He glared at her through the shiny dark glasses that made him look like a cop in a movie about southern bigotry. "All I need is a couple of inches."

"All right," she said, "all right." She leaned forward to move behind the wheel, and now it was her reflection I caught in the rearview mirror. Anger rumbled beneath the surface with seismic force.

She swung her left leg over the hump on the floor to the driver's side of the car and, leaning forward with her left hand on the rich red upholstery of the seat and her right on that dashboard that had made me want to cry when I'd first seen it two days earlier, leveraged herself up out of the seat. Her weight came down on her left leg. The car lurched under me. My head snapped back. The car hit the garage door. My body slammed forward into the front seat, then ricocheted back. My dark glasses had flown off, and I saw Julian clear and sharp in the glare of the sunlight. His glasses had flown off too. His eyes rolled toward the sky. His mouth opened into a black hole. A howl pierced the thin fabric of summer afternoon. Then his body shuddered and slumped forward over the hood. As if he were having an orgasm.

Thirty-seven

ED SNYDER SAT alone in the basement room waiting for the calls to start. You couldn't call the small area subdivided into the chief's cubbyhole, the secretary's desk, and the public waiting area that didn't even have a bench to wait on police headquarters any more than you could label the calls that would start in an hour or two police emergencies. Summer people calling from their BMWs and Mercedeses and Jags because they'd forgotten to turn off the oven or close the skylight or make sure the tank on the gas barbecue was shut and asking if one of the cops could stop by the house and take care of it. Last week Fred Cozzens had called from the LIE to say his wife had forgotten the cat. He hadn't even had the balls to take the rap himself; he had to blame his wife.

It was different in winter. Not so many people. And they were more careful locking up their houses when they left. In winter the housekeeping calls fell off, and the domestics increased. Help, he's going to kill me. Then two of them would drive over, so one could stay with her and say sure he's an SOB, but come on, after all these years you know better than to call him an SOB while he's tying one on, and the other could take him outside to cool off and say sure, she's a ball-cutting bitch, but she happens to be a woman, and you can't go around taking swipes at women. Or else it was the suicides, and by the time they got to those there was nothing they could do except the fucking paperwork. There was always the paperwork.

It was some job. A janitor during the summer; a referee, amateur shrink, and undertaker in the winter; and a paper pusher all year long. If you didn't have a sense of humor, you'd end up in the funny farm.

Then there were the summer weekends when it never stopped. A couple of Fourth of Julys ago they'd had one cigarette boat capsize, one small plane crash, and two heart attacks, not to mention fifteen thousand people on the beach waiting for the fireworks, in a single half hour. That had stopped the talk about cutting the force back from seven men to six.

The phone rang. He could tell by the sound that it was the 911 line. A real emergency. They hadn't just left the oven on and the cat behind; they'd left the cat behind in the hot oven.

He glanced at the computer screen as he picked up the phone. The name Weill flared white against the dark gray background. The address just off Ram Island Drive ran beneath it. That was lucky because whoever was making the call didn't even know where the hell she was on the island. All she knew was that there'd been an accident.

He asked if anyone was hurt.

She said someone was.

He didn't bother to ask how bad. He could tell from her voice.

He was the first cop to arrive at the accident. He'd never seen a more contaminated scene. Neighbors were swarming all the hell over the place. Someone had moved the car. Someone else had moved the victim. He could tell by the line of blood-soaked dirt that ran from the garage to the grass where a hysterical woman was trying to give mouth-to-mouth resuscitation, though it beat him why anybody would think that a man who'd been splattered over the side of a garage would need mouth-to-mouth resuscitation. Only he knew. Even before he asked any questions, he knew the woman who was trying to revive the victim was the wife who'd run over him.

The ambulance and another squad car screeched up seconds later. They did their duty. They checked for vital signs and examined the victim. They went through the motions. But they all knew the minute they arrived on the scene that the man was dead.

The ambulance driver drove to the front of the line of waiting cars and maneuvered onto the ferry. Snyder kept his eyes straight ahead. The boat was crowded with Sunday night commuters, and he didn't want any of them asking what was going on. He didn't want to have to explain, well, we have a stiff in the back of the truck, but procedure says we don't know if he's a stiff or why he's a stiff till the medical examiner in Southold tells us he's dead because his wife stepped on the gas pedal by mistake—at least she said it was by mistake—and pinned him to the garage door like a fucking biological specimen. This wasn't the messiest one he'd ever seen, but it came close.

"So," the driver said, "wha'd'ya think?"

Snyder thought about the question, though he wouldn't say what he thought even if he knew. It looked like an accident. There wasn't any record of trouble, not with them or even with their kids. He knew, because you couldn't be a cop on an island this small and not know about the people who kept coming back year after year. No domestics. No drunk driving. No complaints from the neighbors about noise. Not even the housekeeping shit, unless you counted that time he had to go over to get the squirrel out of the kid's room, and that had been years ago. But you never knew. A year or two ago he'd run into Mr. Weill at the IGA one weekend off-season with a woman who wasn't Mrs. Weill. Buying a pound of hamburger at the IGA wasn't a sin, even if sometimes Grace made it taste that way, but there was something about how they were acting that made him think they were up to more than supper. Still, if all the wives on the island began running over all the husbands who cheated on them, by the end of a holiday weekend the place would look like Gettysburg on the third day. Besides, why would she run him over? Why wouldn't she just throw him out? The money was hers. He still couldn't believe you could make that much writing books for kids, but that was what people said. So the logical thing, if she was pissed 'cause the guy was cheating on her, was to divorce him. But if there was one thing he'd learned in his twenty years as a cop, it was that people never did the logical thing. Not if there was another fucked-up, convoluted thing they could do instead.

"So," the driver asked again, "wha'd'ya think?"

"Beats me. Have to see what the investigation turns up."

"Nah, that's not what I meant. Wha'd'ya think the Giants're gonna do this year?"

Thirty-eight

SUGAR WAS RIGHT. Emma Weill made good copy. She'd made good copy when she was a best-selling, talk show–appearing, have-it-all author, and she made better copy now that she was all that and had run over her husband. Of course, the fact that she'd run over him on a quiet Sunday in August when there was a lull in the various ethnic struggles around the world, Wall Street and Washington were languorous, and no high-level pols had been caught with their hands in a till or under a skirt helped. On Monday morning the accident rated a bite on all three morning news shows, a full column on the first page of the metropolitan section of the *Times,* and a story in *Newsday.* The *Post,* needless to say, carried the most complete coverage or at least gave it the most space. The headline could be read from halfway down the block. MARITAL SPLAT. The photograph of Julian beneath it was almost as bad. At first I wondered how a photographer had gotten there so fast. Then I realized an ambitious amateur had probably snapped it and sold it to the paper. Inside, there were pictures of Emma and Julian in happier days; a photograph of the sweet grandmotherly house on Shelter Island; a fairly inaccurate account of Julian's and Emma's lives; a list of her books, including one that had actually been written by Judy Blume; and comments from the man and woman on the street that ranged from "Tragic" (a self-described housewife in

Queens) through "The statute of limitations on product liability is a gray area that must be tested" (a Manhattan attorney) to "It's time women began to empower themselves" (founder and president of WAP, Women Against Porn).

The networks overlooked my presence fortunately, but I did make the papers. The *Times* identified me as Hallie Fields, a weekend guest who'd summoned the police by calling 911; the *Post* as "the other woman in the house." It didn't say what I was doing in the house, but every reader was free to conjecture the worst. It just goes to show that despite complaints of increasingly graphic depictions of sex and violence in the media, our age is not entirely lacking in imagination.

I missed the television news coverage because after calling Dexter to tell him what had happened, I spent the night on the island with Emma. The doctor, who smacked a little too much of the old feel-good days for my taste, had stuffed Emma full of sedatives to give her a night's sleep and suggested that I hire a car and driver to take us back to town the following morning.

I asked one of the cops if that would be all right. He checked to make sure he had my phone number and address and said he supposed it would be.

The next afternoon the driver dropped us at Emma's town house. Half a dozen friends and relatives had already gathered. I recognized the types from my experience on the sidelines of other semipublic crises. The women brewed endless pots of coffee, and made arrangements for the children's flights home from Europe, and circled the wagons around Emma. The men discussed the situation. One of them, who identified himself as Julian's cousin, was already working up a lawsuit against General Motors. Another whispered the words *criminal charges* and was immediately silenced by half a dozen black looks.

I left Emma in their capable hands. Perhaps that seems like a peculiar thing to do. As a friend—and given the ordeal we'd endured together, I suppose I qualified—I could have stayed. As a journalist I should have. But I was worn out in the first role, and I'd lost my instinct for the second. As soon as I got home, I went straight to my answering machine. The number 37 glowed a hot red on the panel. Every editor I'd ever written for had called, and several whom I'd never been able to get through to in the past; reporters from a good cross section of papers, including the *National Enquirer;* most of my friends; and a variety of strangers, only some of whom mentioned affiliations or credentials. I tried not to think of all the years I'd wasted working and politicking and writing my heart out to make my name, if not a household word, at least a well-regarded product. My fifteen minutes had arrived.

There was also a call from Dexter telling me he'd get there as soon as his meeting was over, and another from Babe. Babe's was the only one I returned. She'd seen the article in the *Times* and was worried about me. It took me a few minutes to convince her there was nothing to worry about.

"The accident had nothing to do with me," I reassured her, though I was still working on convincing myself of the same thing.

I also told her about the thirty-seven calls. "I seem to be sitting on a hot story."

"You're not going to write it!"

Because she talked faster and funnier and wilder, I sometimes forgot that she was, after all, of my mother's era, the golden age of silence. I was the writer, but they were the ones who believed in the power of words. They knew that if you didn't talk about things or, even worse, write about them, they didn't or wouldn't happen.

"Of course not," I said.

It was close to eight when Dexter arrived. I told him about the weekend, or rather told him about it again because I'd given him a fairly hysterical account when I'd called from Shelter Island. He said, as he had then, that it was tragic. It wasn't that he sounded as if he didn't mean it, only that he lived a good part of his life among infants who died of diseases that had been conquered decades ago, and children who died of malnutrition, and men and women who died of natural disasters and human neglect, and so many other tragedies that he could put Julian's death in perspective. It was terrible, but it wasn't epochal. It certainly wasn't worth the fuss that Sugar and everyone else who'd called in the past twenty-four hours were making about it.

I turned on the answering machine and turned off the phones and locked the door. That night I found my way back to that three-o'clock-in-the-morning place I'd discovered in Umbria. And that night I didn't have the dream.

The next morning, before I could even begin returning messages, Sugar called again. It wasn't even nine o'clock. In my experience editors didn't get to their offices until ten.

Before I could explain that I'd just got back the night before and had planned to call her this morning, she suggested lunch. That was unusual but not unprecedented.

I asked her when. She said today. That was unprecedented. I knew a little about Sugar's life. Her schedule was tight, her agenda locked in place and logged into her 512K pocket organizer weeks, if not months, in advance. In order to take me to lunch that day, she'd have to cancel someone else, even if it was only her personal trainer. I figured I was about sixty seconds into my fifteen minutes.

I told her I couldn't have lunch that day. "I'm going to Julian Weill's funeral."

"That's even better. We'll have a drink after it."

"You're not going!" As far as I knew, Sugar had never met Emma or Julian Weill.

"No, the paper said it was private." It was nice to know that some fastidiousness still lurked. "Besides, I don't have to worry about coverage as long as you're there. My eyes and ears, pie. Meet me at six. At my club."

I have never gotten over the fact that when the Century Club finally and begrudgingly decided to admit women, one of the first women they invited to join was Sugar Shapiro. To my mind it was a little like inviting Edith Wharton to a rave, only in reverse. And just because I'm envious doesn't mean I'm not right.

She was waiting for me in the lounge that evening, her expensive clothes glowing like neon in that mellow, musty room, her energy pounding like a rock beat. If she were a man, she would have been shooting her cuffs. As it was, she was tapping her foot.

"How was the funeral?" she asked as soon as I sat down.

"Terrible."

I knew she was waiting for more, but I'd be damned if I'd serve up the bones of Emma's life for Sugar to pick over. I'd be damned if I'd tell her about the teenage girl who'd sobbed with the unrestrained fury of a tantrum-ridden two-year-old or the young man whose physical resemblance to his father had been an innocent rebuke to everyone there. I especially wasn't going to tell her about Emma, who almost overnight had acquired the soiled, squalid aura I'd seen in mental hospital patients. Just because my mind had recorded all those sordid details didn't mean I had to pass them on to her.

When the silence went on for a moment longer, she simply shook her head, whether in sorrow for Emma or annoyance at me, I wasn't sure, and lifted one raucously painted finger to catch the waiter's eye.

"Obviously we'll have to kill the profile," she said after our drinks had arrived.

"Obviously." I agreed.

"This is much bigger than a profile."

I asked her what she meant by "this," but of course, I already knew.

"The unspeakable, the unthinkable, the undreamable. Spouse-icide. I don't mean murder in the heat of passion. I mean an alleged accident involving an alleged loved one. What's happening with the police investigation?"

"There's no police investigation. It was an accident."

"Good, you just keep saying that when people ask you. I can't believe I had my own writer right there at the scene of the crime! Eat your heart out, *New York* magazine."

"I can't write that story, Sugar."

"Are you kidding? All you have to do is turn on your Think Pad. It'll write itself."

"I don't mean I'm not capable. I mean I don't think this qualifies as news—"

"Don't worry about that. You can have all the time you need. Within reason. We're going for the in-depth piece. The thinking woman's look at everywoman's nightmare. There but for the grace of Goddess and all that."

"What I meant was I don't think this qualifies as newsworthy. Or even human interest."

"You're kidding me, right? I mean, this story has so much sex appeal we're going to have to mail the issue in plain brown wrappers. Worst-case scenario. Successful celeb—okay, miniceleb—runs over beloved hubby inadvertently, thereby shattering picture-perfect life. Tell me that doesn't tug at the old heartstrings. Best-case scenario. Famous writer, role model for millions of girls worldwide—the woman's books are in print in

Slovakia, for God's sake—has it up to here"—Sugar lifted her colorfully tipped fingers to her chin—"with codependency and runs down her abusive, womanizing husband. Tell me that isn't a story that sells magazines."

"What I'm trying to say is this is a personal tragedy."

"It's public domain."

"We're talking about a woman's life—and her children's—not a copyright clause in a contract. I can't write it."

"If you don't, someone else will."

I had to hand it to Sugar. She didn't waste time scaling the slippery moral slopes. She went straight to the dank, rat-infested cellar where I lived. Or at least my ambitions did.

"And whoever does"—she went on—"won't do it half as well. It's not just that you were there, pie. On the scene, in the car, at the hot, thumping heart of their life the weekend it happened. But it's your kind of story. It's the story you were born to write."

I thought of Emma's and my childhoods in that stuffy, incestuous town and admitted to myself that Sugar had a point. If I wasn't born to write this story, I sure as hell was brought up to.

Sugar leaned toward me as if she were going to pass on a confidence. "You want to know the trick to being a good editor, pie? It isn't being able to dream up an article, or frame it, or whittle it down to two thousand words. It's knowing which writer is right for which story. It's knowing who can write what." She leaned back in her chair triumphantly. "I'm telling you that you can write this. You're the only writer I know who can write this the way it should be written."

Oh, you smooth-tongued seductress you. "I admit the ambiguities and complexities intrigue me." Ambiguities and complexities, more like prurience and voyeurism. "But that doesn't mean I want to make journalistic capital out of them."

"What do you want to make journalistic capital out of? 'Ten

Things You Should Know Before You Have a Face-lift'? 'Trophy Husbands: Are They a Trend?' "

I was surprised. I hadn't thought Sugar kept up with the stories I ground out for other magazines. I was also stung. It was one thing for me to make fun of those pieces. It was something else for her to.

"I'm not trashing your work. You did a professional job on those pieces. But you're the one who's always talking about taking your work to a new plane."

I was sure I'd never used a phrase like that. But then until a moment ago I was sure I'd never talk about the ambiguities and complexities of a cheap exposé.

She took a sip of her drink. Her small pointed tongue darted over her lower lip. I'd seen reptiles on the Discovery channel do the same thing.

"Look, Hallie, for months now you've been hounding me about the women of death row. Well, this is the same thing, only better. Instead of women who go out and scrub other women's floors, or work on assembly lines eviscerating chickens, or eke out a miserable existence on welfare, you have a woman who's made a fortune. Not inherited it or married it, but made it on her own. So we've got the feminist vote and the traditional woman's envy. Instead of women in prison uniforms with needle tracks on their arms, you have a woman in a Calvin suit with a Tiffany watch on her wrist."

Actually Emma wore a vintage Reverso that I'd envied, which I suppose proved Sugar's point.

"Instead of women with histories of black eyes and broken bones, you have a woman scarred by a lifetime of psychological abuse and sexual betrayal."

"We don't know that."

"The skinny about him in the biz is everything but the garbage disposal. Or maybe it's everything including the garbage disposal. I forget. I can't believe you spent all that time with them and didn't have trouble with him."

Trouble was one word for it, though not the one I'd use.

"But the point isn't the victim, who until the 'accident' was the perp; it's the perp, who until the 'accident' was the victim. Wasn't that the way you described the women of death row idea?"

She knew it was.

"So Emma Weill's story has all the juice of that, plus more texture and subtlety. A woman who has cleat marks on her body can claim self-defense. A woman who has them on her psyche raises more thorny questions. The women of death row was a black-and-white story, pie. Anyone could have written it. This has chiaroscuro. And it's crying out for your brush."

I didn't say anything to that, but I didn't have to. As Sugar had pointed out, she knew her writers. Or maybe she simply knew writers. In the course of a single drink I'd gone from struggling hack to old master.

"I won't kid you, pie. Even as we sit here, there are a dozen writers in my pocket organizer who are dying for this assignment. Some of them have already called me about it." She held up her hand to stop me from arguing, though I hadn't been about to. She might be exaggerating about some things, but I was fairly sure she wasn't exaggerating about that. "Okay, they weren't there when it happened, but they're pros. They know how to interview people. They know how to do research. In other words, they can get the story. But not one of them can write it the way you can. Not one of them can make the reader feel what Emma Weill felt. Not one of them can get into her mind and heart and gut the way you can. I see it all now. The reader starts out envying Emma Weill and feeling lousy about her own life. By the end she's pitying Emma Weill and thinking her husband isn't such a loser and her job isn't such a dead end and at least she hasn't orphaned her own kids. The old hour-glass effect. And only you can pull it off, pie. Say you will and let me die a happy editor."

Do I have to tell you that I did?

Thirty-nine

DEXTER AND I didn't exactly have an argument about the article Sugar wanted me to write—I'd told him Sugar wanted me to write it; I hadn't told him I was going to—but I could tell he was disappointed in me.

"You don't have to do that kind of thing," he said.

"*You* don't have to do that kind of thing. I do if I want to keep my status as a freelancer and my view of the East River."

"That's another reason you don't have to do it. I thought we were looking for a new apartment. Together."

"Terrific. We move in together, and I retire."

"No one's talking about your retiring. I'm just saying that I'm not going to let them foreclose the mortgage on your half of the apartment."

The statement should have reassured me. It scared me.

Maybe that was one reason I let it go. The other was that I knew we weren't talking about the article on Emma or at least only about the article on Emma. Neither of us had mentioned the profile of him, but both of us were thinking of it.

And then, as if that weren't enough, the next morning Emma called.

"I have to thank you," she said.

"For what?"

"Getting me back here. All that."

"It was nothing."

"And one more thing."

I waited.

"Silence. I know they must be hounding you almost as much as they are me. Thanks for not cooperating with them."

I wasn't cooperating with them. I was them. They.

"It's nothing," I said again.

I told myself I hadn't really made up my mind. I could still say no to Sugar. In the meantime, I'd keep my options open. That meant moving ahead with the article.

Sugar wanted me to go to Chicago for a couple of days to get some background on Emma's and Julian's early years together. My first thought since Dexter was in Amsterdam was that I wouldn't have to tell him about the trip. My second was that I was being devious and ought to tell him where I was going and why. My third was damn it, this was my career and I didn't have to answer to anyone.

I spent two days in Chicago and managed to turn up plenty of background on Emma's and Julian's early years together, but no surprises. Not even the part about Julian's departure from academia was a surprise, though it was a variation on the story Julian had told me that day at the Princeton Club. The only surprise about it was that Emma and Julian had managed to keep the incident quiet, but then they hadn't been the only ones interested in hushing it up. Even in those days when student-faculty sex was regarded as a professorial perk and an academic achievement rather than an incidence of sexual harassment, the administration wouldn't have been eager to advertise Julian's record of conquests, which, according to one nostalgic scholar I interviewed, had been inspiring. And then there was the father of the young woman who was too old to qualify as a Lolita but still young enough for grand passion to be mistaken for statutory rape. The father had political connections in an era when political connections still intimidated the press into silence rather than goaded it to libel, and he'd used them. So Julian had been allowed to retire quietly.

The story answered some questions about Julian and raised even more about Emma.

I returned from Chicago to find forty-four calls on my answering machine. I hated to think of what it would have been like if the last shreds of my Luddite convictions hadn't prevented me from owning a fax or having an address on the Internet. Obviously this thing wasn't quieting down. Sugar rang in as number three. She was so annoyed she sounded almost grown-up. Babe was somewhere near the end. She sounded worried. Everyone wanted me to call back as soon as possible.

It was after six, but I took a chance that Sugar might still be in her office. She was.

"Don't ever hold out on me again, pie," she said as soon as the secretary put me through. "I'd be furious with you if I weren't so pleased."

I tried to think of what she might think I was holding out about. It couldn't be Dexter. I hadn't written that profile for her.

"The only question now is whether we go with a first-person account or have you write it as a straight story and tell people who you are on the editor's page."

"Who I am?" I repeated.

"The other woman."

"What?"

"Haven't you seen the *Post*? The woman at the party talked to them."

"What woman at what party?"

"The one who interrupted you and Julian Weill on the deck.

Listen, pie, I'm sorry for that crack about garbage disposals. It was just gossip."

It took me a while to get Sugar off the phone. It rang again as soon as I put the receiver down. I let the machine answer, grabbed my keys and some change, and left the apartment.

My building boasts one of the last elevator operators on the island of Manhattan. Usually I think Felix lends the place a little cachet, not to mention a certain degree of safety. The way he grinned at me as I stepped into the elevator cab and kept on grinning as it descended three floors to the lobby made me long for automation. I wondered if he'd been smirking the same way when I'd come in and I just hadn't noticed.

Felix had nothing on Pasha. Clearly both men were avid readers of the *New York Post.*

I walked one block west to York Avenue. It was another one of those headlines I could read from halfway down the block. SEX MACHINE. Beneath it was a picture of Julian superimposed on one of the Buick and, I saw as I got closer, a small insert of me. It was the photograph I used on the rare occasions a magazine wanted readers to know what I looked like and was meant for slick magazine stock rather than the porous tabloid paper that turned it dark and grainy. The word *hirsute* came to mind. Also *foxy,* not as in *sexy,* but as in *crafty.* In other words, I didn't look good enough to be a home wrecker, but I did look corrupt enough.

I opened the paper to the article. There wasn't much of substance. A woman, who described herself as a close friend of Emma's, had come out on a deck at a party and found Julian and me alone together. The writer made it sound as if she'd surprised us in mid-orgasm. The woman described Emma's mental state as distraught. It was probably the only line of truth in the whole story, which admittedly wasn't very long, though there were plenty of pictures. There was the one of Julian's body again, and an aerial view of the house with marks to show where the accident had occurred, and a picture of the funeral with Emma in the foreground and a circled face in the crowd behind her. I brought the paper closer. I'm not exactly myopic, but the photographs, as I've said, were grainy. The face in the circle was, of course, mine.

Since I hadn't brought my handbag, I had to carry the paper back to my apartment in full view. I folded it in half with the back page out and tucked it tightly under my arm. Pasha's eyes went to it immediately. Felix smirked at it, then at me. I'm not normally a vindictive woman, but I made a mental note to speak to the super about the staff's lack of courtesy. Or, better yet, the president of the co-op board.

When I got back to my apartment, there were several new messages on the machine. An attorney specializing in libel law had left his number. A woman who described herself as a postfeminist disciple of Camille Paglia invited me to participate in a symposium called "The Whore of Babylon: Restoring Women to Their Rightful Powers." A photographer for a magazine called *Down and Dirty* wanted to know how I felt about taking off my clothes in front of a camera for a fee to be negotiated. My first thought was that I ought to negotiate the fee before they saw me without my clothes. My second was that at least I could still laugh about it.

I didn't return any of the calls on my machine that night, but I did make one to Emma. I told myself I wanted to apologize or explain or something.

"I just wanted to tell you," I began, "I feel awful about all this." I heard the fatuousness of my words. Well, yes, who wouldn't feel awful about having her picture on the front page of a sleazy paper under a smutty headline, except maybe Marla

Maples, who'd announced in sixty-point type that it was the best sex she'd ever had.

"Of course, it isn't true," I added.

There was another pause. "It doesn't matter," Emma said finally.

"But it does. At least it does to me. There was nothing between Julian and me."

Her laugh on the other end of the line coughed like an engine that wouldn't turn over. "Look, Hallie, I don't want to offend you, but it had nothing to do with you. I mean, you personally. You just happened to be the guest du jour. So if you were taken in by Julian and now you're looking for absolution, I can't help. But if you're worried that I'm angry at you, I'm not." There was another pause. Then her voice turned gentle. "Besides, you couldn't help yourself. You were just swerving to avoid your own accident. We both were."

I didn't understand what she meant, but I decided not to press it. The word *accident* still made me uncomfortable. Nobody had said it wasn't. But the police still hadn't said it was.

Forty

DEXTER RETURNED HOME the afternoon after the day I made the front page of the *Post,* but he didn't miss the headline. His secretary, who knew me only as the woman who'd followed him around doing a profile for several months, had saved the paper and dropped it off at his apartment with the mail that had been piling up in his office. That was all right. I hadn't planned to keep it from him. I was merely sorry I wasn't the one who'd had the chance to show it to him. Again.

He called as soon as he saw it. "It's a lousy picture," he said.

I appreciated the light tone but wished he didn't sound as if he were straining so hard to maintain it.

"Does that mean you're still coming over?"

"It takes more than a scandal on the front page of the *Post* to queer this deal." He was trying hard all right.

He got there faster than I'd expected. I opened the door to find him leaning against the doorjamb, a question mark of a man. He gave me a light kiss on his way in. I tasted hello but couldn't make out the other flavors. He took off his jacket. He was wearing the shirt with the hole beneath his heart.

We went into the living room and settled on the window seat overlooking the river. When he sat, I noticed that he wasn't wearing socks. Dexter is not a man who bows to or even knows about the whims of fashion. Witness that shirt. His naked ankles were an oversight, not an affectation. He wasn't taking this as calmly as he pretended.

"I suppose we ought to talk about the headlines," I said.

"Only if there's something you want to tell me."

I thought about that for a moment. I didn't know what I wanted to tell him because I still didn't understand what had happened. Not about Julian and Emma and the accident, but about Julian and me and the potential disaster.

I'd gone over it dozens of times. I hadn't particularly liked Julian. I certainly hadn't respected him. Sure, I'd found him sexually appealing, but I also found my neighbor's nineteen-year-old son who rowed for the Harvard crew sexually appealing, and I didn't fall apart every time I found myself alone with him in the compactor room. It was the kind of problem you could spend years or at least several lunches dissecting with another woman, but it wasn't the kind of enigma you could present to most men.

I remembered a conversation I'd had with my mother years ago. "The unexamined life is not worth living," I'd come home from my sophomore year at school and announced.

"Curiosity killed the cat," my mother shot back.

I'd always thought her answer did more than anything else to turn me into a reporter. Now suddenly I recognized the wisdom of it, at least in certain circumstances.

I reached out and put my hand on Dexter's shirt right above the hole. I could feel the faint but steady rhythm of his heart, like an army marching doggedly along. Or maybe that was just my own pulse.

"Nothing," I said.

"Good." The muscles of his chest relaxed beneath my fingers.

I moved my hand a few inches and went to work on the buttons of his shirt. He didn't help. He was too busy at the buttons of mine.

*   *   *

Later that night I sat up in bed watching Dex sleep and remembering the first time I'd done that. I thought about Emma too, as I had that first night. At the time I'd thought that she was the center that held while Dex had set up a powerful centrifugal force. Now Emma was spinning out, and here in my bed Dex was exerting a strong gravitational pull. It was, as Sugar had pointed out, the old hourglass effect. But I wasn't gloating. Life was too fragile for that. Or to quote another of my mother's maxims, sing before breakfast and you'll cry before supper. She used to say that all the time. And it used to drive Babe crazy.

Forty-one

I'D THOUGHT the furor surrounding the accident couldn't get much worse. I should have known better. After all, I was in the profession. The calls continued. Montel Williams wanted to book me for a segment called "I Slept with My Best Friend's Husband." Sally Jessy thought she could milk it more if she put Emma and me on together. But the calls were the least of it.

One night as Dex and I were getting out of a cab in front of the building, I saw a flash of light. "Lucky we beat the shower," I said to Pasha. He looked at me as if I were stupid as well as depraved. Dexter pointed out that the flash hadn't been lightning but a man with a camera and flashbulb standing under the awning of the building.

A waitress in a restaurant, a saleswoman in Bloomingdale's, and a man on the bus who had the crazed concentration of a confirmed stalker recognized me. The man who'd been dry-cleaning my dirty clothes for years, the entire Korean family in my local greengrocer's, and most of my neighbors seemed to be staring at me. The president of the co-op board, to whom I'd planned to complain about the staff, wrote me a letter requesting that I not encourage paparazzi and other assorted members of the fourth estate to loiter in and around the building. I wrote back saying that I happened to be a member of the fourth estate, that one photographer did not paparazzi make, and that in any event, I hadn't encouraged anyone. I also suggested that he do something about the lax security in and around the building, not to mention the lack of courtesy of the staff.

It should have gone away. Emma wasn't a rock star or a professional athlete. She had a loyal following but not a large one, at least by mass entertainment standards. Nobody had ever heard of Julian. And I was, at best, the by-line for someone else's story. But taken together, we somehow added up to inhuman interest, and there was an insatiable machine that worked 'round the clock grinding that out. After all, racks of magazines hanging over the checkout counter in the supermarket had to be filled, talk shows had to be booked, photo ops had to be seized, sound bites had to be bitten, twenty-four hours a day, seven days a week, fifty-two weeks a year.

I told Sugar I couldn't write the story. She marshaled the old arguments, but her heart wasn't in them. As she'd told me before, if I didn't want the assignment, there were plenty of other freelancers who did.

"I'm sorry," I said.

"I think you're going to be," she answered. It wasn't a threat; it was a statement.

"I just can't help feeling that it's nobody else's business." I was still trying to justify myself.

"If you believe that, sweetie pie, you're in the wrong line of work."

I repeated the conversation to Dexter that night. We were making dinner in my kitchen, which the arrival of a few roaches could make seem cramped, and the accidental collisions and murmured apologies made it clear we hadn't got the choreography down yet.

"Maybe she's right," I said.

"Come on," he answered as he grated lemon zest into a sauce he was making. On the rare occasions I followed a recipe, I had a tendency to ignore ingredients called zest or directions that said "garnish with," and I was surprised Dexter didn't do the same.

"That old saw—you'll never work in this town again."

"She didn't say it that way. It was an observation, not a threat."

"Okay, maybe she's right. Maybe you don't have a taste for the jugular." He hesitated for a moment, and I knew he was remembering the profile of him. "Maybe you don't have the instinct to write sensational exposés of lurid accidents." He went on. "Is that something we're supposed to be sorry for?"

What was this "we"? I was the one who was out of an assignment.

I wasn't exactly obsessing about the conversation, but it was still on my mind a few days later when I came home to find a message on my machine—there were only thirteen, so things were looking up after all—from an editor to whom I'd sent the proposal for the women of death row several months earlier. Maybe Dexter was right. Maybe I was meant for better things than lurid exposés.

I dialed the editor's number. "What do you think?" I asked her after we'd exchanged pleasantries.

"It has legs."

That wasn't the way I would have phrased it, but I wasn't going to quibble with wording. "Exactly!"

"Of course, you won't be able to write it yourself."

This was a new slant, but I wasn't going to reject it out of hand. "You mean a question-and-answer format? The women of death row speak for themselves."

"The women of death row?" she repeated as if she'd never heard of them.

"The proposal I sent you."

"Didn't they send that back to you? Thank God I'm out of that place."

"You're not at the magazine anymore?" Voice mail might be a boon to a company's bottom line, but in an era of musical-chairs editors it can be rough on freelancers who're trying to keep up with them.

"I'm in development now."

"Development?" I repeated. It was one of those ephemeral words, like *consultant.*

She must have heard the bewilderment in my voice. "For television movies. That's why I said you can't write it. The networks won't touch it unless we have a real writer."

"A real writer?" I repeated.

"Someone with screen credits. But maybe they'll let you do the treatment. That's twenty or thirty thou over and above the rights to your story."

"My story?" I repeated a third time. Was there an echo in here?

"I won't kid you, Hallie. It would be better if I could get Emma Weill's, but she won't even return my calls. So we'll do it from your POV. It still has all the ingredients. And a terrific locale. If Amy Fisher and some porky grease monkey from Babylon, Long Island, can sweep all three networks, just think what we're going to do with upmarket adultery and vintage car murder on Shelter Island."

"It wasn't murder; it was an accident."

"Whatever. I'm talking production values here."

I'd like to say I hung up on her, politely but firmly, right then. But I didn't. I thought about dollar bills. I thought about screen credits. I thought about made-for-telly movies that weren't trashy. After all, she'd mentioned production values. I thought again that I had no work on the horizon. And after I thought about all that, I still knew it wasn't worth it. Besides, I had no story. At least not one that would play in prime time.

*   *   *

Dexter was delighted with my refusal of the made-for-telly offer. "You don't have to do trash like that," he pronounced. Lie down with God and you get up beatified.

Forty-two

SOMETIMES I THOUGHT it was a conspiracy. Sugar had put out the word. Other times I knew it was merely a slow period. All free-lancers have them. There's even a code of behavior for helping friends in the profession get through them, at least women friends in the profession. Men tend to go out and drink and whore together, or so their self-perpetuating lore goes. Women shore each other up with verbal buttresses. "Remember that time when five pieces fell through and then you got that great assignment for *Psychology Today*?" Or something to that effect.

Dexter, of course, saw the advantages of the situation. Since I didn't have anything more pressing on the agenda—he wasn't being cruel, merely realistic—I could do the preliminary foot-work involved in putting our real estate together. I no longer found the term amusing, but then a lack of work has a deleteri-ous effect on my sense of humor. I've read that it has the same effect on the male sex drive. Not that I had any firsthand experi-ence of that particular problem. Dexter was as busy as ever, though he was making an effort to travel less and turn over more of the running of the fund to his subordinates. He was making an effort, he said, to stop playing God.

One weekend we drove down to Philadelphia and out to the Main Line for me to meet Dexter's widowed mother. She took me on a tour of her garden and told me about her volunteer work for the Women's International League for Peace and Freedom. Dexter hadn't come by his calling accidentally.

I liked her. She seemed to welcome me. The only awkward moment arrived when she asked me if she was likely to have read anything I'd written. Dexter reminded her of the profile of him she'd read the previous summer.

"Oh, yes." She smiled with pride. Clearly the portrait of her son as God struck her as merely factual.

The following weekend I took him to New Jersey to meet Babe. She rose to the occasion magnificently. In fact, she was a little more over the top than I would have liked, but then I was trying to play things down. She told stories about me. She recounted anecdotes about my parents. She waxed nostalgic about the wonderful times we'd all had together. As the afternoon progressed, family pathology became madcap eccentricity.

She even hauled out the photograph albums. There were pictures of infant, and toddler, and childish, and adolescent me, with Babe, with my mother, with my father, and with various combinations thereof. There were pictures of family holidays, and family vacations, and family rites of passage. Dex went through them all dutifully, though I kept telling him he didn't have to. Then one photograph caught my attention. I'm not sure why. There was nothing unusual about it, except perhaps the fact that Babe had mounted it in an album and my mother, who surely must have had another print, hadn't. It was a professional photograph, and in it my parents and Babe and several men and women whose names I no longer recalled were sitting around a large table littered with half-full glasses and half-empty plates and beaded evening bags and matchbooks, which would have been imprinted with the name of a bride and groom and a date, and an unwieldy centerpiece of hothouse flowers that one of the women, maybe my mother would be the lucky one, maybe Babe, would have taken home at the end of the evening. All the men are wearing white dinner jackets. My father's dinner jacket has fallen open to reveal a starched shirtfront and shiny dark cummerbund, because he's leaning back in his chair with one arm on the back of my mother's chair and the other on the back of Babe's. My mother's dress is a pale chiffon with a draped bodice, and I could tell from the way it fell that it was expensive, but Babe is the one who steals the show. Her dark dress is simpler and probably cost a quarter of what my mother's had, but the halter top sets off her beautifully boned athletic shoulders and long neck. She has a cigarette in one hand and a drink in the other and a smile on her face—well, they all have smiles on their faces—but Babe's is like a sweet, juicy slice of melon. My mother's is more a nervous tic, as if she's worried about something. If she looks all right, or whether the gift she sent the happy couple is nice enough, or how long it took me to stop crying after they left the house for the evening. But the smile that struck me as I sat there that afternoon with Babe and Dexter was my father's. It was a wicked grin that cracked open his face to reveal a dangerous fissure running just beneath the surface. My father's smile in that picture reminded me of one of Julian Weill's.

"Your mother was a pretty woman," Dex said on the way back to town.

"I suppose she was." I could see it in the photographs now, though I'd never been able to in the woman when I was a child.

"But Babe," he said, "Babe was really a babe."

The following week I picked up an assignment writing copy for the Christmas catalog of a chain of lingerie stores. The pay was good, and the work easy. All I had to do was come up with a couple of dozen synonyms for *seductive* and *lacy* and remember never to use the word *small* in the bra descriptions.

When Dexter came home and found the piles of illustrations on my desk, he was fascinated. Then I told him what they were doing there, and his face creased in disappointment.

"This is the way freelancers survive," I said. Try to explain survival to a man with an overdeveloped moral sense and a tidy family trust fund.

The woman in charge of promotion for the lingerie chain liked my copy so much that she offered me the entire Valentine's Day catalog.

"You don't have to do that," Dexter said.

"Apparently I do. Unless I come up with an idea for a magazine article that someone actually wants to buy." I hadn't meant to snap, but Kay Meechum had just turned down two proposals I'd sent her, and it was getting harder and harder to convince myself that this was an interlude in, rather than an effective end to, my career in journalism.

"What about the women of death row?"

"Nobody will touch the idea."

"Then write it."

"What?"

"Write the piece the way you want to write it, and make it so damn good that someone will buy it."

"You mean write it on spec?" My voice dropped to a hush on the last two words, the curse of every beginning freelance writer.

"Sure." He tossed off the word with astonishing confidence.

"And what am I supposed to live on while I spend the next couple of months writing this article that no one's going to want?"

"Me."

Last time the suggestion had frightened me. This time it infuriated me. "Don't be patronizing," I snapped.

He let it go, but apparently I couldn't. That night I had the nightmare again.

Forty-three

AT FIRST I was surprised when Emma called and suggested lunch. The accident was in the past. At least I hadn't heard any more from the police about it. And I'd already assured her of my silence. I wasn't going to write the story myself, and I wasn't going to talk to anyone who was. It didn't occur to me until halfway through lunch that it wasn't silence she was after. It was talk. She was desperate for it. And I was the safest person. I was the only one who knew exactly what had happened. I was the only one with whom she didn't have to worry about giving anything away. And I was the only one who could convince her, by believing it myself, that it really had been an accident. The police hadn't brought charges, but that didn't stop Emma from charging herself. It would have been easier if she'd been a believer, in religion, or psychiatry, or any other creed. Then she could have gone to the appropriate practitioner for absolution.

We met at the same restaurant where we'd had our first lunch. This time we weren't dressed alike, though once again I admired her jacket. Her clothes were fine. It was Emma herself who made me uneasy. She no longer had that soiled madhouse aura, but she did look brittle, like a bone china plate that's been shattered and glued back together.

I asked how her children were doing. She said they were holding up. She even managed to joke a little. I suspect that was the wine. Since neither of us was working that afternoon, she'd pointed out in a voice that sounded like the ping that fine bone china gives off, we might as well order a bottle of wine. We were halfway through it when she told me about Becky's school.

"One of the counselors called to reassure me they were monitoring her carefully. That was right after the second *Post* headline. The one with your picture."

"I'm sorry," I said stupidly.

"Not your fault. Anyway, the counselor told me not to worry about the media coverage. 'Her peers are used to that sort of thing,' she said, and you could tell from the way she said it that she was proud. In other words, we're not talking hoi polloi here, we're talking offspring of divorcing movie stars, and substance-abusing socialites, and inside traders." She stopped. "God! I sound like Julian."

She did.

We talked about Julian for a while, or rather she talked and I listened. It was a shame I'd decided not to do the article because I was finally beginning to understand the tangle of needs and fears and convictions that had led her to Julian in the first place and kept her with him all those years. But as I'd suspected when I'd first taken on the story and worried about what Pat O'Dougherty would say, I wasn't in this for knowledge of Emma. Or at least not only for knowledge of Emma.

"I have to ask you something," I said. The level of wine in the bottle was low. The neighborhood matrons at neighboring tables who'd watched it descend with scandalized eyes had gone off to get their toes pedicured, or listen to a museum talk on early American furniture, or suit up in their orange volunteer guard vests to patrol the streets so their children and their children's nannies could walk unmolested.

"That comment you made about each of us swerving to avoid her own accident," I said. "What did you mean?"

She leaned back against the banquette, a lovely, brittle

woman with all the hairline cracks and imperfect repairs show-ing through the shiny glaze. "Our mothers, of course. We were both working so damn hard not to end up like our mothers that we each went to the other extreme. I was terrified of being left by a husband, so I put up with Julian. You were terrified of being trapped by one, so you sabotaged the possibility. I've thought about it a lot, and it occurred to me that was what you were doing with Julian that weekend."

I wasn't exactly angry at the statement, but I didn't like be-ing lumped with her either. I hadn't wasted the past twenty years of my life on a womanizer. I hadn't run over a husband. I hadn't even done anything with Julian that weekend. But I wasn't going to point out any of that. It seemed safer to stay with her original point.

"I thought you thought my mother had a lot of dignity."

"Exactly." She divided the last inch of wine between our two glasses though I'd gestured for her to take it all. "How else could she have carried it off? It wasn't just staying married, though God knows that must have taken courage. But staying friendly with the woman too. What was her name again?"

"Whose name?"

"Your mother's friend. The one she was practically insepara-ble with. From."

"You mean Babe?"

"That's it. Instead of divorcing your father and walking around like my mother with a big red *B* for bitterness on her chest, she acted as if there were absolutely nothing going on. Even that business about his death. She even managed to carry that off. Though that wasn't the way my mother phrased it when she told me about it."

I started to ask what business about his death, but suddenly I knew. My father had collapsed at six forty-five on a Wednes-day night in February.

"He was gone by the time the ambulance got there," my mother had told me.

"Got to his office?" I'd asked.

"To Babe's," she'd said. "He was helping her with her taxes. You know Daddy always helped Babe with her taxes."

"The point is"—Emma went on—"as long as she acted that way, everyone else had to, too. You see what I mean?"

And suddenly I did. There was no shock. There wasn't even anger. There was just a small click, the kind you hear when you turn a camera lens to focus it, and suddenly everything came into sharp relief.

The rage followed. I was furious at my father, and at Babe, and even at my mother, for making me stupid and calling it protection. I was furious at all of them, but there was only one of them left to take it out on. I called Babe and told her I was coming out to see her the next day.

It was one of those blindingly clear autumn mornings when the sky sits like a crystal bell over the world and you think you can see forever. Beyond the grimy train windows the huge tanks of the gas refineries loomed pink and yellow and blue in the distance. Slap a coat of paint on the surface and call it scenery, that's the world I come from. And was going back to.

Babe was waiting for me at the bottom of the stairs to the station platform. I had the feeling she knew why I was there. Maybe she'd heard it in my voice when I'd called to say I was coming. Or maybe I was just seeing her with new eyes. She was leaning against the car again, not a racy vintage Buick but a dusty gray Toyota. The car made me sad. Then I remembered Dexter's comment. Your mother was pretty, but Babe was really a babe.

When I reached the bottom of the stairs, she leaned over to place her cheek against mine. I held back. Her eyes, under age-slackened lids, registered surprise and hurt. I laid my cheek against her parched tissue-paper skin.

We got into the car. She turned the key in the ignition. Her eyes darted from the rearview mirror to the side mirror to the street, once, twice, a third time; then she gunned the motor. The car leaped into the oncoming traffic. My foot came down on an imaginary brake.

"Are you sure you don't want me to drive?"

She shook her head no and asked where I wanted to go for lunch. "The club?"

"Not the club," I said.

Her eyes darted to me nervously, then back to the road.

She listed several other places. I told her I didn't care where we went. "I'm not very hungry." She glanced at me again. I knew I was being cruel, but hell, I had something to be cruel about.

She pulled into a parking lot beside a flat ugly brick and glass building. A sign proclaimed BUSINESSMAN'S LUNCH $6.95, LADIES DRINK HALF-PRICED 5 TO 7.

"Is this all right?" she asked.

"Inspired."

She gave me another nervous glance.

Inside, the hostess greeted her by name. As soon as we were seated, the waitress came over with menus and a pot of coffee and asked how Babe was feeling and if Mrs. Seltzer had got over that nasty cold.

"You're quite a celebrity," I said.

She shrugged. "Some people can get a table at Lutèce or Twenty-one. Eve Seltzer and I cut a swath at the Star Diner. Did you know Henry put up the money to start the original Star? It was down near the port in those days."

I was surprised and annoyed. "No, but then there are lots of things I didn't know about my father."

I waited for another apprehensive glance, but she was too caught up in her memories. "It was a little hole in the wall run by a Hungarian refugee. I forget his name now, but Henry helped bring him over after the war and then loaned him money to start the place." Her eyes were focused on the middle distance. "Your father was generous."

"Generous to a fault, as my mother always said."

Her eyes came back to me. "If you don't mind my saying so, cookie, you have a definite aura today. Like a character in a PMS commercial. Is anything wrong, or is it still the work problem?"

I hadn't realized I'd complained to her about work. And now I was furious that I had. "This has nothing to do with work."

"Then what? Dexter?"

The waitress smiled her way up to the table and asked what we'd have. Babe ordered the Star Salad. I said I'd have the same.

"Dexter's fine," I lied. The more I worried about lack of work, the more he offered to help. And the more he offered to help, the angrier I got.

"I liked him," Babe said. "I liked him a lot."

"The feeling was mutual. He said judging from the old pictures, Babe was quite a babe."

I watched the seventy-four-year-old woman across the table from me preen in pleasure and took my own satisfaction in the way the unforgiving midday light cracked through the tinted windows and cast cruel shadows across her worn face.

"I wasn't bad."

"Don't be modest."

"I'm not. Adelaide was the beauty. I was—"

"Sexy?"

She blinked behind her glasses. "Among other things. At least I hope among other things."

"Men liked you. Even as a child I could see that."

"Happily married men always like an unattached woman. At least they did in those days."

"How come you were unattached? How come you never married after . . ." I hesitated.

She looked across the table at me. She wasn't preening now, but she wasn't cringing either. "After Sydney died?"

I nodded.

"It was too late."

"You weren't that old." It suddenly occurred to me that she'd probably been about my age when she was finally widowed.

"Too late in other ways. I'd become accustomed to a certain kind of life."

"What kind of life was that?" I asked nastily. I was sure I had her now.

"I'd become accustomed to thinking of Sydney off in the wings somewhere. So even after he wasn't, I still had the feeling he was. It's one thing when you live with a man for ten or twenty or thirty years, and he dies. Then every time you walk into a room, or look up from a book, or turn over in bed, you feel the absence. Or so I imagine. But it's hard to believe a man is really gone when he hasn't been there all along. Sydney was sick for a long time."

"Then wouldn't you have . . ." I hesitated. I was ready to have it out with Babe, and it was open season on my father, but her flier was still sacred territory.

"Wouldn't I have what? Been relieved?"

"At least partially. I mean, if he'd been terminally ill or something . . ." My voice trailed off. I didn't know how I'd got on the defensive.

"Sydney wasn't terminally ill. At least not in the conventional sense of the term."

"Then what was wrong with him?"

"You don't know?"

"No one would ever talk about it."

She leaned back against the garish Leatherette banquette. "No, they wouldn't. They were ashamed. I was supposed to be ashamed. After all, physical illness was bad enough. My own mother thought diabetes was contagious. So you can imagine how they felt about Sydney's condition."

"I take it it wasn't physical."

"Henry and Adelaide really never told you? Not even when you were grown?"

I shook my head no.

"You know Adelaide thought I was crazy for marrying him in the first place?"

"Life expectancy and tours of duty?"

"Exactly." She stopped and waited while the waitress put two huge glass bowls overflowing with iceberg lettuce, anemic tomatoes, and a pale substance that could have been chicken or tuna or cottage cheese in front of each of us. The waitress asked if everything was all right. Babe said it was terrific.

"Sydney outsmarted the odds. He came home from the war."

"I know that much."

Neither of us had picked up a fork.

"A few weeks later he announced he was going to get a job as a pilot for a commercial airline. They were scandalized. Henry said he'd never heard of a Jewish man flying for a living. Adelaide said I shouldn't let him do it."

"What did you say?"

"That it wasn't my decision. As it turned out, we didn't have to worry. He never did get a job with the airlines. Henry insisted it was discrimination. At the time I thought he might be right, but later I didn't think so. Later I thought the airlines' tests or Sydney's records or something must have shown what was coming."

She picked up her fork but didn't do anything with it. "He got a job selling insurance. He was good at it too. The man had charm." She glanced out the window again, as if she could see through it back to the past, but this time I took no pleasure in the harsh revelations of the glare. She turned back to me. "I mean, God knows I was impulsive, but even I didn't go around jumping into marriage, or bed, with every man who was about to ship out. Am I shocking you?"

I remembered why I was there. "No."

"At any rate, by the time it happened he'd already been promoted to head of district sales."

"By the time what happened?"

She put down her fork. "Adelaide and I had gone shopping. We were looking for dining room sets. I'd found what I wanted, but she still wasn't sure. Typical Adelaide. We'd taken her car, so she dropped me off. It wasn't late, but it was already dark. This was December. So she sat in the car and waited until I let myself into the house. She'd never drive away until I was inside the house. Even in daylight. Henry too."

"I remember."

"Anyway, I let myself in and walked through the downstairs, turning on lights. Since the house was dark, I assumed Sydney wasn't home yet. Then I went upstairs to the bedroom. I was going to wash my face and put on fresh makeup before he got home. You have to remember this was an era when no self-respecting wife would see her husband off in the morning or welcome him home at night without fresh makeup. The magazines warned us what would happen if we did. I went into the bedroom and switched on the light. To this day I can still see it." She stopped. I waited for her to go on.

"He'd taken my underwear. I don't know why, and none of

the doctors ever explained that part of it. Anyway, the underwear was the least of it. He'd taken it and strung it up all over the room. Across the windows, over the lampshades, even from the overhead light. Stockings, bras, girdles, slips, nightgowns, underpants, you name it, he'd strung them up all over the room. At first I didn't realize it was Sydney who'd done it. At first I didn't even see him. Then I heard him. He was lying on his stomach next to the window, you know, the way you see them lying with rifles in war movies, though thank God he didn't have a rifle. He hissed at me to turn out the light and get down. Before they saw me. I asked him before who saw me, but he just went on hissing at me to turn out the light and get down. Of course, I was too stunned to do anything, and the next thing I knew he'd crawled across the floor on his elbows, you know, dragging the rest of his body behind him. He told me to turn out the light again, and this time I did. Then he pulled me down beside him. We spent the night that way, lying on the floor in the dark, hiding from the enemy. His enemy."

She stopped again, and I could see she was back there again. "The whole time we were on the floor, the whole night, he held me. With his body between me and the window. He held me to shield me from the danger."

She was silent for another moment, and when she finally went on, her voice turned brisk.

"Somewhere around dawn he fell asleep, and I crawled out of the bedroom. When I reached the hall, I could barely stand. I was that stiff. Somehow I made it down to the kitchen. The first thing I did was call Henry and Adelaide. Henry came and drove us to the hospital. The first hospital. There were five by the time it was over. That was twelve years later. In a moment of lucidity —he had them, and they were hell for him—that sweet charm-the-birds-off-the-trees man managed to outsmart the staff and hang himself with a belt they'd forgotten to take away."

She stopped again. "So yes, I did feel some relief. But not a lot. Not compared to the other things I felt, like grief and rage and guilt."

That was my cue, again. Guilt for what? I should have asked. But I just sat staring at her across the hard Formica table. She wasn't preening now. Her shoulders were hunched forward, and her arms were wrapped around her as if she were huddling against the cold, and her face was rigid with the effort not to cry. In the harsh light that broke through the windows and the glare of her past, I saw a woman I'd never seen before. I'd always thought Babe was reckless, but I saw now that the recklessness was merely a response to fear, of the accidents you could worry about and those you'd never dreamed of. And to the knowledge of her own limitations in the face of them.

She straightened her shoulders and stared back across the table at me. Her gaze wasn't defiant, but it was steady. "Henry and Adelaide got me through it. They'd got me through the years when he was sick, and they got me through the years after he died. They were wonderful to me. Both of them." She enunciated the last words clearly, not as a dare but as an insistence on the facts. Then she smiled. It was a small, pinched grimace, nothing like the wide, daring smiles in all those photographs in the old albums. But then maybe I hadn't seen those pictures clearly. Maybe Babe's smiles hadn't been as bright as I'd thought. And maybe my mother's hadn't been as grim. Maybe I'd just been peering at them too closely.

I knew then I wasn't going to say anything to Babe. And as soon as I knew that, I knew something else as well. If I didn't have to avenge my mother, I didn't have to become her either.

Forty-four

A NARROW STREAK of yellow spilled across the dark wooden floorboards. The bedroom got less sun at this time of year. All right, that wasn't exactly news or even symbolic. It was the calendar. She'd spent plenty of October weekends in the house. Julian used to love them. That was all right too. She wasn't going to try not to think about Julian. That was one of the reasons she'd come out to the house. To stop running away from him. No, not him. It.

She lay in bed gazing at the pepperidge trees outside the window. When the sun hit them, they looked as if they were on fire. He'd always predicted which weekend they'd peak, and he'd always been so smug when he was right. Like the crossword puzzles. He'd finished the puzzle that morning. No cheap irony, please. Not when there were real things to worry about. She'd noticed that Becky had begun doing crossword puzzles. The sight of her daughter's slight shoulders hunched over the puzzle and her face screwed up in concentration had stopped her, not just in the doorway to the room but in her life. This is it, the sight said. This is what you have to live with now. You'll never get beyond it.

She kicked off the quilt, got out of bed, and went into the bathroom.

After she'd showered and dressed and made coffee, she took

an oiled sweater from the chest next to the front door—she couldn't even remember whose it had been originally, hers or Julian's—pulled it on, and carried her mug out to the back porch. Light hit the water and splintered off it, but the angle of sunshine was different from then. Then. Her point of reference for everything now. Her own personal B.C.-A.D., antebellum-postwar.

She heard the sound of a car engine and sat clutching her mug and waiting for it to pass. The sound died. Then she heard a car door slam. Her mind raced. The garage door was closed. There were no lights on at this time of day. If she stayed here, maybe whoever it was wouldn't find her. She didn't want to see people. She didn't want neighbors stopping by to make sure she was all right. She didn't want friends inviting her to lunch or dinner to save her from being alone, to save her from herself. But the windows were open, and the aroma of coffee was percolating through the house and out into the morning air. And she wasn't a coward, goddamn it.

She heard the crunch of shoes on the gravel walk, not rubber-soled shoes for boating or running or tennis, but hard-soled shoes for serious endeavors. The gravel exploded beneath them. Then the front porch steps creaked under them. She stood and, carrying her mug, started for the front of the house. As she came around the side, she saw the police car parked in the road.

So they'd found out. She could pretend to fool herself, but she couldn't fool them. It was like the old gun lobby slogan. Guns don't kill, people do. Feet don't come down on gas pedals accidentally. Cars don't shoot out of control on their own. She was almost relieved. At least now she could stop being afraid. At least now she could start paying.

She heard a voice. Not menacing. Not even authoritative. Tentative. "Is anyone home?"

She started walking again and came around to the front of the house. A cop stood at the front door, hunched over a little, peering into the dimness within. At the sound of her footsteps he straightened and turned.

She was surprised. He didn't have the look of a cop who'd come on business. He didn't even have the angry mien of the cops who directed traffic in town or the bored expressions of the ones who dozed in their cars in Central Park. He had a hesitant look, as if he didn't want to intrude. He also looked vaguely familiar. He must have been there that day. Then. There it was again. The point of reference. She glanced at the name plate on his chest. Edward Snyder. She wondered why Officer Snyder had come alone. Didn't they need two to arrest? Didn't they need two even to question, one to play good cop, one bad?

"Morning, ma'am."

Ma'am. Jesus, were they going to play this like some B-level film noir?

"Can I help you?" she asked.

"We've been keeping an eye on the house. No one's been out here since . . . for a while." So he had his point of reference too. Everywhere she went she came up against it. "Except some reporters and photographers and those guys, and we've been keeping an eye on it." Was he serious? "I saw the doors and windows were open this morning, and I just thought I'd check and see that everything was okay."

"Everything's okay." Not exactly. Not by a long shot.

She saw the way he looked at her. He was older than she'd thought at first. Not one of the baby cops who still got excited at the St. Patrick's and Puerto Rican Day parades in town, but not one of the tired alcohol-flushed over-the-hill ones either. Somewhere between. And from the look on his face, not stupid, or at least incurious. He was after something.

"Everything's fine. Thanks for keeping an eye on things. I appreciate it."

He was still staring at her. Did he think he could unnerve her that way? Did he expect her to come out and say it? You're right, Officer Snyder, it wasn't an accident. If you've read your Freud, and from the look of you, I wouldn't be surprised if you'd come across him in some criminology course, there are no accidents. I was mad as hell at my husband. I'd been mad as hell at him for years. That's why my foot came down on the gas pedal.

"How about you?" he said. "You okay too?"

So she was right about the Freud. Forget the B-level film noir. This was a television series starring a cop with a heart of gold and a Ph.D. in psychology.

"Fine," she said, and then, because she heard the chill in her voice and knew exactly how her chin had lifted as she'd said it, went on. "Thanks. It's nice of you to ask."

"Yeah. Your small-town police in action. I also deliver babies and get cats out of trees."

Suddenly she remembered him, not from that day but from before. Really before, when Matt and Becky were small. She'd been out here alone with the kids—God only knew where Julian had been—and a squirrel had got trapped in Becky's bedroom. She'd called the police, and this cop had turned up. He'd stood on the porch in that classic pose, legs wide apart for balance, arms outstretched in front of him with one supporting the other that was training a red plastic water pistol on the door. "Come out with your paws up, squirrelface," he'd growled, and Matt and Becky had squealed with excitement.

She asked him if he'd like a cup of coffee. He said he would. She led him around to the back porch, got a mug from the kitchen, and brought it out to him.

He took it from her but, instead of sitting, stood leaning against the porch railing. She wondered if that was a ploy, if he was trying to intimidate her. Or maybe he just thought he looked more macho positioned against the railing that way, with his big shoulders silhouetted against the police-blue sky and the worn fabric of his fly hitting her at eye level. Her friend

Charlotte, who wrote mysteries, was always talking about how sexy cops were. Of course, in the eighties Charlotte had insisted the same thing was true of arbitrageurs, so the statement obviously said more about Charlotte's attraction to power and its abuses than about cops.

She pulled herself up. What was wrong with her anyway? She'd come out here to lay the demons to rest. Instead she was sparring about her guilt with a strange cop and having weird fantasies about him to boot, despite the fact that . . . Her eyes moved to his hand on the railing. Sure enough, a thick gold band cut into the tanned flesh of his third finger.

What was wrong with her?

She was alive, that was what. More than alive. Once or twice since—since then she'd felt dizzy with freedom, lightheaded with possibility, as if she were breathing pure oxygen. And every time she had the feeling, the shame followed right after. Then the two emotions chased each other around in her chest like unruly children. Shame, the bully, always won.

She forced her eyes up to his face. He was still making self-deprecating jokes about small-town cops. Something about the psychological side of the job, like trying to look innocent or at least dumb when you ran into Mr. and Mrs. Jones at the IGA on Sunday morning after Mrs. Jones had called you on Saturday night because Mr. Jones was using her as a punching bag. She thought cops were supposed to be laconic. This one couldn't stop talking. She wondered if that was another ploy.

He was putting his mug down on the table now and thanking her. She put down her own mug and walked with him around to the front of the house. The porch groaned under his big boots. She thought of Julian's soft rubber boating shoes. Julian had come on stealthy feet. She couldn't believe this cop was as straightforward as he seemed. She couldn't believe he'd come just to check on the house.

"Thanks for the coffee."

"Thank *you*," she said, and held out her hand. "For keeping an eye on things." She hesitated. "And for your help." She hesitated again. "That day."

He shook her hand. "That's what we're here for, ma'am. Trouble. Emergencies. Accidents."

"Some accident." The sound of her voice shocked her. Was she crazy? She hadn't meant to say that. Not to him, certainly. To a properly certified Upper East Side therapist, maybe. To a friend in a moment of weakness, perhaps. But to a cop who'd come snooping, never. Especially not to a cop with a threadbare fly and an unfortunate manner of addressing her. She pulled her hand away.

He smiled. Actually he laughed. "Don't worry, Mrs. Weill. We don't work that way. If I was questioning you, you'd know it."

He was peering down at her, and she realized that unlike the cops in movies, he wasn't wearing dark glasses.

"We closed the investigation a couple of days after the accident. I thought you knew. And it was an accident. A pretty weird accident, but then most accidents are weird. Were you around when that lady ran herself over? Seems to me you'd already bought this place by then, but I could be wrong. You remember that mess at the town dump?"

She shook her head no.

"Well, this summer resident drives to the dump. Gets out of the car and goes around to the trunk to get out her trash. All presorted. Wet garbage. Paper. Clear glass, green, brown. Plastic containers. Aluminum cans. We get a lot of heavy-duty Greens on the island. No offense intended. So she takes out her bottles and cans and begins recycling. Only when she got out of the car, she was so busy thinking about how she was saving the planet she forgot to pull the hand brake. So while she's standing there tossing her chardonnay bottles into the green glass receptacle and her Bass ales into the brown, she looks up and notices that her car has started rolling. Naturally she drops the bottles and begins to chase it. The planet's important, but a late-model Beemer's nothing to sneeze at. Now unfortunately a car's not like a boat. It doesn't head into the wind automatically. The wheel must have been turned because the BMW begins to circle. So the car's cruising around the dump in circles, and the lady's chasing it. Pretty soon the car begins to pick up speed. Lady does same. So there they are going around the dump in circles, lady chasing car or maybe it's car chasing lady. Only problem is the dump isn't paved, and it being summer and all, she's wearing sandals. So the next thing you know, she trips. Now she's on the ground, but the Beemer's still cruising. Ran right over her. DOA." He was still staring down at her, and now he raised his eyebrows. "So what do you think? You think it was an accident, or you think she had some kind of death wish?"

"You weren't kidding about the psychological aspects of your job, were you?"

"I never kid, ma'am. Thanks again for the coffee."

"Thank you for the absolution."

"Now you're kidding."

"Only a little."

"Okay, but I'll make you a bet."

"What's that?"

"I bet some night when you're lying in bed at three A.M. staring at the ceiling, you'll remember that story."

"You think it'll make everything all right?"

"All right, no. A little better, maybe."

He gave her a mock salute and started down the porch stairs. "And don't worry, ma'am. We'll keep an eye on the house."

Forty-five

THE FOLLOWING SUMMER Emma invited me out to Shelter Island again. She invited Dexter too, and this time he managed to make it. He was traveling less these days, though he was still traveling a lot. As he'd pointed out in that convoluted story about the man whose daughter had died, human change is a sometimes thing. The point applied to both of us. Once or twice during the past year my mother had stirred in me, and I'd panicked at the thought that he wouldn't come home. A couple of other times I'd panicked at the knowledge that he would. But for the most part I was happy with him. And I was working again, though I'd given up on the women of death row. Every now and then the idea tugged at me; then I'd remember the long list of editors who'd turned it down and put it out of my mind.

Emma was doing as well as could be expected. At least her career was flourishing. All her books were still in print, including *Happily Ever After,* which her publisher, who knew a good thing when he saw it on the front page of the *Post,* had reissued in the nick of time. And she was finishing a new novel. She told me about it at the beach on Saturday afternoon. Neither of us had suggested taking out the Sunfish.

We were sitting side by side in folding chairs. I was admiring the way Dexter's body sliced through the water as he did laps back and forth across the bay. I wasn't sure what Emma was looking at.

"You'll approve," she said about the book. "It's dark. Probably the darkest thing I've ever done."

I asked her what it was about.

"An adolescent girl whose mother goes to prison after shooting her abusive father in self-defense."

I was surprised. I'd told Sugar anger was rampant, but I'd never thought Emma would write about it.

"Dark is an understatement," I said.

"Julian gave me the idea."

My head swiveled to her. "You mean . . . his . . . accident?"

She turned from the water too, and I could see from the dismay on her face that she really hadn't made the connection. "I hadn't even thought of that. I meant Julian himself. He came up with the idea. That weekend, as a matter of fact. He called it 'a woman of death row.' At first I didn't want to do it—I didn't want to do anything grim—but the more I thought about it, the more I realized that was the reason to do it."

I turned back to the water. Dexter's wake lay like a foamy ribbon on the surface of the bay. His arms flashed in the sunlight with each stroke.

"What do you think of it?" she asked.

"I think it's a great idea."

She smiled. "I figured you would. Given your reaction to *Happily Ever After*. But you're in good company. My agent loves it. My editor says it's the best thing I've ever done." She turned back to the water and sat staring at the horizon for a while. "And I owe it all to him."

"Not exactly."

"I knew you were going to say that. But it really was his idea. I'm not saying I couldn't have done it without him. Obviously I did. And I'm not saying I owe him everything. But he did help. In lots of ways. I have to give him that."

I let it go, and we sat in silence for a while. I was still watching Dexter's progress back and forth across the bay. It seemed to me he should be getting tired. I suppose she was thinking of Julian, of what she owed him, and what she'd wasted on him, and what she could never make up to him.

I turned to look at her. She no longer reminded me of a patched and fragile piece of china. If I had to compare her to anything, it would have been to one of those women carved on the prows of old sailing ships. She was weathered, but she still had a bold forward rake.

I turned back to the water. It lay flat as a mirror. There was no line of foam, no flash of wet arms, no kick of spray. Something inside me that I didn't know was movable lurched.

"Can you see Dexter?"

Emma glanced out over the water carelessly. "He's out there somewhere."

"I can't see him. He was there a moment ago, and now he's gone."

I stood, shaded my eyes with my hand, and scanned the bay from one side to the other. Children played in the shallow water. A small boat moved across the horizon. That was all.

"It's only the bay, Hallie. There's no undertow. There aren't even any waves. You can practically walk across it."

She was right, of course. But there were also cramps. And there was sudden exhaustion. And everyone knew sharks loved shallow water. There were a dozen things I could think of and God only knew how many I couldn't even imagine.

I was still squinting into the sunlight when I felt a hand on my shoulder.

"Looking for someone?"

I turned. He was grinning at me. Some people might have called it a boyish grin. I thought it was mean or at least callous.

"You scared me."

"You should know I'm indestructible. Gods don't drown."

"I told her there was nothing to worry about." Emma was sitting behind me, but I could tell from her voice that she was laughing at me too.

"It's not funny."

Dexter bent, picked up a towel from the sand, and began drying himself. "It's nice to know you care." He was still grinning at me, and now he glanced over my shoulder at Emma. For one awful moment I thought he was going to wink at her. He didn't, but I still couldn't help remembering that joke from my childhood. I could kill him, the women used to tell one another, but I could never divorce him. I still didn't think it was funny, but I finally understood it.